ONE LAST DAY OF SUMMER

SHARI LOW

Boldwod

First published in Great Britain in 2022 by Boldwood Books Ltd.

A CIP catalogue record for this book is available from the British Library.

Paperback ISBN 978-1-80048-744-4

Large Print ISBN 978-1-80048-743-7

Hardback ISBN 978-1-80426-797-4

Ebook ISBN 978-1-80048-745-1

Kindle ISBN 978-1-80048-746-8

Audio CD ISBN 978-1-80048-738-3

MP3 CD ISBN 978-1-80048-739-0

Digital audio download ISBN 978-1-80048-741-3

Boldwood Books Ltd
23 Bowerdean Street
London SW6 3TN
www.boldwoodbooks.com

To the wonderful Caroline, Jade, Rose and the brilliant Boldwood Books team,
who work miracles every time I turn in another pile of pages.
And to JL, who has known a miracle or two of his own.
Everything, always, my love xx

WHEN WORLDS COLLIDE...

Bernadette's World

Bernadette Manson, 54 – devoted nurse at Glasgow Central
Hospital A&E, loving mum, former wife of eminent cardiac
surgeon, Kenneth Manson.
Nina Kerr, 33 – Kenneth and Bernadette's daughter, married to
Gerry, their children, Casey (7) and Milo (5) are the lights of
Bernadette's life.
Stuart Manson, 26 –Bernadette and Kenneth's son, a lawyer who
lives with his partner, Connor.
Sarah Delaney, 60 – Bernadette's best friend, who found happiness
with second husband, Piers, after divorce from her first husband,
Drew. Accident-prone daughter, Eliza, 28.

Tadgh's World

Tadgh Donovan, 28 – born and bred in Dublin, by day he's a

graphic designer and by night he's the lead guitarist in the rising Irish rock band, Home.

Cheryl Downey, 28 – Tadgh's fiancé and childhood sweetheart since they were fourteen years old.

Shay Donovan, 29 – Tadgh's older brother and the lead singer in their band.

Conlan, 28 – Tadgh's best mate since school, bass guitarist and best man at his imminent wedding to Cheryl.

Jean Donovan – Tadgh and Shay's late, much beloved, mother.

Jack Donovan – Tadgh and Shay's widowed father.

Hayley's World

Hayley Ford, 32 – a high-school dance and drama teacher. Once a free-spirited surfer chick, now she's the wife of a top fertility doctor, yet she has been unable to get pregnant, and hates the irony in that.

Lucas Ford, 35 – Hayley's husband, a work-obsessed, leading IVF specialist on Harley Street.

Dev's World

Dev Robbins, 30 – a sports writer and aspiring novelist.

Lizzy Walsh, 30 – Dev's flatmate and best pal since they lived next door to each other as children, Lizzy is now a successful artist and Dev's oracle of common sense.

12TH AUGUST

8 A.M. − 10 A.M.

1

BERNADETTE MANSON

The ring of the phone cut through the peace of Bernadette's morning like a cheese grater through cheddar, drowning out the sound of the gentle ripples of water from the stream at the end of the lawn. The stream was one of the things that had made her fall in love with this cottage. She'd been here five years now and the joy and peace it gave her had never diminished – except when it was being disturbed by a phone barking out the Stormtrooper theme from Star Wars. Her best mate, Sarah, had set that ringtone up on Bernadette's new phone and – technophobe that Bernadette was – she didn't know how to get rid of it. The only silver lining was that it made her seem cool to any children who had the misfortune to end up in the A&E ward and gave them a giggle.

On the screen, Bernadette saw Sarah's name, noticed the time, then skipped the 'hello's when she answered.

'Is that you outside, lovely? I'll be right out. I knew you'd be half an hour early, so I'm all prepared.' As she spoke, Bernadette dipped back into the kitchen and put her mug in the open dishwasher. This wasn't her first holiday rodeo with Sarah. On Sarah's insistence, they'd once shown up at the airport four hours early for a flight, despite Bernadette pointing out that the pilot probably wasn't even out of his bed yet. Today, they only had to check in an hour before the domestic flight from Glasgow to Gatwick, London, where they'd have ninety minutes before catching the next flight to the sunny paradise of St Lucia.

'Bernadette...' It came out like a strangled sob. 'Bernadette, I can't...' Sob. 'Can't...' Sob. 'It's Eliza, she's...' Sob.

The nerve endings right under Bernadette's skin tingled, sending a wave of anxiety around her body. Not that she showed it. Thirty-five years as a nurse at Glasgow Central Hospital, most of them in A&E, had instilled in her the absolute need for calm in the face of a crisis. And this sounded like a bloody big crisis.

'Sarah, what's happened? What's wrong? Take a breath. Just breathe, honey, try to explain...'

'It's Eliza. She's been in an accident.'

Bernadette's blood ran cold. Eliza was Sarah's twenty-eight-year-old daughter. She was on holiday with her girlfriends in Crete right now.

'I'm on my way, Sarah. I'll be there in fifteen minutes...'

'No! I'm sorry. I didn't mean to panic you. She's going to be okay.' A large sniff restored a little strength to Sarah's voice. 'Daft thing was climbing up a drainpipe outside their apartment because they'd lost their keys. The whole pipe came away from the wall and she fell...' Another large sniff. 'She's broken both legs and one arm, pretty much battered the rest of her body too, but she's alive and... oh God, Bernadette, I got such a fright. I can't stop shaking.'

'Oh honey, I'm so sorry. I'll come now.' It wasn't even a decision. Sarah. Best friend. Distress. That was all Bernadette needed to drop everything and go to her.

'Thank you, but, oh, Bernadette, I don't know how to tell you this – Drew is on his way now to collect me.' Drew was Sarah's first husband, and she was his first wife. They'd split right after Eliza was born and he'd had two more wives since then. Or was it three? Sarah had stayed single for two decades, until she'd met Piers, an absolute sweetheart, on a cruise a few years ago. Despite their re-marriages, Sarah and Drew had somehow remained close friends throughout all the ups, downs and dramas of divorce and extended families, so it was no surprise that they'd immediately sprung into action together when their daughter was hurt. Sarah was still gushing out all the details. 'There's a flight from Prestwick in two hours. Eliza's travel insurance doesn't cover a flight home, so we're going over to be with her and bring her back when she's discharged. Don't hate me. Please don't hate me. I need to be with her, so I can't come away with you.'

A hundred thoughts were ricocheting through Bernadette's mind, but not one of them contained a shred of resentment. Like Sarah, she would also drop absolutely everything if one of her kids were in the same situation, even if it did mean missing a two-week, all-inclusive holiday in St Lucia with her closest friend.

'Of course, I don't hate you. I would do the same. Are you sure you don't need me to come?'

'Positive. We'll only be hanging around the hospital until she's ready to come home. Oh Bernadette, our trip was non-refundable though, so you won't get your money back. I'm so sorry.'

'Stop apologising!' Bernadette said, nothing but kindness in her voice. 'You know I don't care about the money. Obviously.' In more ways than one, that was so true, not because she was careless with cash, but because in this case, it wasn't hers to begin with. Her ex-husband, Kenneth, had originally paid for this holiday, but by an unexpected sequence of events, it had become hers and she'd then invited Sarah along. But that was another story and not one that she was even going to think about now. 'All that matters is that Eliza is going to be okay, and that you're going to get her home. We can go away any time. Don't worry about a thing. Just take care of you, give my love to Drew and give Eliza a very gentle hug from me. Poor thing. Keep me posted and...'

Bernadette heard a loud beep at the other end, and Sarah blurted, 'That's Drew here. I need to go. I'm so sorry, Bernadette. I love you.'

With a click, she was gone.

Her mug made a clink against the door of the dishwasher as Bernadette retrieved it. She rinsed it out, then poured in what was left of the pot that was still on her shiny new coffee machine. Her son, Stuart, and his partner, Connor, had bought it for her at Christmas – cream and silver, to match the rest of her kitchen. She wasn't much of a gadget person, but this was her very favourite new toy.

She hadn't even taken the first sip when the phone rang again.

'Mum! I'm so glad I caught you.' As always, her daughter, Nina's voice came with a cacophony of noise in the background that was completely disproportionate to the size of the people making it. Big noise, little guys. At seven and five, her grandsons, Casey and Milo, were higher up the decibel scale than a brass band. 'These two have been up since five o'clock and I just lost track of time. And my sanity.'

Bernadette sat on the window seat that overlooked the garden. 'Actually, you could have called me at noon and I'd still be here, my love. We've had a slight change of plan.'

She went on to fill Nina in on Sarah's call and a few gasps later, Nina groaned, 'A *slight* change of plan? Mum, that's like me saying these two are *slightly* high energy.'

That made Bernadette smile. It was a family joke that the boys were like mobile phones that just recharged themselves for a few hours overnight, then pinged awake for another day of noise and activity.

'You might have a point there. Anyway, love, I guess it just wasn't meant to be. I've got lots of things I can be doing over the next two weeks. This garden could do with some attention, and I could watch the boys for you or—'

Nina cut her off. 'Or you could still go and have a lovely time in St Lucia.'

Bernadette tried to process that suggestion. It hadn't even crossed her mind. And no wonder. There were so many reasons that she couldn't do that. Problem was, none of them were coming into her mind right now. Total blank.

'But...' she began weakly.

'No "buts", Mum. It's not as if Sarah would lose out on anything if you went ahead with it – the whole holiday is going to be lost. You said yourself that you've got two weeks off work anyway. You're staying in a lovely resort, so it's perfectly safe. And most of all...'

'Your dad would hate it if I went alone,' Bernadette said, not even realising she'd spoken the thought out loud.

'Yep, dad would hate it. He'd tell you that you were ridiculous to go by yourself. That there was no way you could do it.'

'That I'd have a terrible time. I'd be incapable of getting there without him, of sorting it all out, of enjoying it with just my own company,' Bernadette added, both of them on exactly the same page. 'You're right. Nina, honey, I need to have a quick think. I'll call you back in a minute.'

She hung up. Bernadette Manson made snap decisions on the ward day in, day out. She was respected there. In control. Confident in her management and her work. But that confidence and ability to think on her feet evaporated the moment she set foot outside the hospital doors. When it came to her personal life, Bernadette liked to run things through in her head. Thirty years married to a man who controlled every move she made, every decision, every action, had done that to her. It had been a gradual process to leave those constraints behind, but since her divorce four years ago, she'd taken so much joy from slowly savouring possibilities, weighing things up, and then making her own decisions for the first time since she'd walked down the aisle. She'd married when she was barely out of her teens to someone she thought was the man of her dreams. It had taken her a while to learn how wrong she'd been.

To the world, he was Kenneth Manson, the brilliant, esteemed cardiac surgeon and a pillar of the community. A shining light in the medical profession. A devastatingly handsome, debonair man who could charm anyone. To Bernadette, he was a cheating, lying, abusive, vile excuse for a human being.

Nina was right. He'd never believe she would go on a trip like this on her own. If he could see her now, he'd be waiting for her to crumble, to back out and retreat into her corner.

Maybe he was right. Some people were natural solo adventurers, but Bernadette wasn't one of them. When she'd left Kenneth, she'd had a vision of who the new Bernadette was going to be. As fearless, strong and independent outside the hospital as she was when she had her uniform on. The kind of woman who would fly off to Paris for the weekend, after a long week on the ward, just because she could. However, that Bernadette was still missing in action. Instead, she'd slipped into a quiet life, a peaceful one, taking care of anyone who needed her, staying very firmly in her comfort zone. She liked it there. No risk. No drama. No unpredictability.

St Lucia was a whole world of uncertainty. What would she do all day on her own over there? What if something went wrong? If there was a problem? Look what had just happened to Eliza, and she was a young, vital, strong woman with a good head on her shoulders. Not that Bernadette would be climbing drainpipes, but still, anything could happen. She'd be over four thousand miles, and at least two flights, away from home, and there would be no one to help.

No. Going on her own was a crazy idea. Much better to wait and book another break when Sarah was available again. They'd had such lovely plans for long, luxurious days by the pool, some exploring in their rental car, lots of cocktails and sampling the local cuisine. And chat. Lots and lots of chat. Much as Bernadette loved living alone, there was no denying that sometimes she missed having someone to share the day with. Not that Kenneth had ever been that person. He'd created a world paved with eggshells and Bernadette had walked on them every day of their marriage.

Another sip of her lukewarm coffee warded off the shudder that was a frequent accessory to memories of her married life. The chill she felt was enough to make her remember that was then, this was now. She'd broken free of that life. Made a new one. It had taken every single ounce of her strength to do it. Going on holiday alone would prove once and for all that she was no longer constrained by him, his opinions or his power.

But... Oh, bugger. She was flip-flopping back and forth by the second here. Did she really want to go on holiday alone, an idea that filled her with absolute dread, just to spite him, just to defy him, just to prove to herself that she could do anything and everything without him? That was ridiculous.

Sighing, she reached over for her phone and picked it up, then pressed the top name on her favourites list.

Nina answered on the second ring. 'Well then? What's it to be? Are you unpacking your beach ball or are you going to go for it?'

The pause seemed to last for ages, but it was probably only seconds.

What was it to be?

Was today going to be the day she finally broke free of the man who had almost destroyed her?

2

TADGH DONOVAN

Tadgh groaned as the early-morning light came through the blinds of the hotel like a laser beam and focused on a spot right in the middle of his forehead. Either it was the start of a new day or a sniper had him in his sights and could blow him away at any moment. The roaring pain in his head was so crushing, he wasn't sure which option he preferred.

Why? Just why?

Booking a room in a hotel at Dublin airport so they'd be handy for their early-morning flight had been a great idea, so why had they thought it was a good move to go to the hotel bar last night? Why did they have to sink enough Jack Daniel's to intoxicate an army? Why had they stayed in the residents' lounge until 3 a.m.? And why, oh dear God why, did they not consider the fact that they were going to be sitting on two flights today, one of them for almost nine hours on the way to his very own wedding in St Lucia?

Tadgh rolled over, groaning, and caught sight of his two best men, one of them on the other queen bed in the suite, one of them on the couch, both, like him, still fully dressed in the clothes they were wearing the night before.

'Ah, shit,' Tadgh muttered, to no one in particular. 'I think my liver is on its knees. I need something to drink. Or maybe just cut out the middleman and get orange juice fired into me on an IV.'

His brother, Shay – dutifully appointed as best man number one– managed to get one eye open, but it was clearly a struggle. If that man's adoring fans could see him now.

Shay was the lead singer of Home, a rock band that was gaining a huge following in Ireland and a bit of a fanbase in Europe too. They were already popular on the festival scene, and the big record companies were showing interest. Tadgh and his other best man, Conlan, played lead and bass guitar. According to the Irish music press, they were tipped to be the biggest thing since The Script, and Tadgh understood the comparisons. They both wrote their own material and had the same contemporary rock, feck-off big-anthem vibes.

For Shay, the band was a full-time job, but Tadgh and Conlan still worked for a living – Conlan as a tattoo artist and Tadgh as a freelance graphic designer, a job he'd always planned to give up if the music tipped the financial seesaw and began to earn more than the day job.

Shay coughed up a chunk of his lungs before he spoke. 'You're a really shit rock star, you know that? Last night was your final shot at a wild night before you're off the market and there wasn't a lap dancer in sight. Fecking lightweight.'

With that little pearl of wisdom, he stretched up and pushed his long brown hair off his face, and there he was again. Shay Donovan, lead singer, all chiselled jaw and lean, gym-honed body. Since they were teenagers, everyone said that he was a dead ringer for Michael Hutchence from INXS. Tadgh had looked Hutchence up on the internet when they were about fourteen, and even then he could see it. Crazy thing was, they said that about Tadgh now too. Both brothers had the same unruly chocolate hair, the same sallow skin, the same brown eyes. The similarities between them stopped with physical appearance though. Tadgh was laid-back, preferred to fly under the radar. Shay had Noel Gallagher's self-esteem and Liam Gallagher's gob.

Ignoring his brother, Tadgh tossed a pillow and smacked Conlan in the face, causing him to splutter and sit bolt upright, then crease in pain. 'Jesus, I feel rough. Shoot me. Hurry up. It'll be a mercy.'

His best mate since they were kids, Conlan was the guy who could make Tadgh laugh without even opening his mouth. 'I can't shoot you, because then I'll be down a best man and Cheryl will have my balls for messing with the wedding plan.'

'Och, well, if it'll save your balls, I'll find a way to suffer through this.'

'Good man. Right, boys, let's get moving. It's... It's...' For the first time, Tadgh squinted at his watch. 'Feck! It's ten past eight. The flight is in an hour. How the hell did we manage that? I set four alarms on my...' He reached over and snatched his iPhone off the bedside table. '... dead fecking iPhone! Shit. Shit. Shit.'

He jumped out of bed, ignoring the wave of dizziness that almost had him collapsing back down again and grabbed his black leather backpack. Thank God they hadn't unpacked last night. The whole point of staying at the airport hotel was so that they would avoid the rush-hour traffic from the flat they shared just off Grafton Street. He'd be moving into a new home in the same block with Cheryl as soon as they got back from honeymoon. Anyway, they'd reckoned that the hotel plan gave them 100 per cent surety that they'd be on time for the flight to Gatwick, which would mean that – as long as there were no delays – they'd definitely make the connecting flight to St Lucia. He hadn't factored in getting wrecked the night before. What a colossal lesson in stupidity that was turning out to be.

Tadgh checked his watch again. They could still make it if they got to the terminal in the next half-hour. And it was a ten-minute drive away.

'Move, move, move!' he hissed at the other two, who were gradually emerging from their daze and joining the human race.

Shay was typically laconic about the state of emergency. 'Och, if you miss it, it's a sign that you shouldn't be doing it. No idea why you're even thinking about tying yourself down anyway. It's an—'

'Outdated and completely fecking stupid tradition,' Tadgh added for him, repeating the mantra Shay had been spouting since they were about thirteen and he began preparing for a career in rock. Although, back then, he could only play three chords and his voice hadn't dropped, so no matter what he sang, he thought he was Bono, but in reality, he sounded like Aled Jones singing 'Walking In the Air'. 'But, shocker – I couldn't give a crap what you think, so can you just move your arse so I don't get dumped before I even make it up the aisle.'

Tadgh could just imagine Cheryl's reaction if he had to call and tell her he'd missed the flight. Back in those heady teenage days when Shay was channelling Bono – and by 'channelling' Tadgh meant wearing wrap-around sunglasses and spouting pish about how he was going to save the world – fourteen-year-old Tadgh was plucking up the courage to ask Cheryl Marie Downey out on a date. In the end, he only managed it because Conlan was dating her older sister, Cindy, and it was easier to make a foursome than for Cheryl to be third wheel to Conlan and Cindy's Friday nights at the youth club. Almost fifteen years later, the landscape was slightly different. Conlan was now single – his adolescent fling with Cindy had ended after about a month and a half. Years later, she'd gone on to marry Jay, their other school mate and now the road manager of the band. It was all pretty incestuous, but it worked just fine.

Tadgh and Cheryl had outlasted the childhood sweetheart

bracket, and he'd finally got around to proposing to her a few years ago. Not exactly a surprise that she said yes. She'd been dropping engagement hints since they left high school. They'd already postponed the wedding once, a couple of years before, when Tadgh's mum had a heart attack the week before the ceremony. Fifty-two years old. She didn't survive. The following weeks and months had been spent trying to put themselves back together again. Shay had hit the drink pretty hard, and Tadgh had moved back in with his da a few nights a week to keep him company.

Their mam and da had been happily married for over thirty years and they'd had pretty set roles in their relationship. Mam was the whirlwind, the one who laughed the most, danced the longest, loved the fiercest, but would shout the loudest if you put a foot out of line. Their da was the strong, grounded grafter who you could rely on to be a rock of strength, but he was a quiet man and not prone to sharing his emotions. That was fine by Tadgh. After Mam passed, it was enough just to be with him, to work on truck engines in the garage of his da's haulage company, or to sit and watch some rugby on the TV. Gradually, they'd healed, papered over the hole in their hearts. But it was a flimsy cover that blew off sometimes to expose the raw wound underneath.

Their fans thought their biggest hit, 'Everywhere Without You', was written about a broken romance, but the truth was, Tadgh wrote it for his mam and da, trying to put into words the pain of losing her, and how his da had to go on now without the love of his life. The first time Tadgh played it for Jack Donovan was the one and only time he'd ever seen the big man blink back tears.

It had taken a while before Tadgh could even think about rescheduling the wedding again, and when he did, he knew it couldn't be in Dublin. Too sore. Too many memories. So instead, they'd decided to go for a destination wedding and Cheryl had been up for it in a big way. She'd planned the whole thing and had been determined to make the most of the occasion. He'd barely heard from her since she'd gone out to St Lucia a week early with a squad of girlfriends to have a prolonged hen party that, according to their Instagram posts, had consisted mostly of a night out in London on the layover between flights, and then lying in the St Lucia sun with cocktails, and having massages at the spa. However, no amount of alcohol was going to soothe the pain if her bloody groom didn't turn up.

He didn't fancy the bollocking he'd get from her parents and his da either. They'd flown out there yesterday, so they'd be over the jet lag by the ceremony. The one that would only go ahead if they got a fecking shift on.

Tadgh was on his feet, ushering the other two out of the door, dragging his suitcase with one hand and, with the other, hooking his iPhone up to the power bank he kept in his backpack. Pity he hadn't thought about that last night.

Shay belted out the first line of 'Nowhere To Run To' by Martha and the Vandellas as they hightailed it to the elevator, making Tadgh laugh despite the panic. His brother could be an arse, but he loved him beyond words. Most of the time. Right now, he'd love him even more if he could shift a bit faster.

Downstairs in the lobby, Tadgh bolted over to the one receptionist who didn't have guests in front of her. He turned his best smile on the grey-haired woman who hadn't noticed him, too busy concentrating on the screen on her desk. 'Excuse me, I need to get over to the airport in the next ten minutes, or I'm going to miss my flight and my life will be over.'

As she raised her head, her eyes widened in surprise. Tadgh could see that she was forty-ish, with large leopard-print rimmed glasses and dimples in her generous cheeks. 'Dear Lord, you're Shay. From Home. I saw you at a festival last summer...'

Tadgh's spirits rose and fell at exactly the same time. Getting mistaken for his brother was depressingly familiar, but he quickly realised that the recognition could help them out here. 'Nope, I'm Tadgh. But Shay is over there,' he gestured to the sofas in the middle of the lobby, where Shay and Conlan were now parked. 'And we're in a bit of a state here. We need to get to the airport in ten minutes and—'

'Tickets to your next concert and I'll get you there in nine,' she said, a twinkle in her eye, already picking up the phone.

'Done!' Tadgh replied, relief consuming him. 'Send me a DM on Insta and I'll get you sorted. Front row. And I'll tell everyone you saved my life.'

'I suppose marrying me is out of the question?' she chirped back, with a wink.

'Ach, I'm taken. But I'm pretty sure Shay has a free Saturday...'

'Excellent!' She was giggling now as she spoke into the phone. 'Ted, I need the shuttle bus to get my future husband and brother-in-law to the airport, pronto. There's a drink in it for ya later.' As she replaced the phone, she gestured to the front doors. 'Shuttle bus will be at the door in thirty seconds.'

'You are a gem...?' Tadgh fished for the obvious.

'Catriona,' she said.

'Catriona. I love you already and yer not even family yet. Thank you.'

Still grinning, he ran for the doors, signalling for the others to follow.

As promised, Ted was there in a heartbeat, and they made it to the terminal with minutes to spare. They rushed to the luggage drop and checked in their cases just in time, then, with Tadgh finally exhaling and beginning to relax, they made their way to the gate. In the departure lounge, heads rose and eyes stared as the three good-looking, slightly dishevelled guys, all in beat-up jeans, T-shirts, boots, tattoos, steel chains and silver rings, rushed in, just as a ground-crew member announced on the tannoy that they were about to commence boarding.

'Ladies and Gentlemen, our flight to London Gatwick is now preparing to board. Would passengers with small children or those requiring assistance, please make your way to the boarding area now.'

'We won't be called for a while and I'm not standing in that queue. There are some seats over there,' Tadgh announced, forcing Shay and Conlan to do a ninety-degree pivot in the direction of the empty seats, while Tadgh followed right behind them. He saw Shay throw his carry-on holdall over his shoulder, and as he did, the mobile phone in his back pocket worked its way free and fell on the floor. Swooping down, he picked it up, the pause allowing a couple of people to cut in front of him, separating him from the other two. No worries. He could give the phone back to Shay as soon as they got to their seats. Tadgh was just about to tuck it into his backpack when it vibrated. Instinctively, his gaze went to the screen. A new text message. The first lines of it were right there for anyone to see.

I don't think I can do this. We need to tell him as soon as you get here. It wasn't a mistake for me. I love you.

Aw Jesus, what had Shay got himself into now? Honestly, when it came to relationships, the guy was a nightmare. It was a standing joke that his penis had been causing complications and unscrupulous decisions since the minute he learned to use it.

Tadgh was about to laugh it off, to store it up as ammunition for taking the piss out of his brother later, when the next few letters made him stop dead.

Cxoxo.

What? It was so familiar to him that he had almost missed the significance of it. He glanced up again at the top of the message. There was no name in the sender space, just a... a 'C'.

What the fuck?

He read it again.

I don't think I can do this. We need to tell him as soon as you get here. It wasn't a mistake for me. I love you. Cxoxo

That was exactly how Cheryl signed her texts and emails. He'd seen her do it a thousand times. But this couldn't be from Cheryl. His Cheryl. The woman he was going to be marrying in less than forty-eight hours. No. It was a mistake. Hang on, not a mistake, a coincidence. It had to be from someone else who signed their emails the same way. Because the alternative was unthinkable. Something had happened between Cheryl and Shay? That may or may not have been a mistake? She loved him?

No, it definitely couldn't be his Cheryl. Could it?

Clearly, Cxoxo couldn't live with whatever had happened, so it sounded like he was going to find out soon enough.

What the fuck was going on here? Was he about to fly to the woman he loved, the one he wanted to commit to for the rest of his life? Or was today going to be the day that his whole world exploded?

3

HAYLEY FORD

Hayley quickly switched off the track that was playing on her iPhone when Lucas marched into the dressing room of their Richmond upon Thames penthouse, realising that he didn't need to hear Jessie J, Ariana Grande and Nicky Minaj singing 'Bang Bang', or see Hayley doing her best moves, while he was on a work call. It was one of her favourite retro hits. Reminded her of a party on Bondi Beach that had lasted two weeks. Of course, that was before... Before marriage, before respectability, before she had a husband who had perfected the snappy, no-nonsense tone he was using now to shoot out orders on the phone. In her mind, she could picture his ever-efficient secretary, Mrs Banks, taking down notes.

'Okay, Anne, let's schedule in the first egg retrieval for Mrs Jackson on the fifteenth of September. No, make it the sixteenth, just in case there are any flight delays on the way back from this trip. And let's slot in Mrs Smyth and Miss Gold's embryo transfers for the nineteenth. That's the Monday, right? Okay, any changes to that, just update my calendar or call me. Sorry, what was that?'

The whole time he'd been speaking, Lucas had been pulling shoes from one of the shelves on his side of their dressing room. As he listened, he put his hand over the mouthpiece of his mobile phone, so Anne wouldn't hear him speaking. 'Hayley, where are my cufflinks?' he asked, clearly irritated by the fact that they weren't in the brown leather case on the middle shelf of his centre wardrobe.

Dr Lucas Ford hated disorganisation, as witnessed by his side of the room compared to his wife's. On every rail, his clothes were organised into purpose – work suits, casual suits, standalone jackets and trousers, jeans and chinos, polo shirts, and on the column of shelves to the left, perfectly folded jumpers and T-shirts. Within the categories, his religion of order went even further, with each section colour-coded, dark to light. God forbid she ever hung a blue jumper in the middle of the white polo shirts. There was every chance his head would explode.

Hayley's mother, a practising psychologist specialising in the field of sex – always a little nugget of mortification to share with new friends when she was a kid – had told her many times that Lucas's extremely precise, rigid uniformity came from a need for control that wasn't unusual in very successful surgeons and top level consultants in the medical field. Something to do with having other people's lives in their hands. At this point in her analysis, Hayley would mentally switch off just in case her mum, as she occasionally did, would expand on her theories and delve into hypotheses about her son-in-law's sex life. However, on the subject of the relationship between control and success in life-or-death occupations, she probably had a valid point, because in the medical field, Lucas Ford was one of the best. He'd originally trained in general surgery, then found his specialty in gynaecology, before leaving the NHS and taking up a partnership in a prestigious London fertility clinic. Now, he was regarded as one of the top reproductive consultants in the country.

Hayley's side of the wardrobe, however, reflected her personality. It pretty much looked like the high street and a few choice designers had got together and shot all her clothes out of a cannon. It drove her husband crazy. As did her love of loud music, her fondness for eating custard out of the tin and the fact that her long black waves clogged up the shower, no matter how careful she was and how many times she cleared out the drain.

When they'd met on a beach in Ibiza a million years ago, Lucas just out of med school, and Hayley just one year qualified as a teacher, he'd loved her carefree, surfer-chick attitude to life. How long ago that seemed now. And how different those two people had been.

'I've already packed them,' she answered his cufflinks question, then watched as he sighed and returned to his conversation. Sometimes she wasn't sure if she was his wife or his assistant. She told herself he didn't mean to speak so sharply to her – it was difficult to go from spending seventy hours a week being in charge, to coming home and being one equal half of a couple.

As soon as he hung up, he returned his attention to her. 'And my sunglasses? I need the Armani and the Boss ones.'

'Both packed too. All you need to do is throw your electronics into your carry on and we're good to go.'

'Fine. Okay.' His phone began to ring again, and he took the call, marching out of the dressing room as he spoke. Something about damaged ovaries. Hayley didn't listen any more. Once upon a time, she'd found his work totally fascinating. But that was before...

Blocking the thought, she turned her music back on. Not 'Bang Bang' this time. She needed something a bit more raucous. A bit of... Pink. Yep, that would do it. 'Get The Party Started'. If only.

A text came through, letting her know that the car was outside, and she did a final sweep of the room, hoping that if she'd forgotten anything it would suddenly come to her, like some kind of divine message. Nothing. Okay. She checked her packing notes on her phone. Everything had a tick next to it. It wasn't in her inherent personality to be this organised, but, as always, she'd made a massive effort, knowing that Lucas would be severely pissed off if she missed anything important. A forgotten iPhone charger had once caused him to ignore her for a full day in Barcelona.

She caught up with Lucas in the lounge. 'The car is here, darling.' His call over, he actually smiled for the first time since he'd come back from his 5 a.m. run this morning. Who goes running on the day they're flying out on holiday? Surely that meant you were off the clock, ready to relax and have a good time? Or, in her case, check, check, and check again that everything was done. Hayley just didn't get his obsession with running every morning, but she knew better than to question it. He was under so much pressure at work and also at home with their... *situation*... that if he didn't get some endorphins going first thing, he'd be wired tighter than the knot that was in her stomach right now.

Breathe, she told herself. *You haven't forgotten anything. The car is here on time. It's all going to be fine. This holiday is just what you need. What you both need.*

The travelling time from their home in Richmond to Gatwick Airport was close to an hour on a day with no traffic, but at 9 a.m. on a Friday morning, they'd catch the tail end of rush hour. Lucas had suggested booking the car for two hours before they had to be there, just to be on the safe side, so, of course, that's what Hayley had done.

As it turned out, the traffic wasn't too bad, and half an hour in, they were already on the M25 and making good progress. Not that Lucas noticed. His head was buried in his laptop, and his fingers were flying across the keyboard. He never missed an opportunity to get some work done. It was that kind of commitment that had seen him rise through the ranks to become a partner at one of the most respected fertility clinics on Harley Street. The irony still stung.

Watching him now, she had the familiar thought that, on the

face of it, Lucas Ford was the full package. Devastatingly handsome, successful, driven, smart, sociable and – thanks to a massive bonus payout after his first year as partner at the clinic – wealthy too. Three years ago, they'd moved from a small but gorgeous one-bedroom flat in Barnes that Hayley adored, to a glass-fronted pent-house overlooking the river. Of course, Lucas had already said that they'd have to buy a house with a garden if... when...

He snapped his laptop shut and slipped it into his carry-on case. 'Okay, I'm officially on holiday,' he declared, making Hayley smile as she reached for his hand.

'We'll see how long that lasts,' she said, teasing him. 'I bet the laptop will be open again at least twice before we board.'

'Well, excuse me. Sorry if my urgent matters are slightly more critical than your daily traumas of dealing with a squad of first years that can't master a dance move.'

Ouch. Hayley ignored the barb. Her job, teaching dance and drama at a comprehensive school in Ealing, was one of her very favourite things about her life and she adored every day of it. Even the tough ones. The school was underfunded, short-staffed, and in the last week of term she'd had to accessorise a scene from the sixth form's production of *Romeo and Juliet* with a bucket to collect the rain that was pouring through the roof, but still she loved it, because she truly cared about the kids she taught. Even the one who'd spray painted, 'I'd shag Mrs Ford' on the back wall of the school hall, three hours before the parents arrived for the lower school's end-of-term production of *Calamity Jane*. The Deadwood Stage had to hustle down to B&Q quick-style to get a pot of white emulsion to cover it up.

Without thinking, Hayley dropped her head down onto his shoulder, then lifted it again almost immediately as Lucas reached forward into his bag for his mobile phone. Of course. Because God forbid he should be without an electronic device for more than ten seconds. It wasn't as if they were going on holiday for the first time in two years. It wasn't as if he could even consider relaxing and just being them, the way they used to be before careers, pressures, adulting got in the way. It wasn't as if he could just love her. Right now. Right here. Just the way she was.

The movement of his finger told her he was scrolling through the phone calendar, making calculations.

'Okay, so I was thinking that we come back on the twenty-sixth, your period is due second of September, so we can test that day if you're late and if it's...' he paused, and Hayley felt a massive stab of guilt as she saw yet again how difficult this was for him.

'Negative,' she added gently.

'Yes. Although I'm sure it won't be. But if it is, then we can start the next round of IVF immediately afterwards.'

He was speaking in his very best sympathetic and caring bedside manner, but it didn't sting any less. There it was. The guilt. The shame. The anxiety. The utter devastation. Dr Lucas Ford, eminent fertility specialist, and his own wife had been trying and failing to get pregnant for five years now. Four rounds of IVF. Dozens of tests. Countless natural remedies. Every single old wives' tale. A whole lot of desperate hope. Yet, nothing.

The hardest thing was, as all the tests had confirmed, there was no identifiable cause. Naturally, he'd been tested and his sperm were high achievers, just like the rest of him, so the issue was down to her, but the problem was that... well, there didn't seem to be a definitive reason. Unexplained infertility. Nothing they could fix. Her ovaries started the party every month, but the rest of her reproductive system just refused to accept the invitation. Every month, Lucas would monitor her stats, check her cycle, they'd have sex at peak ovulation and yet... nothing. And every month she had to see the crippling disappointment on his face when her periods came. He barely spoke to her in the days after it now, and she'd come to terms with the fact that she was no longer just his wife, she was the patient that let him down, month in and month out.

That's why they were taking this holiday. Lucas had never taken more than a week off, but this was a last-ditch attempt to get pregnant naturally before the next round of treatment. Two weeks of sun, sand and sex. A chance to reconnect and just be them again, without all the pressure and the highs of hope and the lows of disappointment.

'Darling, are you even listening to me?' Hayley was sure that it just came out a bit more brittle than he'd intended.

'Sorry, yes. I'm listening. That all sounds fine, but I just hope that... well, you know. I'm telling myself this is going to work.'

He took her hand, finally showing a bit of tenderness, and for a moment he reminded her of the old Lucas, the one she'd met on that beach in Ibiza.

'I hope so,' he said. 'For both our sakes.'

She wasn't sure what he meant by that, but she didn't push it, a firm believer in the old saying that you should never ask a question that you don't want to hear the answer to. She had a horrible feeling that this whole conversation was straying into 'better left unsaid' territory.

A silence descended as they both sat with their own thoughts until the moment the car pulled up outside the terminal building.

This was it, Hayley told herself. Positive thinking. It was all going to work out. They were going to go to St Lucia and by the time she came back she would already be pregnant.

Today was the first day of the holiday that was going to change their lives.

4

DEV ROBBINS

Dev tossed four pairs of Calvins, three random T-shirts and some shorts into his carry-on case. He was pretty sure they were clean. Although, he might have worn one pair of shorts when he was playing basketball with some of the lads down at the sports centre the other night. Sod it. He could get them washed when he got there. Or maybe he wouldn't even be there long enough to run them through a spin cycle.

Over on the bed, his flatmate, Lizzy, was watching him with mild amusement. 'You're really doing this?'

'I'm really doing this,' he confirmed, scratching his head as he cast a glance around the room looking for some kind of miracle to occur. *Dear God of Shite Packing Skills, let everything I need find its way into this suitcase in the next ten minutes, otherwise I'm bound to leave without something vital.*

'Do you want me to tell you that you've lost your mind now, or will I wait until we're on the way to the airport?'

Dev lunged towards the pair of trainers peeking out from under the base of the bed. 'Tell me when we're on the way to the airport.

Right now, I'm in "Packing" mode. "Castigation and Prophecies of Doom" mode will have to wait.'

That made Lizzy laugh. It had always been the way with them. Next-door neighbours since they were kids, Lizzy was a year younger, but somewhere around the age of five, her maturity level had fast-forwarded at least ten years and he'd never quite caught up. She was the sorted one. The one who knew what she wanted, had the courage of her convictions and who made her dreams happen.

The perfect example of that was a cold night in 2008, aged around sixteen, when they had sunk a whole bottle of cider in her parents' shed before she went in and announced that she wasn't entering the family business and was going to be an artist instead. 'But we're lawyers, darling,' her mother had replied, aghast. Lizzy had launched into an argument that a Crown Court barrister would have been proud of and eventually won the battle. Now she made really cool digital art that she sold around the world on every online platform you could mention, and her annual profit was more than Dev had earned in the last two years writing sports features for the *Essex Tribune*.

Going into journalism had seemed like such a great idea when he was thirteen and choosing the subjects he wanted to study at school. It was an even better plan after a few ciders in Lizzy's family shed, when he'd waffle on about all the world-class sporting events he'd get to write about. Not such a great idea when he was twenty-one and got an entry-level job on the paper that mostly involved making tea and phoning irate pensioners to discuss their dispute with their neighbours over a thirty-foot leylandii. It got a little better at twenty-five, when Bob, who ran the sports desk, retired and Dev got his job. But by the time he was thirty, Dev knew without a doubt it had been the crappest life plan ever, because by then newspaper circulation had been dropkicked out of the park. Sure, the website that had been developed a few years ago had helped make it slightly more interesting and brought in more readers, but management had yet to work out how to make it generate a profit. The result was more cuts, more work for less pay and a staff morale that was so low they'd cancelled the Secret Santa at Christmas because they couldn't be arsed.

Not that Dev would be there much longer, because, well, he had a plan. Somewhere in between watching approximately three thousand four hundred and forty-seven romantic comedies and every episode of *Friends* at least ten times with Lizzy, he'd started writing about things that didn't involve two teams of sweaty men chasing a rubber ball. Romantic stories. Sweet beginnings. Slushy endings. All the clichés that no one cared about because when the titles rolled at the end, or the last page was turned, you felt a bit better about yourself.

A romcom novel. That's what he really wanted to write. Sure, there were not many blokes in that line of work, but as far as he was concerned that was a plus, because it made him unique. That was where his confidence ended though. When it came to actually writing the book, he was racked with self-doubt. Over the last few years, he'd made at least a dozen stabs at it, but he'd abandoned every one of them because they weren't original enough, or didn't have a shock twist, or a storyline that would keep readers guessing.

Not surprising really, given that his entire romantic history consisted of a few one-night stands, several casual relationships that never made it past the one-year anniversary, and his most recent debacle, a ten-month engagement to Poppy on the entertainment desk that had ended after he found out she'd slept with Robbie Williams. Not the one from Take That – the one from a Take That tribute act who'd charmed the knickers off Dev's fiancée at a girls' night out in a nightclub function suite in Basildon. Dev had no idea what they were called, but in his mind, they'd be forever known as Fake Twat. It had taken a solid, self-pitying, beer-soaked week with Lizzy and the whole of Jennifer Aniston and Sandra Bullock's back catalogues to even begin to restore his faith in love again.

'She didn't know the real you, anyway,' Lizzy had told him gently, in the middle of *The Proposal*. 'All she saw was the blokey, footie-playing journalist who could pass for Ryan Reynolds on her Instagram.'

'Only if the pics were taken in a dim light,' he'd muttered. He got that all the time though. There were three little kids in the next street who were convinced he was Deadpool. He was pretty sure their noses were pressed up against their windows every night, waiting for him to race past them in red and black Lycra.

Anyway, with such a tragic relationship history, it was no surprise that he couldn't write the great romantic novel.

Until now.

Because, last weekend, the answer had, quite literally, dropped in his lap.

His packing slowed considerably as, for what might have been the hundredth time that week, he replayed the previous Saturday night in his head.

He and Lizzy had been up in town with a group of mates from their college days. They'd had a great time at a Greek restaurant, doing some highly therapeutic plate smashing, then Lizzy had dragged them all to a swanky new country-themed bar that had commissioned her to design all their wall art. She'd immersed herself in the theme and had been wearing bootcut jeans, big buckle belts and silver bangles up both her arms since she'd started working on it. The place was mobbed, the music was loud, and after a few more beers, he'd finally decided that Poppy deserved the bloke from Fake Twat and he wasn't going to care. Time to stop feeling shit and move on.

'What are you smiling at?' Lizzy had barked over the sound of Chris Stapleton grinding out 'Hard Livin', when she'd returned from the bar with another round of drinks.

He'd knocked back the shot of tequila she'd just placed in front of him. 'I'm smiling at the decision to not give a fuck about what happened with Poppy.'

'Ooh, that's an excellent decision. I'm very happy to drink to that,' she'd agreed, picking up her shot and throwing it back too. 'What's the plan then? Single life? Taking a break? Tinder?'

Her words had drifted off as he'd stopped listening, suddenly aware that the most beautiful girl he'd ever seen was walking towards them, presumably on the way from the large group of riotous ladies who were celebrating something at the table on the right of where Dev and Lizzy were sitting, to the bar on the left of them. If that was indeed where she was going, she was about to walk straight past him. She was three metres away, when Chris Stapleton left the building, and the opening bars of Miranda Lambert and Elle King's 'Drunk' had struck a beat so loud, it had bounced off the wall.

Two metres. Lizzy had shrieked, 'I bloody love this song. Come dance with me!' as she'd jumped off her stool.

One metre. Lizzy had somehow managed to accidentally elbow the approaching goddess, who'd then stumbled on her skyscraper heels and begun to go down. Dev had reached over, trying to save her, she'd grasped his outstretched arms, and in what could only be described as a startling feat of acrobatics crossed with a miracle, she'd twisted around, swayed and fallen right onto his lap. Or, rather, his right knee, but it was close enough.

It had taken a moment for all three of them to process what had just happened, but the stranger got there first and broke into a low, sexy laugh. 'I do apologise. I seem to be invading your personal space.'

Dev had shrugged, acting nonchalant. 'Not at all. This happens to me all the time. I'm pretty much public property.'

That had made her laugh even more, her long sheet of ash blonde hair falling behind her as she'd tipped her head back.

'Maybe I'll just park myself here for a minute then. I mean, take advantage of the public property.'

Out of the corner of his eye, he'd registered Lizzy rolling her eyes, then summoning their mate, Mike, to the dance floor. Nothing ever stood in her way when she wanted to dance. Not even the sudden arrival of a five-foot-eight-inch tall woman with an incredibly intoxicating Irish accent.

Dev had fallen in love at that second. Everything that had happened over the next few hours only confirmed it. She was his person. At the risk of sounding like a complete twat (not the Fake variety), he'd always known that his true love was out there. For a while, he'd thought it was Poppy, but he'd been kidding himself, because he'd never felt like this. This was like a shot through the heart. And yep, he did realise that Jon Bon Jovi might have come up with that line first.

His legs had gone numb after about twenty minutes, but he didn't care. Despite lots of hollers and nudges and knowing nods from her friends at the other table, they'd swapped brief stories of how they'd come to be in that bar at that moment. She and her mates were flying out the next morning to St Lucia, to prepare for a wedding the following weekend at a swanky resort. He'd recognised the name of it, because one of the former *Love Island* contestants, a fellow Essex boy, had taken his last showmance there, and the paper had run some pap pics.

Not that Dev cared, because all he could do was sink further into her eyes.

After a couple more hours of drinking, dancing, and being glued to each other's sides, she'd come back to his place and spent the night. It had been mind-blowing. If it was a romcom, there would have been fireworks. And they'd have been followed by a heartbreaking violin solo when he woke up the next morning and discovered she was gone, with only a note left behind to make him smile and convince him the previous eight hours had been real.

'Hello! Yo!' Lizzy's insistent demand for his attention took his mind off the twist of his guts, the one that happened every time he thought about how wonderful that night was, and how terrified he was that she might not feel the same. He tossed a pair of pool sliders into the holdall and then looked around the room for his charger. He was almost done. Bag packed.

'Are you even listening to me?' she prodded, amused.

'Of course, I am. I always listen to you. You're on the same "must listen at all times" level as my mother and Reese Witherspoon. I like you the best though.'

'Aaaaw, do you mean that?' she chirped, grinning.

'No. Reese probably wins it. But you're definitely second... Unless it's Mother's Day.'

Lizzy cackled with laughter and threw a scrunched-up pair of socks at him. He picked them up and shoved them in his bag. 'You never get less annoying.' She'd been telling him that since they were about eight, so it wasn't a newsflash.

'I realise this. It's a gift. Anyway, what were you saying before, when I was trying to mentally escape back to the giddy bliss of that last Saturday night, to a woman who didn't think I was wholly irritating?'

Lizzy's bangles rattled as she pulled her wild mane of blonde curls up into a high ponytail and secured it with a band that she slipped off her fingers. 'I was asking what her full name was. I just realised that all this week you didn't say. I just need to know so that I can give the information to Interpol and the *Crimewatch* team when you vanish during this completely fricking insane mission to find a stranger you picked up in a bar a week ago.'

Again, thinking about her made him smile. Everything about her had that effect. Her voice. Her touch. The incredible, mind-blowing sex they'd had that night. Twice. And of course, the note she'd left the next morning.

It was written on the top of the Nike shoe box that had been lying at the side of his bed.

Had to go for flight. Thanks for catching me last night. Cxoxo

The box had made it to the recycling bin, but he'd torn off the lid with her words on it and stuck it to the fridge, where he'd read it a thousand times as his plan of what to do next had unfolded in his head.

'I only got her first name. Cheryl,' he replied, the corners of his mouth turning up when he said it. 'She never told me her surname. I didn't ask.'

This was bonkers. It was so out of character for him. It was impulsive. Daring. Bold. And the perfect romcom twisty tale, complete with drama, suspense and, of course, happy ending.

Because today was the day that Dev Robbins was going to St Lucia to track down the Cheryl of his dreams.

10 A.M. – NOON

5

BERNADETTE

There was still time to back out of this nonsense. What was she thinking? Why would she want to go away for two weeks, entirely on her own, when she could spend the time at home relaxing in the garden and having the kids over in the afternoons to give Nina a break?

The beeping horn of one of those little terminal transport vehicles made her jump as it moved past her, a smiley couple on the seat facing backwards. Bernadette briefly contemplated hitching a ride, but changed her mind. She could do this, even if she could feel the sweat buds popping out on her forehead.

The connection between her flight from Glasgow to Gatwick, and then the next one to St Lucia was always going to be tight, but, bloody hell, she hadn't realised it would require a sprint. Yet another sign that she should just park her arse, get a cup of tea, then book the first flight back up to Glasgow.

She'd kept her earphones in, just in case Sarah tried to get in touch with her with news, so, feeling very trendy and high-tech, she just pressed a button on the left one when it began to vibrate. Her son, Stuart, had taught her how to do that. It had taken a whole afternoon, and a couple of accidental calls to people in her contacts list, but she'd mastered it eventually. And the people in her local Chinese takeaway had been very understanding about the six calls in the space of an hour. She'd ordered a chow mein for two on the last call by way of apology.

'Hello?'

'Dear God, Mum, why are you breathless? Are you being chased? Should I hang up and call the police?' The very same Stuart who had taught her to use the earphones. If she'd known they'd become weapons of sarcasm and teasing, she wouldn't have bothered.

'No, son, I'm in training for the next Olympics. Middle-aged speed walking. It's a new category.' People passing her probably wondered why she was grinning. Stuart had that effect on her. A newly qualified criminal lawyer, he worked at a legal aid firm, defending everyone from shoplifters to a bloke who was being prosecuted by the council for having sheep in the garden of his terrace house.

'Glad to hear you're getting new hobbies. I believe solo travelling is on the list now too.'

Bernadette panted. 'Honestly, you and your sister can spread news quicker than CNN. I'm at Gatwick. Just going from arrivals to departures. I've got less than an hour, and I'm going to have to stop soon for oxygen in case my lungs explode.'

There was a warm chuckle at the other end. 'I'm glad you're still going, Mum. How many times have you changed your mind in the last hour?'

'I reckon I'm in triple figures.' She sighed. 'Am I being crazy? I was just thinking I could come back and have a nice relaxing holiday in my garden. I mean, what am I going to do in St Lucia for two weeks?'

'Think how wonderful it is and how far you've come in the last five years.'

'I don't need twenty-quid cocktails in the Caribbean to know that though,' she protested.

'Mum, do you remember the last time we went on holiday? All four of us?'

Bernadette's body was charging forwards, but her mind was rewinding. Of course, she remembered. Kenneth had cancelled the trip to Barbados two or three times due to his work, so when they'd finally managed to go, Bernadette had mixed feelings. She was glad for the kids that they were going to get to spend a couple of weeks on holiday with their dad. By then, Nina was about seventeen and Stuart was ten and Kenneth worked such long hours that he barely saw them most weeks. On the other hand, though, it meant that she had to spend fourteen days with him too. In a row. With no escape. Keeping up the appearances of a happy marriage was just about bearable at home. She'd been doing it for so long, that she was well-practised in the art of Pretending You Still Love The Man You Married, of keeping the peace, of tolerating his rants and his ego. It was worth it, she'd told herself. He loved the kids and they worshipped the ground he walked on. He always had a kind word and a hug for them. Great father, terrible husband. Now, Bernadette knew that they saw the other side of him too, but back then, she thought she'd shielded them from it. No one could shield her though.

On that flight, Nina and Stuart had been sitting in the two seats in front of them in business class. Bernadette would have been perfectly happy with economy, but the great Dr Kenneth Manson wouldn't travel any other way. He'd completely ignored her for the whole flight, keeping his head in his book, except for when the very attractive flight attendant came by with a drink from the bar or their meals. She was tall, slim, glamorous, with her rich tawny hair in an elegant chignon at the nape of her long, thin neck. Bernadette had felt herself improve her own posture every time she saw her coming, then had watched as Kenneth flashed her his beaming, perfect white smile. She didn't blame the attendant for flirting back. Kenneth didn't wear a wedding ring and he had barely acknowledged her since they'd taken their seats, so the poor woman probably had no idea that he was sitting next to his wife.

Bastard.

Still, Bernadette had kept her cool. It wasn't worth it. And, truth be told, by that time, she honestly didn't care. As long as he didn't upset the kids, he could do whatever he wanted. If he was giving someone else attention – of whatever kind – then he was leaving her alone.

He'd disappeared a couple of times during the flight, presumably to stretch his legs, but Bernadette had just kept her headphones on so she could listen to some retro eighties tunes, while losing herself in the latest Danielle Steel novel. Living in Ms Steel's world was inherently more enjoyable than living in Kenneth's.

Their first day at the resort was a beauty, with sun, sea, golden sands and squeals of laughter from Nina and Stuart as they attempted to master windsurfing and failed for the first hundred or so times. Kenneth was out there with them, the perfectly formed Alpha male, his body chiselled to perfection with his daily gym workouts and cycling. There was no denying they'd aged differently. Kenneth could pass for someone ten years younger, but Bernadette... she was realistic about what two children and twenty years of night shift on a busy A&E ward had done to her. She'd gone from stunning to... softer around the middle. Comfortable. Pretty. She looked exactly like what she was – a middle-aged working mum who didn't have time for a whole lot of self-care. But she was happy with that. She didn't mind. She loved her job, adored her children and she'd found a way to deal with Kenneth – she just told herself that every passing day was a day closer to the kids leaving home and then she'd pack her bags and be free of him.

That day at the beach, she wasn't letting Kenneth get under her skin. When the afternoon sun had faded, they'd showered and changed, then the kids went off to the resort's teenagers' disco, Nina sulking a little because, at seventeen, she felt far too mature and sophisticated. Didn't stop her spending an hour doing her make-up, right enough. As soon as they were gone, Kenneth had announced he was going for a walk, and Bernadette had felt the strands of tension in her shoulders loosen. If he was with her, he'd only ignore her, criticise her or want to have sex, and none of those options appealed. Instead, she'd got a couple more hours of peaceful bliss on her own, sitting out on the terrace with Danielle Steel and a gin and tonic. Heaven. So much so, that she'd lost track of time until Nina and Stuart had returned, faces beaming, all full of chat and plans they'd made with the people they'd met at the disco. It was only then that Bernadette had realised Kenneth had been gone for hours. She was about to suggest they go find him, when Nina got there with the answer first.

'We saw Dad,' she'd blurted. Bernadette had spotted a slight flicker of apprehension in her daughter's eyes and braced herself. Something wasn't right. She was chewing her bottom lip, a sure sign that she was worried about something.

'Did you, love? Where was he?'

'He's... erm... in the bar with that lady from the plane. We passed them on the way back, but he didn't see us.'

Do not react. Do not react. A career in A&E gave her every tool for masking her feelings and being calm in the face of a crisis, heart-break or fury.

Bernadette aimed for nonchalance. 'The lady from the plane?'

Nina's hands were fidgeting and there was a line of worry between her eyebrows. Bernadette could see that she knew exactly what this all meant. 'Yeah, the air hostess.'

Bernadette had wanted to close her eyes. There was no shock. No surprise. Of course, that's where he was. She should have guessed. The man couldn't help himself – just one of the many reasons she despised him. That didn't matter now though, because there were two choices: go over there and announce to everyone within earshot that he was a lowlife cheating bastard, tip the largest beverage she could find over his lowlife cheating head and tell his chirpy date that she could shag him until his lowlife cheating penis fell off... or bluff it out and reassure the kids that everything was fine. The first one was oh so tempting, but...

'Ah, yes, she was lovely and invited us for drinks, but I fancied a couple of hours of peace. It was nice of your dad to go, though.'

The relief in Nina's face was instant and Bernadette had watched as her beautiful girl processed that it was okay. There was no big drama. This was fine.

Bernadette had felt her rage rising further, but again, covered it flawlessly. How bloody dare he? It was one thing risking their marriage and humiliating her, but to stress the kids like that? Selfish git. How could he risk hurting their family? Because he was a spoiled, egotistical, nasty bastard, that was why. The ultimate narcissistic control freak, who thought of himself over everyone else. Right at that moment, she had never hated him more.

Now, years later, as Bernadette bustled towards the departure gate for the flight to St Lucia, sweat running down her back and into the waistband of the trendy skinny jeans that Nina had talked her into buying, her opinion of Kenneth hadn't changed, even though the hatred was long gone. He couldn't hurt them now.

Couldn't damage their lives. He'd done that time and time again, but she'd survived him, beaten him, lived to tell the tale.

Now it was time for her.

Stuart's voice sat somewhere between amused and concerned as it blasted into her earpiece. 'Mum? Mum?'

'Sorry, son, think I had a dodgy signal there. Yes, I remember that holiday. Every moment of it.'

'Then you'll remember that Dad was a complete tosser to you.'

She'd been so sure back then that she was protecting them, but she knew now that they'd seen far more than she'd ever realised.

She tried to keep it light and teasing. 'I do remember that, thank you, son. Good of you to remind me.'

'Well, that tells you everything,' he said. 'That's why you need to do this, Mum. He took all those incredible experiences away from you. Don't let this one go, either.'

Bernadette groaned. 'Och, I much preferred you when you were a huffy teenager who kept his thoughts to himself. All this wisdom is so overrated.'

His laughter made her smile. How lucky was she to have somehow made these two incredible adults? Not perfect, because no one was, but wonderful all the same, in their very own perfectly imperfect way. Yes, she'd hated Kenneth, but she would always be grateful for the family they'd raised together.

'Right, you can stop nagging me. I'm pretty sure I've lost five pounds and my lungs could explode at any moment, but I'm at the gate.'

'And you're going to get on the flight?'

Bernadette was momentarily distracted by three tall blokes in jeans and leather jackets, two of them wearing dark glasses, who were sitting on the row of seats to her right. They looked like rock stars. Miserable rock stars, but pretty cool all the same. Exactly the kind of guys that Kenneth, her uptight, self-important conformist ex-husband, would be horrified by. For some reason, that made her smile.

'Yes, I'm going on the flight, son. I agree with you and your sister. It's definitely time I had a little adventure of my own.'

6

TADGH

'What's up with you today, bro?' Shay asked him, digging his elbow into Tadgh's ribs. 'You're acting like a bloke on his way to his funeral, not his fecking wedding.'

Tadgh fought back the urge to grab his brother's intrusive elbow and snap it in two and instead he shrugged and moved to the free seat on the other side of Conlan. However, his brain was still back at the moment he'd seen that text.

I don't think I can do this. We need to tell him as soon as you get here. It wasn't a mistake for me. I love you. Cxoxo

Shay had turned around a split second after Tadgh had retrieved the phone from the floor, but Tadgh had already clicked the button to clear the screen, so his brother wouldn't know he'd read it. In some ways, he wished he hadn't. It had been on a permanent loop in his mind for every minute of the flight from Dublin to Gatwick, during the transit from arrivals to the departure gate, made longer by having to go through security for a second time. They'd made it to the gate with only a few minutes to spare before boarding was due to start. Every single second of that time, he'd wanted to say something, wanted to challenge his brother, to make him read the text aloud and get some kind of explanation, but it was so unfathomable, so absolutely shocking, that Tadgh was desperately trying to absorb it, to excuse it, to find some way that this could be something other than the very obvious first conclusion, that his fiancée was shagging his brother. He felt himself retch at the very thought of that, and Conlan backed away slightly and dealt out a warning. 'Man, don't puke on me. I just got this jacket cleaned.'

In any other moment, his best mate's priorities would have made Tadgh laugh. Not today.

The irony was that if the tables were turned, Shay would have punched Tadgh's lights out first and asked questions later. That had always been his brother's way. They'd been in school scrapes and bar fights on too many occasions throughout their lives, and every single one of them had been kicked off by Shay's temper. It used to drive their poor mam crazy, God rest her. She hated it when her boys fought. Jesus, what would she make of this? She'd drag Shay out of here by the ear and berate him, then pray all the way to the chapel for his mercy.

Despite every reservation, and every cold chill of dread, Tadgh was going to have to say something though and there would be one of two outcomes – either there was a simple explanation, in which case he could stop freaking out, or Shay would admit something had happened, in which case... in which case... Tadgh had no fecking idea what he would do.

Fuck it, he couldn't sit next to him on a plane for nine hours and not say anything. 'Shay, what was...'

Bing-bong. The sound of the tannoy drowned out Tadgh's words and made his hung-over brain rattle inside his skull. If his head was in a cartoon, there would be a close-up of his eyeballs shattering like windows after a ramraid.

'Would Mr Tadgh Donovan make himself known to one of the gate staff as soon as possible please.'

What the hell? The three of them looked at each other to check if they'd all heard the same thing. The puzzled faces on the other two told him they had. What now? Had Cheryl texted the airline too?

Please don't let my fiancé on that flight because I'm shagging his brother.

And how could his brain even joke about this? Self-preservation. He couldn't take it seriously. There was no way this could be happening. He'd been going out with this woman since he was fourteen years old. She wouldn't do that to him. If she had those kinds of flaws in her personality he'd have spotted them, surely? This was all a mistake. It had to be.

At that very moment, Shay's phone beeped again, and he glanced down at it, then flushed, his eyes darting from side to side. Tadgh had seen that expression before: every single time Shay had been in trouble since they were kids. Every single time he was about to lie. Every single time he'd fucked up.

That's when Tadgh knew. Or got as close to knowing without hearing it with his own ears, or seeing it with his own eyes. Shay and Cheryl. Holy fuck.

'Who's that?' Tadgh asked him through gritted teeth, daring him to say it. *Come clean. Be a fucking man about it.*

'Eh, just a... eh... promoter about a gig I'm trying to arrange for next month. Down at the Loading Dock,' Shay blustered, mentioning a club in Cork that they'd been trying to get into for a while.

He was lying. Tadgh knew it. Shay knew it. Conlan had no idea, but if his newly cleaned jacket got messed up in an altercation between the two men on either side of him, he'd know it then.

Bing-bong.

'Would Mr Tadgh Donovan make himself known to one of the gate staff as soon as possible please.'

He'd almost blocked that out the first time, too focused on what was going on right in front of him. This time, though, he suddenly welcomed the excuse to get up, to get some air, to have a distraction before he did something that he would absolutely regret. Or maybe he wouldn't.

Maybe there was still some innocent explanation. He could hear his mother's voice in his head the minute that thought left. 'Och, Tadgh son, you always see the best in people,' she'd said to him once, after Shay had been brought home for shoplifting three packets of Monster Munch and a bottle of Coke from the supermarket in town. Tadgh hadn't been with him, but still he'd insisted his brother was innocent. 'It's your biggest blessing. I just hope you never find out that sometimes people don't deserve the benefit of the doubt,' his mam had added, before marching back into the living room and reading the riot act to his brother.

'Hi, I'm Tadgh Donovan,' he said to the very attractive lady in the blue suit at the departure gate desk. Her dark hair was tied back in a low bun, her lips the same bright red as her scarf. Tadgh didn't even notice that her smile was a little flirtatious as she spoke to him.

'I'm afraid we've had a slight problem with the seating, Mr Donovan,' she said, and for a second Tadgh felt a ripple of relief. He was being offloaded. Delayed to the next flight. Or maybe cancelled altogether. Which would solve absolutely nothing, but it would give him breathing space to think and time for his Tennessee-whisky-soaked brain to stop throbbing and start processing the morning's curve balls.

'That's okay. I can wait until the next flight,' he shrugged, registering her surprise. Clearly passengers didn't normally react in that way when the rug on their flight to an exotic holiday destination was whipped out from under their feet.

'No, no,' she protested gently. 'We still have a seat for you, but I'm afraid we're going to have to separate you from your fellow travellers as the seat you were allocated when you checked in is no longer available.'

'Oh. Okay.'

Pros and cons.

Cons. He was still on the flight and would be in an aluminium tube hurtling through the skies while in close proximity to his brother for the next nine hours.

Pros. At least he wouldn't be sitting next to him. He didn't care if he was stuck up the back somewhere, wedged in between two strangers who swapped stories about their medical history over the last three decades (that had happened to him once on a flight to New York – he'd learned more than he ever needed to know about irritable bowels and gastric reflux). He actually felt sorrier for the people he'd be stuck with, since he hadn't had a chance to shower since their epic bender last night. He probably smelled like a bar room floor after a St Paddy's Day lock-in and he definitely didn't feel like making up for it by being scintillating company.

'We've actually found you a seat in premium economy, to compensate for the inconvenience. Here's your new boarding pass. Seat 13F. It's right at the front of the cabin. A passenger on that row upgraded to first class on check-in, so we have a spare seat. Is that okay with you?'

Typical. He'd never flown anything other than basic economy in his life and now he was getting upgraded on the one flight he was seriously considering bailing out of. On any other journey, on any other day, he'd be well chuffed. For a second, his eyes gazed upwards, wondering if this was his mam trying to keep the peace. She always said that if there were miracles to be done after she passed, she would be the very one to do them.

'Yeah, sure, that's okay.'

'Actually, we're just about to start boarding now, so you can go on through if you'd like to.'

'Sure. Just let me grab my bag. And thank you.'

'You're very welcome,' she said, with a genuine smile that he reciprocated. She'd never know what she had just saved him from, and he was grateful.

He strolled back over to where Shay and Conlan were looking up at him expectantly. 'Well?'

'Problem with my seat so they've moved me.'

'Not a bad thing, you smell like a skip,' Shay fired back, with a grin that Tadgh was suddenly desperate to punch right off his face.

Down at his sides, his fists were clenching. Tadgh distracted himself from the violent urges by reaching down and picking up his backpack.

Shay was oblivious to his latent fury. 'Result for us,' he said, fist-bumping Conlan.

Conlan laughed and returned the bump.

Emotional awareness and detection of undercurrents had never been one of his brother's or his mate's strengths. Probably just as well.

'Right back at ya,' Tadgh said, slinging his backpack over one shoulder and heading back over to the desk, just as they were beginning to board the first group of passengers. The woman he'd spoken to spotted him and beckoned him over, running his boarding pass through the scanner as she checked his passport.

'Have a great flight, Mr Donovan.'

'Thanks,' he replied, as she handed back his documents.

He carried on moving, down an escalator to the entrance to the gangway, then along the steel tube on to the plane.

The flight attendant at the door checked his boarding card, then gestured to his left. 'Straight across here, and then turn right – it's the first row of the next cabin.'

Tadgh gave him a nod of thanks and headed on through. He was the first to arrive in that whole section, so he detoured into the toilet, opened up his backpack and pulled out a fresh T-shirt. He stripped last night's one off, washed his face and his torso, brushed his teeth and ran some water through his hair. He felt a solid 30 per cent better. He stuck on some deodorant (the stick one he always travelled with), then pulled on the new black T-shirt, which, to the untrained eye, looked exactly like the old black T-shirt. He ran his fingers through his long hair again, as he stared in the mirror. Had he really been a complete tit? Was he about to get crapped on from a great height by everyone he loved? Or did he have all this completely wrong? Never, not for a single second had he doubted Cheryl in the years they'd been together. Never. Now he had no idea whether that was blind faith or stupidity. And if it was true, what would it mean for them, for his family, for their lives, for the band... He had to force himself not to go down that hole.

He blew his cheeks out as he sighed and got his stuff together, then headed back out to his seat. The row was still empty. Maybe it would be that way the whole flight. God, he hoped so. The last thing he wanted to do was to make small talk with strangers. All he wanted to do was sleep, but first, he pulled out his phone. Maybe he could get some answers from the other side of the situation. He began to type out a text. It took him a dozen false starts before he settled on,

Hey babe, how's the sun?

No point in going in strong when he didn't know the facts. This had to be a misunderstanding. It just had to be. And if it was, the last thing he needed to do was piss off his bride by displaying a rampant lack of trust, forty-eight hours before their wedding.

He carried on typing, trying desperately to think what he'd have said if he hadn't picked up Shay's phone that morning. It would have been something like...

On the plane, taking off soon. Just thinking I can't wait to marry you.

Not strictly true at this point, but he had to act normal until he knew for sure that there was definitely something *abnormal* going on here.

Just checking you've no plans to jilt me at the altar?

It was an old standing joke between them. She used to say she'd definitely be there as long as Adam Levine from Maroon 5 didn't swoop in and snap her up first. He was her rock star hall pass, the one person she could have a fling with if the opportunity ever presented itself. His was Rihanna.

He hadn't realised that Cheryl might have another hall pass a bit closer to home.

He'd know. Whatever she texted next would tell him the answer.

...

The three little dots that popped up showed she was texting back.

She'd fess up or she would say something that would reassure him that this was all going to be okay. Fine. Completely good.

'Excuse me, I think I'm in the seat next to you...' A voice distracted him, and he glanced up at the woman who had appeared beside him, just as his phone pinged with the incoming text.

Tadgh stood up, then instinctively offered to help the new arrival with her bag, while trying not to show that all he wanted to do was ignore the world until he'd read Cheryl's answer, words that were, right now, in the palm of his hand.

7

HAYLEY

Hayley could see that Lucas was already bristling with irritation within five minutes of waiting to check their bags in. He despised waiting for anything. Changed days. When they'd first met, and in their first couple of years together, he'd been so much more laid-back. If they got held up, they'd just plonk themselves down on their backpacks and chat or listen to music while they waited. Delays hadn't pleased him back then, but, at least, he didn't go straight to grinding teeth and darting eyes, searching out someone important he could complain to. Sometimes the change in him still surprised her. It had started as soon as he began getting a bit of power at work, and sometimes Hayley wasn't sure any more which Lucas was the real one – the cool guy she'd met back then, surfing at the beach, or the one who was so wrapped up in his own mind that he was wound tighter than a drum. Although, she knew which one she preferred.

'Why the fuck are we not in business class?' he hissed, staring at the priority queue for first-class and business-class passengers.

Hayley's heart sank. They'd already had this argument when

she'd booked it, but he'd probably forgotten. He had so much other stuff on his mind.

'Because business class was fully booked,' she told him, keeping her voice calm and even. It was like trying to defuse a bomb before it went off, never sure if you were about to cut the right wire. Red or blue? Fury or understanding?

This time, she didn't have to find out, as one of the furthest away desks freed up, and the agent behind it beckoned them over, defusing Lucas instantly. To strangers, he was all charm and suave Alpha male.

They both handed their passports to the agent and waited as he checked them. Or rather, Hayley waited, while Lucas turned on the charm.

'Can I just check if there are any upgrades available? We tried to book business class, but it was full. I'm more than happy to pay for it – I'm not looking for a freebie.' He finished that with the smile that she'd seen him turn on with every patient, every restaurant manager, every highbrow colleague, his mother and just about anyone else he wanted to impress, reassure or get something from.

'I'll just check, Mr...' The agent glanced at Lucas's passport. 'Sorry, *Doctor* Ford.'

Another blinding smile and Hayley felt her heart sink a little as she saw that the agent was genuinely trying to help him. In term time, and in the summer holiday camps she ran for children in struggling areas, she spent all day, every day, with kids who could never dream of jetting off to St Lucia for their holidays, and yet here he was, totally dissatisfied because he didn't have a fold-down bed and china plates. This was yet another example of how Dr Ford always got what he wanted. At least, almost always. Her reproductive system wasn't being quite as co-operative as the bloke who was currently trying to shift them to better seats.

'Sir, I'm very sorry...' The agent paused, squinted at the screen again, then sighed. 'I'm afraid first class is full, and we only have one seat available in business class. It's a very busy flight.'

Ah, that was that then. Nothing ventured. They could just sit in the seats she'd booked in premium economy, order a couple of glasses of good wine and make the most of it. It wasn't exactly a hardship.

'Not to worry...' Hayley began, then realised that, although he'd turned to look at her, Lucas wasn't listening to what she was saying because he was talking over the top of her.

'Darling, would you mind?'

'Would I mind what?' It should have been obvious really, but he completely caught her off guard. He couldn't possibly be going there with this. Could he?

'Would you mind if I upgraded? It will give me the chance to do some work and to rest before we get there.'

The guy behind the counter was watching her reaction, one eyebrow raised in surprise, and Hayley knew exactly what he was thinking. *Don't do it, love. Don't let him take you for a chump.*

Lucas was still arguing his motion to proceed. 'It's just been such a long week.'

And there she'd been, skipping through daisies all week as she spent forty hours teaching at a dance and drama summer camp for special needs teenagers – although, in fairness, she'd loved every minute of it – and then the rest of her waking hours getting the house sorted and the packing organised for this trip.

She was still way too conscious of the glare of the man behind the desk. It sat somewhere between pity and disapproval and it was making her cheeks burn. Or maybe that was down to her husband being a complete and utter dick.

She did the only think she could possibly do in that moment – she tried to save face. 'Of course I don't mind.' She did. 'I've down-loaded some great books on my Kindle that I'm dying to read.' She hadn't. 'I probably won't even notice you're gone.' Oh, she definitely would.

He leant down and kissed her on the top of the head. 'That's amazing, thank you.'

That's amazing. Not *you're* amazing. Hayley felt hot tears spring to her bottom lids, but she blinked them away. She damn well would not cry. She wouldn't. No way. Neither Lucas bloody Ford... Sorry, *Doctor* bloody Lucas bloody Ford, nor Mr Judgement behind the desk were going to get the satisfaction of seeing her weep. Instead, she kept a 100 per cent fake smile on her face while the desk agent printed off a new boarding pass for her husband, replacing the one he had on his phone.

'There you go, Dr Ford. I see you're a member of our executive club, so I'm happy to waive the upgrade fee on this occasion. And, of course, you're welcome to use the club lounge before your flight. You can sign Mrs Lucas in as your guest at the desk.'

His guest? The check in guy was trying to be nice and smooth the situation over but he had probably just unwittingly summed up this whole bloody situation. It was Lucas Ford's world, and she was just a bloody guest in it. Hayley felt her face begin to burn. Her husband was acting like a prize asshole and she was just having to smile and go along with it.

'Thank you, you've been excellent.' Lucas fired back his most sincere nod of appreciation, then practically skipped away from the desk. 'Right, let's go grab a drink and maybe a bit of brunch before we board,' he suggested, with not even so much as an apology for ditching her.

Why? Why did she let him do this to her? When had he become this guy, this unbearable tit? She was absolutely sure that the man she fell in love with was under there somewhere, but it was getting harder and harder to dig her way through to him.

But then, he hadn't got what he bargained for either in this marriage. She had enough self-awareness to know that her guilt and devastation over being unable to get pregnant had changed her and caused a shift in their relationship. It was only natural that he would pull away from her. She'd read somewhere that 30 per cent of couples struggling with infertility end up in the divorce courts and she believed it. The stress was incomparable.

They'd be fine, though. She'd get pregnant, Lucas would check back into their marriage and go back to being the sweet guy she'd fallen in love with. Okay, maybe he was never sweet. Let's just say, the incredibly sexy, fun guy she'd fallen in love with.

* * *

Barely more than a few sentences were exchanged between them in the two hours they were in the club lounge. Lucas had a glass of wine – his one concession to being on holiday was a decadent daytime vino. Normally Hayley would decline – she wasn't much of a drinker and she'd abstained altogether since the beginning of her fertility treatments. Today, though, she was making an exception to the alcohol ban, because right there and then, she'd decided that she bloody deserved it.

Lucas obviously noticed her glass of Prosecco. She could have opted for champagne, but this didn't feel like anything worth celebrating. Besides, she'd never developed a taste for it. Just like some other aspects of her life now.

'Darling, remember, I talked about this. We recommend staying away from alcohol when you're trying to get pregnant.'

She wanted to point out that in the annals of history, there were probably billions of women around the world who had only got pregnant because of alcohol. She didn't engage in the argument.

'I'm sure just one will be fine,' she replied through a tight smile and gritted teeth. He responded with a disapproving shake of the head, which made her want to take her Prosecco and tip it over his bloody head. But she didn't. Waste of good wine. Instead, she gave herself a talking-to.

Okay, so not the start you were hoping for here. But he's stressed, he's preoccupied and he's trying his best. The whole reason you're both on this holiday is to give you the time and space to cut off from the world and hope that the sun, sea and sand will help you to relax.

He's taking the time off for you and he's doing it because he loves you. It doesn't matter a toss what seat you sit in to get there. What matters is that tonight you're going to go to bed in a bungalow on the shore, with the waves crashing on the sands outside, and he's going to be very naked, and so are you, and you're going to make love until the sun comes up. Just you and him. The way it used to be.

You're going to be the carefree spirit that you used to be and he'll be that guy again, the one you fell in love with, the one who adored you and swept you off your feet. Those two people are going to emerge from all the strains and stresses of the last couple of years and you're going to find each other again. And then you're going to go home and in two weeks, three weeks, maybe a month, you're going to see a second line on a pregnancy test.

That was what was going to happen. She just had to keep believing it.

Lucas glanced up from his newspaper and checked his watch. 'Time to go.'

She still had about a third of her glass of Prosecco sitting in front of her, but she didn't argue. Instead, she picked it up and knocked it back, ignoring his tight jaw of disapproval. Sod him. The speech she'd just given herself might not have sanded off all the spikes of resentment she was feeling. She was an understanding, accommodating wife, not a fricking angel.

They made their way from the club lounge to the departure gate and got there just as a boarding call was being announced for groups one and two. She checked the boarding pass on her phone. Group five. They could just grab a seat and…

'Ah, that's me, darling. Group two.' He reached over and gave her a kiss on the cheek. 'I'll pop back and see you as soon as we're in the air. Thanks for being so great about it. Love you.'

And off he strode, leaving her standing there on her own.

Hayley could feel her heart rate increase, her anger beginning to rise, her outrage working its way through every single cell of her body.

He. Wasn't. Even. Going. To. Wait. With. Her.

There was a group of three ladies sitting over to her right, and she suddenly realised they were watching this play out in front of them, wide-eyed and intrigued. The suave, incredibly attractive tall guy in the casual suit kissing the woman goodbye and striding off onto the airplane. She could hear the questions they were asking themselves in their own minds and she didn't like the answers to any of them.

Something inside her snapped. From her bag, she pulled out the second mini bottle of Prosecco that she'd slipped in there when they were back in the club lounge, opened the top and took a swig. Fuck it. If that's how he wanted to play this, that was fine by her, because right now she was sick of being the good wife. For this flight, she wasn't going to be Dr Ford's wife. Nope. She was just going to be Hayley. The old version. The one who didn't wake up with a knot of anxiety in her gut and then feel it grow by the hour throughout the day. For the next nine hours, she was just going to chill out, maybe drink a little, watch some movies and enjoy every minute of it. She was going to be Hayley Parker, the old version, before Dr Lucas Ford had married her and her ovaries had gone on strike.

'Ladies and Gentlemen, thank you for your patience. At this

time, can we ask all passengers in groups four and five to come forward for boarding.'

Hayley threw back another slug of wine, caring not a jot that the three women who'd been watching her goodbye with Lucas now had their eyes on sticks. Let them judge. She reached down, grabbed her huge white Valentino tote bag, grinned, winked at them and headed to the gate. She bleeped her mobile boarding card through the scanner while the nice lady at the gate checked her passport and wished her an enjoyable flight.

'Thank you. I'm sure it'll be wonderful,' she told her, meaning it, while hoping that her wine breath didn't knock the poor woman out.

There was a minor traffic jam on the airbridge at embarkation, but when she reached the front, the attendant directed her to the right. She didn't even glance left, no desire to see her husband living it up in business class. *Keep moving, Hayley, keep moving.*

She followed the directed path, across the galley, turn right, first row in the next cabin. When she got there, she saw that there was already someone else in the row. A guy. Shoulder-length, tousled hair. Black T-shirt. Beat-up jeans and boots. A couple of silver rings on his fingers. A whole 'rock dude' thing going on. She almost laughed. If you could imagine a guy who was completely opposite to Lucas in every way, this was probably it. Excellent. The last thing she needed was a reminder of the husband who was currently missing in action. Or, at least, missing in business class.

'Excuse me, I think I'm in the seat next to you,' she said.

He glanced up, then nodded. No smile.

Fine. She couldn't care less.

While he was standing up, she grabbed her wine, her Kindle and her phone out of her bag and then stretched up to put it in the overhead bin. One of the perils of being five foot four – overhead bins were a stretch.

The unsmiling bloke reached out towards her. 'Let me help you with that.'

'Nope, I'm fine,' she snapped. Shit, where had that come from? She was never rude. She was just altogether sick of men, of being told what to do, of the whole fricking world.

The guy... he reminded her of a young Jim Morrison, maybe? Her slightly hippy, sex therapist mother had loved The Doors. Played their music all the time when she was younger. Anyway, he just shrugged, stood back and waited until she was organised.

When they finally sat down, him on the outside, her on the seat inside him, she realised he smelled of toothpaste. At least he was hygienic, because by the look of his stormy face, he wasn't going to be the chatty fun type. Suited her fine. For the next nine hours, all she was going to care about was herself. But still...

'I'm Hayley,' she told him. Duh. She blamed the Prosecco and her complete inability to be impolite. 'Sorry if I snapped there. Rough day.'

'No worries,' he shrugged. Irish accent. The 'Bang Bang' summer of Jessie J, Ariana and Nicki on Bondi Beach had been with an Irish guy she'd adored. Long hair, a bit like this one. Colm had been a laugh a minute though. Somehow, she wasn't getting the same vibe here. This guy barely smiled. He gave off no sense of friendliness at all. Hayley disliked him already. In fact, she barely reacted when he finally reciprocated her introduction in a dismissive tone that made it quite clear that he had no interest in chatting.

'I'm Tadgh.'

8

DEV

'You're really doing this. Like, really?' Lizzy asked for the hundredth time, as they fired down the motorway to Gatwick in her sporty Tesla Model 3. It had been her treat to herself when her fledgling company had turned its first profit. Environmental awareness combined with sexy wheels, she'd said, as they tore around the streets like teenagers, blaring music and singing at the top of their lungs the first night she got it. It was a lot more fun than his clapped-out Mini, with the slow puncture and the dodgy starter motor.

'I'm really doing it. Look, I'm owed two weeks' holiday anyway, so what would you rather I do? Stay at home wondering if I'd just let the woman of my dreams slip through my fingers?'

Lizzy wasn't placated. 'Tell me again, what do you actually know about this woman?'

'That she's a goddess,' Dev answered.

'So is Margot Robbie, but I don't see you jumping on a plane to stalk her.'

'I'm not stalking,' Dev argued. 'Okay, maybe slightly. But there's no ill intent. I just need to see her, to find out if she felt the way I did and if she didn't—'

'You'll come back and we'll drink mojitos until you black out?'

'Absolutely,' he agreed, while refusing to allow himself to consider how that would feel. 'Look, either way, it's the story for my book. I know it. This is research. Life experience. The one where the everyday normal bloke gets the goddess in the end.'

'I think a few of the Jennifer Lopez romcoms did that storyline first.'

'Yeah, well, I'm doing it again. Only this time, the bloke is from Essex and he takes a totally insane leap of faith that ends up with him getting the girl. Or not. But, at least, he tries.'

Lizzy sighed. 'I think I liked you better when you were a dating nightmare with zero motivation. Or when you were moping over Poppy. This new optimistic, proactive you is taking a bit of getting used to. I think I need to find a new friend, one who doesn't make me roll my eyes a lot.'

Dev opened the window a little. He should have eaten before he left the house, but he had been slightly distracted by the whole 'spontaneous act of romance' thing. 'You know what you really need?'

Lizzy kept her eyes on the road as she answered. 'I've got a horrible feeling you're going to tell me.'

'Love. That's what you need.' He was teasing her, knowing it would send her into orbit. Taking the piss and jokingly winding each other up had been the mainstay of their relationship since he stuck chewing gum on the bottom of her favourite wellies when they were six.

'Aw, bugger off. What I really need is to stop and pap you out on the hard shoulder and leave you to... Oh shit. Shit. Shit.'

'What?' He was watching her, but followed her gaze, turning to look out of the front window as she applied heavy pressure to the brake. In front of them, the whole of the M25 had ground to a standstill. Fuck. Fuckery fuck. 'Nooooooo,' he groaned, grabbing his phone and frantically typing Gatwick into the maps. He zoomed in on the route and saw a solid red line in front of him with the little signal for roadworks.

Again, fuck.

His eyes flicked up to the arrival time: 11.30 a.m. How the hell could that be right? It was a half-hour drive. And yes, they'd been running a bit late because Lizzy had insisted on organising a bag for the gym and then making a pitstop for coffees for the journey, but there should still have been plenty of time to get there before the gate closed. Shit. Shit. Shit. And why was his brain only capable of repetitive sweary words right now?

Lizzy was tapping the wheel now, massively frustrated that they were down to a 10 mph crawl.

'This is what happens though...' he heard himself swerving back into the desperate optimism lane. 'In every movie, every book, it always seems like the whole thing is going to go tits up before it even gets started, but somehow, they make it work.'

'Yeah, well, you'd better call the coastguard, because the only way this is going to work is if a search and rescue helicopter comes and winches you up and drops you at the front door of Gatwick bloody airport.'

Dev's stomach was beginning to churn. He checked the map again. 'Lizzy, it says this blockage only lasts for a mile. You need to do something. Can we come off the motorway and get back on again?'

'Nope, no slip roads. Shit. Okay, buckle up—'

'I am buckled up.'

'I know, but they always say that in *Fast and Furious* before they—'

She didn't finish the sentence. The car suddenly swerved to one side, and Lizzy Walsh, upstanding citizen and successful entrepreneur, a woman who had never so much as had a parking ticket, veered onto the hard shoulder, switched on her hazard lights, and – at an admittedly non-*Fast and Furious* thirty miles an hour – drove up the inside of the jam, yelling an anxious, 'Shit, shit, shit,' the whole way.

Dev didn't know whether to laugh or just be bloody terrified. Every scenario played out in his mind. He only had hand luggage, and he'd already downloaded his boarding pass to his phone, so he didn't have to check in and could go directly to security and then on to the gate.

But still, if they'd sat in the traffic, it was almost certain that the gate would have closed by the time he got there. By passing this gridlock, they should get there with time to spare. Unless, of course, they got arrested for violating at least a dozen rules in the Highway Code and spent the rest of the day in the clink.

That thought made him pale. Reality check. 'Lizzy, you don't need to do this—'

'Oh, I do. I really do. I'd never hear the end of it. This traffic is not going to be the reason that you lose the woman of your completely unrealistic, lost-your-mind dreams.'

Dev did the only thing he could possibly do in that situation. Laughed and squeezed his eyes shut, ignoring a cacophony of beeping horns from the cars stuck in the queue, the ones who didn't have a reckless pal willing to risk an encounter with the law to get him to the airport on time.

He kept them shut for what was only a couple of minutes, but seemed like an hour and a half, until he felt the car swerve back to the right. He opened one eye to see complete normality. Standard traffic flow. Blockage behind them.

'Lizzy, in case I forget to tell you this, I fricking love you.'

'Yeah, tell me again when the police track me down from the

motorway cameras and I have to phone you at 4 a.m. to bail me out.'

'I'll be there,' he vowed. 'I'll even bring you a coffee and a hotshot lawyer.'

Lizzy glanced towards him, laughing. 'Do you know any hotshot lawyers?'

'Nope, but one of the Chelsea players just got off with his second drink-driving charge, so I'll find out who represented him and get him on the case. You might need to sell the Tesla to pay for it, though. I blew the bank on this ticket. They had no economy seats left, so I had to buy the next grade up.' He paused. 'Jesus, Lizzy, what am I doing? I just want you to know that there's a part of me that realises this is completely fricking insane.'

'And what is that part of you saying you should do?'

'I've no idea. I've tied him up, gagged him and left him at home in a cupboard.'

Lizzy's cackle of laughter made him grin.

'I wish you were coming with me,' he said, truthfully. 'At least that way, if I land on my arse, we can go drown our sorrows and have a laugh.'

'No chance. I'm the kind of person that always looks away when there's a car crash up ahead. You're on your own with this one, pal. But I do want texts every half-hour to keep me amused. The least you can do is entertain me while I'm sitting in some Sussex nick doing hard time for being a menace on the M25.'

Their chat kept them going all the way to the drop-off zone at Gatwick, which, thanks to Lizzy's driving, they made with time to spare. They both jumped out of the car, and Dev pulled his bag out of the boot, then hugged her. 'Sure you don't want to come?'

'I'd rather poke my eyes out with a fork.'

'I'll take that as a no then,' he deadpanned.

He was about to go, when she said, 'Dev, if it doesn't work out –

and I reckon that's about a 99 per cent probability – don't worry about it. You'll be fine. I'll have those mojitos waiting for you.'

'It's going to work out,' he countered. 'But thanks, Lizzy. I love ya. Now drive carefully and stay on the main lanes of the motorway all the way home. If I ever write an action movie, the last hour of my life will definitely be in it.'

'I think that would be a lot more interesting than this romcom,' she told him tartly, then softened. 'See you later, pal. Let me know what flight you're coming back on, and I'll be there. And I love ya back.'

He gave her a last kiss on the cheek, then walked briskly into the building. Security was packed, but he got through it in time to stop off for a beer before going on to the gate. The whole boarding process was quick and efficient, and luck was on his side when he got onto the plane and found a space for his bag in the overhead bin right above his head. He took a snapshot of the moment in his head, so that he could recreate it in his book.

He was in a row of four, right at the front of the premium economy cabin. There were already two people in the furthest away seats. A man and a woman. He had no idea if they were together, but if they were a couple, they definitely weren't feeling the love today. Nah, not a couple. Their vibe was too different. The guy looked like someone you'd see in a documentary about rock bands doing arena tours: battered boots, jeans, black T-shirt, and – not that he was an expert in these matters – he could even see that he was the kind of guy that would have fans throwing their knickers at the stage. The woman...? Maybe thirty, long dark hair, dressed casual but smart in black silky trousers and a white shirt. Nope, definitely not together.

He smiled at them as he climbed into the seat right next to the woman. She returned his gesture, the guy didn't even look up, just stared straight ahead. Not the friendly type then.

Dev pulled his seatbelt on, and just as he did, another woman stopped by the empty seat beside him, checked the number above it and nodded.

'Think I'm in here,' she said, her Scottish accent soft and cheery.

Dev took another snapshot. She was maybe in her fifties – he was hopeless with women's ages – red hair, cut in a mum-type bob, wearing a flowy, flowery jacket over skinny jeans. She didn't seem to have a carry-on case, just a large handbag that she dropped on the floor, then scooted under her seat with her feet when she sat down.

'Och, for a minute there I didn't think I was going to make it. Sorry, I promise I'm not one of those passengers that wants to chat to a stranger for the whole flight. It's just been a bit of a morning. I'll be fine when I'm sorted.'

'That's okay,' Dev told her, thinking this was the second time in a week he'd met a stranger whom he'd liked on sight. In a very different way, of course. This woman seemed like the kind of lovely person that his mum was always chatting to on buses and in the queue at the bakers. 'I've had a bit of a morning, too.' Understatement of the year.

'Well, I think we both deserve a drink and a snooze then,' his new row mate informed him, before following up with, 'I'm Bernadette. Pleased to meet you.'

'Dev,' he said, reaching his hand over to shake hers.

She clocked the laptop he'd just opened on his knee. 'I'll keep quiet and not disturb your work,' she reassured him.

'Oh, don't worry, it's not work. It's just notes for...' Woah, was he really doing this? Was he about to blurt out the secret double life that only Lizzy knew about? Bugger it, he was. 'For a book I'm writing.'

'A book?' Bernadette's eyes widened. 'Oh well, forget what I said about not disturbing you. This is something I want to hear all about.'

'Me too,' said the stranger on the other side of him. 'Sorry. Shouldn't have been eavesdropping, but I love a good book.' She gestured with her Kindle and a smile. 'Hayley,' she said. 'Me, not the book I'm reading. Sorry. I've had a glass or two of wine.'

That made his new friend, Bernadette, chuckle. 'I intend to catch up with you. Pleased to meet you, Hayley. I'm Bernadette. This is Dev.' He then watched as Bernadette leaned forward and caught the eye of the sullen passenger at the other end of the row, in that way that only a friendly middle-aged face could get away with. 'What about you, son?'

For a moment, Dev thought the guy was going to ignore her, but he didn't.

'Tadgh,' he said, managing to grudgingly make the corners of his mouth turn up.

'Okay,' Bernadette nodded. 'Tadgh. Hayley. Dev. Very happy to meet you all. Right, Dev, let's hear all about this book then.'

10 A.M. – NOON

9

BERNADETTE

Okay, so far so good. Bernadette was on the plane. It had taken off on schedule around 12.30. She was going. She was doing this. Even if the slight apprehension of it all was making her chirp like a budgie to the poor chap next to her. A handsome bloke, probably about the same age as her Nina, so around thirty. He seemed quite happy to chat back, and so did the lass to his right. The guy at the other end of the row – Tadgh, he'd said his name was – clearly wasn't interested in chatting, but, dear lord, if she was twenty years younger and forty pounds slimmer, she'd be in love with him by now. She chided herself for the political incorrectness of that thought. There was none of that objectifying nonsense allowed any more and quite right too. However, it was absolutely fine as long as it was just a wee nugget of amusement in her own head and never passed her lips. She'd wasted the best years of her life on a man who didn't deserve it – the least she could do now was have the occasional moment of appreciation for a drop-dead gorgeous stranger, in the same way that her and Sarah had a cheer and a good old round of applause every time that big bloke, The Rock, took his shirt off in a movie. They'd been hoarse by the end of that *Baywatch* film.

Bernadette switched her attention to what that nice Dev next to her was saying. Apparently, he was writing a book about a guy who went off to track down a stranger after falling in love at first sight.

'What do you think?' he asked, when he'd outlined the plot. A sports journalist. A blokey guy. Single. Falls in love with a woman who is about to get on a plane with her friends. The resort that she's going to sticks in his head. He can't shake off the thought that this woman is the right one for him. He has no other way of tracking her down, so he gets on a flight to go there, to see if she felt their connection too.

'And is this based on a real-life experience? You know, since you appear to be heading off to St Lucia on your own?'

Bless him. Bernadette watched as he went all red and got a bit flustered.

'Maybe a bit,' he murmured, shrugging, the embarrassment written all over his face. 'But please don't think I'm a weirdo, because I've never done anything like this before in my life. My best mate thinks I've lost my mind and I think she has a point.'

On the other side of him, the lass – Hayley – was gleefully hanging on every word. 'No way! Oh my God, I love that. It might be the best thing I've heard in a long time. I mean, definitely weird,' she teased him, making Bernadette laugh, 'but bloody brilliant all the same. Did I mention I've had wine?'

Just at that, the seatbelt sign clicked off and the bloke at the end got up and went to the toilet.

'So what are the names of the characters then?' Bernadette asked, needing more details.

That put him on the back foot. 'Well, for the work in progress version I'm going with Dev for the bloke and Cheryl for the girl, because in real life...'

'You're Dev and the girl you met was Cheryl?' Hayley finished for him, setting all three of them off again.

'I know. It shows a stunning lack of creativity,' he conceded ruefully.

This was one of the most bizarre meetings and conversations Bernadette had ever had – actually, cancel that. She'd spent most of her career on an A&E ward and there had been many, many crazier conversations than this one. Difference was, in this one, no one was hurt and the only risk of injury was the breakage of this poor guy's heart.

They were interrupted by the flight attendants, a very glamourous lady who must have been in her fifties and a young man with a dark tan and smart blonde highlights, reaching the end of their row with the trolley.

'Would you like a drink from the bar?' the female attendant asked with a warm smile.

Bernadette thought how lovely it was to see a woman her age still out here looking so glamourous and serene. Most days, Bernadette struggled to get a brush through her hair and slap on a bit of lippy. Nina had been telling her for ages that it was time she started making a bit of effort, hence the skinny jeans, but Bernadette didn't see the point. Kenneth's last fling before their divorce had been with a thirty-year-old blonde who looked like a forties movie star, with her flowing waves and flawless figure. What was the point of even trying to compete with that? The truth was, Bernadette didn't want to. She wouldn't care if she never had another relationship with a man in her life.

Sure, there were some things that she missed, and a wee bit of excitement would be nice, but she had no time for all the other stuff that came with it. She'd been married to Kenneth for over thirty years. If she spent the next thirty single, that was fine with her. In the meantime, she had a smashing job, a wonderful family, great friends, and she was at a stage in her life that came with true peace and contentment. Oh, and she was also on a flight to St Lucia with some new travel buddies that were chatty and making her laugh.

She realised she hadn't answered the attendant's question. Usually, she'd have just gone for a soft drink, aware of the dehydrating effects of alcohol on flights, but bugger it. She was on her holidays. And she'd promised that young Hayley that she was going to catch up with her.

'I'll have a gin and tonic, please,' she said, then watched while the woman went on to ask the rest of the passengers in the row what they wanted, while the younger, male flight attendant at the front of the trolley plonked some ice into a plastic glass, then added a stirrer and put it down on her tray, swiftly followed by a miniature bottle of Tanqueray and two mini cans of tonic water.

'Would you like crisps or pretzels, madam?' he asked, a row of gleaming white teeth almost blinding her.

'Oooh, crisps please.'

He delivered them with a flourish and another flash of his pearlies. Happy days.

Dev asked for a beer, Hayley requested another small bottle of Prosecco and the bloke at the end (she kept forgetting his name) got back just in time to shout up a Jack Daniel's on the rocks. Bernadette smiled to herself. If she'd had to guess what that guy would be drinking, that was exactly what she'd have gone for.

There was a pause in the conversation as all the drinks were served and Bernadette took advantage of it to slip her phone out of the bag underneath her seat and text Sarah.

Bugger. Of course, there would be no signal. Dev saw what she was trying to do and offered help.

'There's Wi-Fi on the plane if you need to send messages,' he told her. 'It's twenty quid though. Bit of a rip-off, but I guess it's a captive audience.'

'Twenty quid!' Bernadette was outraged. In normal life, she'd have stuffed her phone right back into her bag and waited until she could text for free, but she stopped herself from doing that. This was her first proper holiday in years. She could afford it. And besides, if she had Wi-Fi, it meant that if Sarah, or Stuart or Nina were trying to get hold of her, their messages would get through. That was all she needed.

She followed Dev's instructions and signed into the Wi-Fi, then fired the message off to Sarah.

How are you doing, lovely? I've got Wi-Fi on the flight, so you can message me any time. Any word from Eliza? Stay strong, my love, you'll be there soon. I'm here if you need me. Xx

She followed that up with a quick message to the group chat she shared with Stuart and Nina.

In the skies. Have Wi-Fi. Feeling very technological. Pretty sure Bill Gates would be proud of my achievements. Love you two, Mum xx

She waited to see if any responses came in straight away, but nothing pinged. Might take a while. She had no idea how Wi-Fi worked thousands of feet in the air.

Phone still silent, she slipped it back into her bag, then took a sip of her gin and tonic. Ah, that was a little slice of wonderful. Although, she could feel her ankles swelling at the first taste of the gin. Or maybe that was the new wedges cutting off the circulation. Either way, she did a few rotations of her feet just to be on the safe side and wondered if now was a good time to fish her flight socks out of her bag.

She glanced to the side. One handsome aspiring novelist, a gorgeous lass and a hunk of burning love who had no right being that bloody miserable when he had a face like that. So no, her green stretchy flight socks could stay in her bag, along with her Gaviscon indigestion tablets, her inflatable neck pillow and the stretchy old leggings she'd brought to change into on the plane.

For the purposes of this flight, she was a new Bernadette: a high-tech, glam, carefree one, and if she temporarily lost all feeling below the waistband of these bloody jeans, then it was a small price to pay for the fun she was having.

She let the conversation lie for a few moments while everyone sorted out their drinks. The chat so far had been fun and interesting, but she didn't want to be the pain in the arse who disturbed other folks' journeys with incessant talking. Maybe they just wanted to chill out and keep to themselves, and of course, that was absolutely fine. Much as she'd enjoyed chatting to them, she didn't have it in her nature to be pushy, so she let it be, taking a sliver of satisfaction in the knowledge that Kenneth would have hated this. He despised being in close proximity to people he had no interest in, and the reality was that he'd have no interest in the two gents, because they could do nothing to further his career or social standing. Hayley was a different story. She was around thirty and beautiful, so no doubt there would be a bit of intrigue there on his part, but she was wearing a wedding ring, so that would turn him off completely. He didn't have the stupidity, or maybe it was the balls, to go after another man's wife. Not exactly a redeeming feature in his character, but it was as close as he got to having a decent bone in his body.

Bernadette felt a buzz at her ankles and after reassuring herself that it wasn't an alert to warn of an impending DVT, she reached down into her bag and pulled her phone out. Three new messages. The first was from Sarah.

No more news to share. Just want to get there and hug her. Glad you're
still going and will make this up to you, pal.

She immediately texted back.

Nothing to make up, my love. Hugs to you all.

She thought about inserting an emoji, but that might be taking
her new-found technological genius a step too far. She'd been
perfectly contented with her flip phone back in the old days.
Kenneth got a brand new, up-to-date model every year, which made
her almost stubbornly determined to stick to her Nokia. She'd only
upgraded when the grandchildren were born, and Nina wanted to
send her photos and videos of Milo and Carson. A little pang of
longing rose inside her and she pushed it back down. She'd see the
kids when she got back. She was only going for a fortnight, not a
six-month sabbatical.

Talking of which, there were a couple of new texts on the family
chat too.

The first was from Stuart.

Proud of you, Mum. First day of a brilliant trip. Wish we were there.

Which was immediately followed by a comment from Nina.

But yer not, bro, so can you come take the kids to footie tonight so I can
stay home and watch Chicago Fire?

She was a chancer, her Nina, but in the loveliest way. The fact
that her offspring were so close, despite a seven-year age difference,
was a constant source of joy to Bernadette.

Sorry, sis, I don't do ball sports. And whatever innuendo came into your head when you read that, keep it to yourself.

Nina replied with an emoji of a face with zippered mouth. Bernadette's thumbs got involved.

Play nice, you two. Love yous xx

Bernadette put her phone back in her bag. The conversation with her fellow passengers still hadn't started up again. Ah well.

She was about to switch on her TV and find something to watch, when Hayley leaned forward so she could see her around Dev.

'So, Bernadette, are you travelling on your own to St Lucia?'

Bernadette nodded. 'I am. My friend Sarah was supposed to be with me, but she had to call off an hour before we were due to leave for the airport this morning. It's a long story.'

Hayley gestured to her watch, almost tipping over her new glass of bubbly. 'Well, we've got nine hours to kill if you fancy sharing it.'

Bernadette smiled. 'Okay. As long as Dev promises not to put it in his book. So what happened was...'

10

TADGH

The people beside him had been chattering away since the minute they'd all boarded the plane, but Tadgh just blocked them out. He hated being rude. It wasn't in his nature. But right now, he had zero headspace for anything except the complete head fuck that was being presented by the potential that his fiancée might have shagged his brother. Christ, every time that thought ran through his head he wanted to vomit.

He checked his phone again.

The three little dots that had come up after he'd texted Cheryl earlier had disappeared to be replaced with... nothing. What the fuck did that mean? She'd read his messages, but she hadn't replied? Or maybe she had replied, but it hadn't come through for some reason. Maybe this really was just a whole big domino chain of misunderstandings and miscommunications.

Yeah, that had to be it. He'd heard the others in his row talking about the Wi-Fi and for a moment his heart soared. Of course, that was the problem! He had a quick look in the card in the pocket on the wall in front of him, followed the instructions to get online, then stared at the screen, willing a text to come through. Nothing.

Come on, babe, don't do this.

Still nothing.

Not. A. Fecking. Thing.

None of this was making sense. If Cheryl wasn't madly in love with him, why had she been the one to push for them to get married? He'd have been perfectly happy just rolling along, moving in together, having a cool time with no official contract.

And Shay... sure, he was devoid of many scruples when it came to women, but his brother's fiancée? No. Surely that was too far even for him?

Tadgh stood up, unable to sit any longer. Earlier, he'd thought he saw some guilt on Shay's face. But maybe he'd been wrong? He needed to see his brother again, to check if there really was something there, a hint of shame because he'd done something wrong.

He worked his way back to the economy cabin and scanned it for Shay and Conlan. There they were. Standing right at the back, chatting to a flight attendant and, by the smiles on all their faces, having a grand old time.

'Hey, hey, hey...' Shay greeted him. 'Thought you'd be way too high-class to associate with us plebs back in the cheap seats.'

'Nah, Mam always told us to be nice to people less fortunate,' Tadgh shot back, immediately falling into the usual sarcastic banter between the two of them. He didn't want Shay to think he suspected anything, so he had to play this smart.

'Lisa, this is my less attractive brother, Tadgh. Tadgh, this is Lisa from Dublin. She saw us when we played the festival in Wicklow last month.'

The cute dimples on Lisa's cheeks creased as she greeted him. 'You guys were great. Anyway, I'd better get back to work before the old dragon who's in charge gets riled up. I'll slip you lads some more beer in a while.'

With that, she went off to answer a flashing light further down the cabin.

'Tired of slumming it up there, then?' Conlan asked him, before taking another slug of his beer.

Tadgh briefly wondered if Conlan would sense his irritation, but then corrected himself. He adored his mate, but he had the emotional awareness of the beer can he was holding. Tadgh would have to write his feelings in fireworks on the fecking sky for Conlan to notice them. Music, beer, Jack Daniel's, rugby and occasionally women pretty much completed the full scope of their discussion subjects.

Conlan handed Tadgh his beer, then excused himself with a 'back in a minute,' and took a few steps forward before going into the toilet just in front of them, leaving Tadgh and Shay.

Now. This was his moment.

Tadgh took a deep breath. *Act normal. Don't make a big deal of this. Don't warn him that something is going on. And definitely don't suggest that he saw the text.* The last thing he needed was the flight to be diverted to Alicante to offload two brothers who were rolling around the floor, battering each other with beer cans. They hadn't been in a physical fight since they were about fifteen, but going by the way Tadgh was feeling now, it wasn't too late for a rematch.

'Bro, have you heard from Dad at all?' Tadgh started, kicking it off with something completely innocent. That's how they always did it in the *Godfather* movies. Right now, Shay was Fredo Corleone, and Tadgh was Michael Corleone.

Christ, what was he thinking? None of this came naturally to him. Up until a few hours ago, Tadgh would have said he was the most laid-back, easy-going guy he knew, one who had absolutely no time for macho bullshit and who would love his family until the death. Now he was Al Pacino and on the verge of the first meltdown of his life.

Shay shook his head, in response to Tadgh's question. 'Nah, bud. Not since he called you last night to say that he'd landed and was in the bar with the entire hen party. He's probably lying down in a dark room, traumatised.'

Even given the circumstances, that made Tadgh smile. Since their mum had died, their dad had made an effort to get on with his life, because he knew it was what Mam would have wanted. He still had no interest in meeting anyone else though, despite no lack of interest from the single women in their home town. Jack Donovan was a mountain of a man, almost six foot four and, as their mam used to tell them regularly, the best-looking of them all in his day. He didn't look too bad even now, in his mid-fifties. In fact, Cheryl's mother swore he looked like a younger Clint Eastwood, and she had been flirting with him mercilessly since her divorce came through, but Jack Donovan was having none of it. He'd had a great love once, he said. That kind of luck didn't happen twice in any lifetime.

'You heard anything?' Shay returned the question.

Tadgh saw the opening and he took it. 'Nah. I'm beginning to think my phone is fecked. I've heard from no one all day. I texted Cheryl earlier, but she hasn't got back to me either.' It was taking every single ounce of strength he had to keep his voice casual and normal. 'Don't suppose you've heard from her, have you?'

Shay's denial was instant. 'Nope, why would I have heard from her?' Hasty. Defensive. Especially as it wouldn't have been out of the ordinary for Cheryl to drop Shay a text if she couldn't track Tadgh down. She'd done that countless times, on the many occasions his phone had died while they were rehearsing or in the studio. Cheryl had pretty much been a part of their family since they were kids, so she'd always had that brother/sister vibe with Shay... At least, that's what Tadgh had always thought it was. Now there was a distinct possibility that it was all a bit more incestuous.

Tadgh shrugged. 'Just thought she might have texted you if she couldn't reach me.'

'I'm not your fucking secretary, mate,' Shay sneered, and Tadgh was about to go right back at him when he realised they were no longer alone.

'Sorry to disturb you, boys,' Lisa, the flight attendant, purred and Tadgh saw that she was flirting in Shay's direction. 'But we've got a bit of turbulence up ahead and the seatbelt sign has just gone back on. I'm afraid I need to ask you to return to your seats.'

Shay gave her the Shay Donovan smile. Was it Tadgh's imagination or was there a tightness there now that hadn't been there before? Maybe. But Shay was still acting like the big-time joke he thought he was. 'No problem. My brother was just leaving to go back to the upper classes.'

Tadgh didn't even bother responding, just turned on his booted heel and made his way back to the premium economy cabin. The whole way there, he ran his conversation with Shay back in his head.

His brother had had no contact with Cheryl whatsoever. None. That's what he'd just said.

Did Tadgh believe him?

Yes.

He did.

He definitely did.

A pause. Who was he fecking kidding?

The slight tick in Shay's right eye when he was speaking. The almost indiscernible but very real thickness in his voice. And the absolute giveaway – the fact that Shay went on the offensive with the comment about not being Tadgh's secretary. That was how he rolled. Any time Shay was backed into a corner, he came out swinging, determined to bully the problem into submission.

And this was definitely a problem.

Tadgh couldn't remember when he'd ever been more certain that his brother was lying through his fecking teeth.

Question was, what was he going to do about it? And when?

And was there any way, any chance at all, that he – someone who had never thrown a punch in his life - was going to get through the rest of this flight without going back to the cabin behind them and knocking his brother out?

Jesus, this was killing him. It felt like his guts were being ripped up through his throat. His own brother. His fiancée. Two days before his wedding. The only time he'd felt pain like this before was when he got the phone call to say his mam had been taken from them.

How could Shay do this to their family? Hadn't they been through enough? Or... was Tadgh completely wrong about the whole thing? The confusion was kicking in on top of the hangover to make every bone in his face hurt.

When he got to his seat, he saw that someone else was sitting there already. The woman next to him, Hayley, glanced up over the top of the new arrival's head and smiled apologetically.

He managed to do something with his face in return, but he wasn't sure what it was, because now, every single muscle seemed to have snapped so tight it could barely move.

'Excuse me, mate?' Tadgh said.

The guy in his seat turned and looked up at him. 'Two seconds.'

Tadgh did not have the patience for this. Not right now. Still, he took a step back and waited, until he saw the flight attendant who'd served their drinks earlier sashay towards them. She didn't look impressed.

'Can I ask you to take your seat, please? We have some turbulence ahead.'

Tadgh put his hands up. 'I'd be very happy to take my seat, but it appears to be occupied.'

The woman's gaze went from Tadgh to the guy in the hijacked seat, before she leaned forward, her hand resting on the top of the headrest. 'Excuse me, sir, could you please return to your own seat?'

Tadgh watched as the guy gave the attendant the same response he'd given him a few moments ago.

'Can you just wait a moment?'

The flight attendant, her badge said she was called Marian, wasn't as patient as Tadgh, and she wasn't for taking any nonsense. 'I'm afraid we cannot wait, sir, because the seatbelt sign is on and we're about to hit turbulence.' Tadgh decided her tone was professional, with a hint of forthcoming headlock, and the thought somehow cut through the tension in his head and amused him.

'I think you'd better go,' he heard Hayley say.

'I think you should take the lady's advice, sir,' Marian the muscle agreed. 'We need to get everyone seated immediately.'

With an explosive sigh, the bloke finally got up and, without so much as an apology or a backward glance, stormed off in the direction of the business-class cabin in front.

Marian seemed satisfied that her job there was done and, with the resurgence of her perfectly hospitable smile, gestured to Tadgh to take his seat. She then glanced over to make sure everyone in the row was wearing their seatbelts and began working her way back through the cabin doing the same.

Tadgh clipped his belt on and made eye contact with Hayley. The difference in her expression from before he left was startling. A few minutes ago, she'd been smiley and having a chatty conversation with the others in the row. Now she was staring ahead, and even at this angle Tadgh could see that her teeth were clenched tight and there was a line of strain across her brow.

'I'm sorry I left my seat open for so long,' he heard himself say. He hadn't planned on speaking to her, but she looked so pissed off he couldn't help it. 'Was that guy bothering you?'

He saw she was chewing her bottom lip and wondered if she was trying not to cry. Oh God, he hoped not. He was hopeless with anyone who cried. His mother rarely shed a tear, was always so stoic and positive that he had very little training in that department. Still, he felt a responsibility to check she was okay.

There was a barely discernible nod, but no words came out. So yes, the bloke had been bothering her. It was none of his business and he would normally avoid getting mixed up in someone else's drama, yet he felt somehow responsible, so he couldn't let it go.

'Do you know him? Or shall I let the flight attendant know? I'm pretty sure she could take him out using just her thumbs.'

Another smile. Then she shook her head. 'Thank you, but you don't need to say anything to the scary lady. I know him.'

'You do?' he asked, puzzled, not understanding the dynamic here. Mr Flash Suit was all arrogant business and not her vibe at all. Maybe he was a work colleague. Or her boss. Or – long shot – her brother who had just slept with someone she loved. Yeah, that was it. That was the theme for the day.

'I do,' Hayley said, with detectable weariness. 'He's my husband.

11

HAYLEY

Oh God, she was absolutely mortified. Close to fatal-level embarrassment. Even the brooding Irish guy on her right was feeling the need to be nice to her and he hadn't even seen the extent of what had just happened. God knows what Dev and Bernadette were thinking. She couldn't look at them. She didn't want to see the shock that was bound to be there. Maybe disgust too. If there was another empty seat on this plane, she was going to find it, so she didn't need to spend the next... she did a quick calculation... eight hours burning with shame.

Her mind rewound to the start, trying to suss what had gone wrong and what she could have done differently. She'd been deep in conversation with Dev and Bernadette, listening to Bernadette's story about how her friend, Sarah, had to cry off at the last minute this morning, and how she'd decided she was just going to come on her own. Hayley totally respected that. 'Well, I'm so glad you came, because it's been lovely to meet you. I used to fly solo all the time and I loved it,' she'd said wistfully. 'The great thing about travelling alone is that sometimes you meet really lovely people like you, Bernadette. And you know, weirdos too, like aspiring novelists who are off chasing after a one-night stand.'

'They're the worst kind,' Dev had nodded, completely deadpan, making the two women dissolve into laughter.

Hayley had nudged him with her shoulder, which seemed like a very overfamiliar thing to do to a guy she met an hour ago, yet strangely not overfamiliar at all. They'd been chatting constantly for an hour and a half and he was just one of those very likeable guys who put you at ease the moment you met him. No wonder Chastity... no, not Chastity. Was it Cherry? Cheryl! That was it. No wonder Cheryl had fallen in his lap and decided to stay there. If Hayley had been a single woman, she might have done the same.

'Hayley.' The oh-too-recognisable voice had come from the other side of her, from the space vacated by the jeans and boots guy who had disappeared right after the drinks had been served. It wasn't a friendly greeting. Or a warm one. If it was a perfume, it would be full-bodied disapproval with top notes of irritation and ire.

Both Bernadette and Dev had stopped speaking as Lucas sat down in the empty seat on the other side of her.

'Someone was sitting there,' she'd said weakly.

Lucas had acted like she hadn't said a word. 'What the hell are you doing?' he'd hissed under his breath, but she'd had a horrible feeling that Dev and Bernadette could hear him.

'I'm talking to the nice people in the row beside me. You know, the ones who didn't upgrade to business class and leave me to fly alone like a total chump.' She was provoking him and she knew it, but he bloody deserved it. And if he was any kind of decent guy, he'd have a sense of humour about the whole thing and recognise that a bit of gentle ribbing was in order for doing that to her.

Unfortunately, he wasn't in the 'decent guy' frame of mind. Not exactly a shocker, these days.

'For fuck's sake, how much have you had to drink?'

Okay, so right then she should have pacified him. Gone full-scale submissive and acknowledged that she shouldn't be drinking. Unfortunately, though, her submissive genes had strapped on armbands and were busy having a wee swim in her last glass of bubbly.

'No, no, no, you don't get to do that,' she'd whispered. 'You don't get to desert me, then come back here and tell me what I should be doing. I'm a grown bloody woman, Lucas. Go back to business class and have another canapé.'

She had no idea if they were even serving canapés up there, but in her head that had seemed like a perfectly logical thing to say.

'Christ, you're an embarrassment.'

The harshness of his words had made her reel back as if she'd been slapped. Not that he had ever laid a finger on her and she was certain that he never would. That didn't take away the sting of the last attack though. Maybe it was the altitude, or the vino, but for once she couldn't let his rudeness lie.

'Well, my new friends don't seem to think I'm an embarrassment. And if you're up there in another cabin, you can pretend that I'm not back here, shaming you. You know Lucas, I'm doing nothing wrong. I'm having a couple of drinks on the first day of my holiday. Don't you remember when we got completely plastered on cheap cocktails on our first day in Bangkok? Or when we had a few too many tequilas in Mexico? You used to think it was fun to have a drink or two on holiday. I don't see what's changed.'

'What's changed is that back then we were barely adults...' His voice was still low, and she'd prayed again that no one else could hear. 'And what's also changed is that you have a medical issue and drinking doesn't help that.'

A medical issue. Had he really just said that? Why didn't he just shout it to the entire bloody plane – hey, my name is Lucas and my wife's fricking lady bits don't work.

She'd fought to keep some semblance of calm dignity.

'It's one day, Lucas. One day out of a whole year of nothing. And I've had a few small glasses of wine, it's not like I'm mainlining vodka straight into my veins. But look, if it makes you happy, I won't have any more.'

She'd meant it. Before today, it had been over a year, maybe even two, since she'd had a drink and it honestly hadn't bothered her. All that had mattered in that time was trying to get pregnant. One IVF cycle after another. Endless rounds of fertility drugs to stimulate her ovaries. Disappointment after disappointment. The irony was, the occasional glass of wine would probably have helped to deal with all that, but she'd been so hopeful, so determined not to disappoint him, so absolutely desperate to get pregnant, that she hadn't even considered it.

'Yes. It will make me happy.' His words had shot out like bullets, and she'd seriously doubted that anything could make him happy right then. What had happened to him? Where was the man that she married? Or the man she thought she'd married? 'Don't have any more,' he'd added, like a father telling his kid to lay off the jelly beans.

That should have been the end of it. She should have left it there. But there was something in his tone that had really irritated her and before she could stop herself, she'd murmured a defiant, 'Or what?'

He'd been starting to get up, but now he'd reversed that action and swung to face her. 'What did you just say?'

'I said, or what? Will I be grounded? Have my allowance taken away? Only I don't get an allowance because I'm a fully-fledged adult who is more than capable of making her own decisions.' Oh bollocks, this was getting worse. What was she doing? She never fought with him like this. In all honesty, she'd decided years ago that it just wasn't worth it. It was so much easier to keep the peace. Especially when the thing that caused the most friction between them – just like today – was her inability to get pregnant and that was her fault.

To make matters worse, not only was she arguing with him, but she was doing it in a public place, something she hadn't done since she'd tossed her engagement ring back at him after a dinner at his parents' house where he'd acted like a possessive dick, accusing her of making eyes at his brother. It was ridiculous. She'd just been nervous and his brother, Ralf, was being kind to her, so she'd found him easy to talk to. On that occasion, she'd quietly left the house and he'd chased after her, apologising profusely and swearing it would never happen again. Since then, any disputes had been behind closed doors and just a raised eyebrow of warning from him was enough to make her clamp her mouth shut in company.

Well, today she wasn't clamping. And the fury in his eyes had told her that he wasn't thrilled with that line of action.

He'd bit back at her, still keeping his voice low. 'What the hell has got into you? You're being totally fucking irrational.'

Behind her, she'd heard a sharp intake of breath, which pretty much ruled out her hope that her fellow row-mates couldn't over-hear their discussion. She wasn't sure, but it sounded like it had come from Bernadette.

'Where has all this attitude come from? Is it because you're getting a bit of attention? Are you flirting? Is that it? Are you flirting with the guy next to you?'

Hayley had felt a red rash of embarrassment creep up her neck and conceded defeat. *Kill me. Kill me now.* The whole 'flirting with other people' thing wasn't new either. Ironic, considering he was the one that metaphorically charmed the knickers off everyone he met.

This couldn't go on. It had to stop. It was going to make everyone around her feel so uncomfortable and they weren't going to be able to look her in the eye for the rest of the flight. Yet still she'd felt the need to stand up to him. She was having an out-of-body experience and both bodies were pissed off with him and refusing to take his nonsense.

Before she could say anything else, though, it had taken a turn for the worse and the Irish bloke had returned to reclaim his seat. For a split second, she'd hoped that he'd punch Lucas in the face for being an arrogant prick to him, but he didn't show even a hint of aggression, just acted like he couldn't care less. That probably annoyed Lucas even more.

The flight attendant wasn't so amenable. Hayley wished she had a fraction of the woman's grit. She hadn't even hesitated to over-rule his objections and dispatch Lucas back to his seat. He was probably sitting up in business class now, fuming over that canapé. Anyway, with Lucas removed, Tadgh had sat back down and she'd had to confess that Lucas was actually her husband. As the kids in her first-year drama class would say, she was pure morto.

Now she was left sitting beside three people who probably thought she was a complete idiot at best, and certifiable at worst. This plane was starting to feel way too small and way too claustrophobic. There wasn't even an option to escape to the toilets, because she was terrified of Marian the Scary Flight Attendant returning and putting her right back in her place.

It took Hayley a few moments before she could even flick her eyes to her right, and when she did, Tadgh caught her glance and returned it with something approaching a half-smile. It was probably just his way of masking his terror at being sat next to an unhinged woman. Whatever the reason, though, he should do that smile thing more often, because it suited him.

She flicked her gaze to the left this time and saw that Dev had earphones in now, and his eyes were closed. She sent up a silent prayer that he'd put those in the second Lucas sat down and he hadn't heard a word of their conversation. Or maybe he'd put them in afterwards, because he thought she was pathetic and didn't want to make conversation any more. The thought made her cheeks burn, but she told herself that at least he'd have another chapter for his book.

That's when her gaze went past Dev and locked on Bernadette's and the other woman regarded her with an expression of so much compassion that Hayley almost burst into tears.

'I used to know someone just like him,' Bernadette confessed.

'Really?' Hayley's voice was shaky with emotion. 'How did you handle it?'

'That's a long story. I think before we go there, I'm going to need another drink.'

Hayley smiled, a little emboldened by the other woman's empathy. 'Make it two.'

12

DEV

All Dev could hear was the chorus of 'Crazy' by Gnarls Barkley blasting in his ears. It was one of his favourites. It reminded him of the school disco, circa 2007, and hitting the dance floor with Lizzy because she had just been chucked by the school footie captain. The bloke was a complete wanker anyway. Last time Dev saw him was about a year ago, and he was ferrying three young kids into the soft-play area at the local Harvester. About six hours of that was probably suitable punishment for ditching Lizzy.

He made a mental note to fish out his phone and send her a text just as soon as Hayley's angry husband had vacated the area. When the guy had arrived, he and Bernadette had given each other knowing looks, and then he'd slipped on his headphones and shut his eyes. Whatever was going on there was none of his business. Surprising though, because despite only having known her for a sum total of less than two hours, Hayley seemed like a really cool person. The husband, not so much.

What was really cool about her was that she didn't want to change seats when she heard his story about crossing the globe to track down a one-night stand. That would have had most people commando crawling out of the area to get away from him. Although, granted, that wasn't a great option when you were 38,000 feet in the air, but still... He couldn't quite believe that he'd shared that story within an hour of meeting them. It was the very definition of TMI. Yet, their sheer enthusiasm for the whole caper gave him even more faith that this was going to work out. It had to. He wasn't going back to Essex with his tail between his legs, to spend the rest of his life in perpetual singledom, with the highlight of his year being the opportunity to write about the giddy drama of the regional lawn bowling tournament of 2022. There had to be more to life. Correction. There *was* more to life. Cheryl.

He conjured up a snapshot of last Saturday night in his mind. When the music had switched to a slow dance at the club (Luke Combs singing 'Forever After All' – how prescient was that?), she'd curled her arms around his neck and she'd moved in time to the beats of the song, her hips touching his.

'Can we go somewhere?' she'd murmured, and for a second, he was a tad flustered on the inside. This was new territory to him. He'd never had someone hit on him like this before. He'd always been the guy who was friends with someone first, then let it escalate to occasional benefits, before graduating to a relationship that fizzled out and went to shit shortly after. He just didn't have the skills. He could talk for three hours about the merits of the offside rule, but had not a single scooby when it came to how to keep a woman interested. Lizzy claimed it was because he was too nice. No intrigue. 'I mean, no offence, but you're maybe not edgy enough. Most women want a bloke that keeps them on their toes, not someone who wants to spend Sunday afternoon on the couch rewatching the episode of *Friends* where she got off the plane.'

It was Dev's all time favourite TV scene and he knew it verbatim. Rachel is on a flight, leaving Ross. Ross wanted to stop her going, but he missed her at the airport, so he's back in his flat when he hears a message on his answering machine. It's Rachel, saying she was trying to get off the plane to come to him. Ross is in his room having a berzy and yelling, 'Did she get off the plane?' Cut to a voice behind him. Rachel. 'I got off the plane,' she says. It got Dev every single time.

'Yep, don't think I don't hear you sniffing all through that scene. You're a pushover, Dev Robbins,' Lizzy had told him.

The fear that hadn't been far from his guts since last weekend began to tighten around his abs again. What if Cheryl had no interest in a guy like that either? What if she thought the bold, spontaneous bloke from last weekend was the real him?

He had to admit, most of his behaviour that night had been fairly out of character. When she'd whispered the suggestion in his ear, he'd brushed his lips against her cheek and murmured, 'Let's go to my place.'

Then he'd had a ten-minute internal panic because he was sure he'd left his washing draped over every chair and radiator. And pizza boxes – a consolation prize from Lizzy the previous night, to try to get him out of the fugue he'd been in since Poppy broke off their engagement – were still piled up on the coffee table, where they'd been since he'd bitten into his first slice of deep-pan pepperoni and pressed play on *There's Something About Mary*.

Thankfully, as soon as they got back to the flat, Cheryl had gone into the bathroom (always kept spotlessly clean at Lizzy's insistence), giving him time to tornado around the open-plan kitchen and lounge, toss all the drying washing into the laundry basket and shove the pizza boxes into the first available hiding place. Looking back now, he was pretty sure they were still under the couch. He'd forgotten all about them, thanks to having an existential crisis and deciding to embark on the most insane trip of his life this week. He should probably text Lizzy about that too.

He pulled his memory back to that night again. Cheryl had

come out of the bathroom and for a moment he thought she'd changed her mind about being there. She almost said as much. 'Look, I shouldn't have come. I'm... seeing someone,' she'd said. 'I should probably go.' His hopes had dropped like a lift with a snapped cable, but it made him feel better that there was definitely some reluctance in her voice. Now that she was walking towards him in the light of his flat, he could see that she was even more beautiful than he'd realised. She was tall, maybe five foot eight or nine, and she was wearing the tiniest white mini dress, her long legs were tanned to a dark shade of caramel and ended at skyscraper silver strappy heels. Her thick glossy hair was in a side parting and fell in waves, halfway down her back. She was just stunning and, he was pretty sure, way out of his league. It was absolutely no surprise that she'd realised her mistake and wanted to bail, he'd thought.

'Look, it's no problem at all. Let me call you a cab. Or you can stay for a coffee and then I'll call one.' He'd put his hands up in a genuine surrender pose. In all honesty, he'd expected her to see sense and bail out long before now. It was close to miraculous that she was still there. 'No pressure at all. Whatever you want to do.'

She'd leaned against the doorway as she thought that one over, all the time watching him, as he pulled himself up on the kitchen worktop. He was starting to get a bit puzzled as to what was going on when she said, 'Has anyone ever told you that you look like Ryan Reynolds?'

He'd nodded and laughed. 'Yeah. There's a couple of kids in the next street who are convinced I'm keeping the neighbourhood safe from bad guys.'

That had made her laugh and she began walking towards him, like a model coming down a catwalk. He'd sent urgent messages to his anatomy to behave itself. She was leaving. Going back to her hotel. She'd already said that. So why was she now standing right in front of him, and why were her arms going around his neck, and why were her lips now on his, and why, oh holy fuck, why was her tongue now doing a serious investigation of his tonsils?

'I think I'll stay for the coffee,' she'd whispered.

Okay, coffee. He could do that. As long as she didn't want a cappuccino, because he only had some of those Americano ones that Lizzy bought for their Dolce Gusto machine. Or rather, *his* Dolce Gusto machine. Lizzy had bought it for his last birthday, despite the fact that he'd never drunk coffee in his life. They both knew that it was only there because she drank twenty cups of coffee a day and had been trying to seduce him into the habit for years, but for the purposes of their friendship, neither of them mentioned this when she gave it to him, gift wrapped, while singing 'Happy Birthday'.

'I'll make you that coffee,' he'd said, when she moved from kissing his mouth to his neck, her hands wandering down his back.

'That's okay. I think I've changed my mind,' she'd said.

Oh. Okay. So a taxi then. But why was she still kissing him, and why, bloody hell why, were her hands now under his T-shirt at the back?

Sliding off the worktop, he'd put his hand on her face and rubbed her cheek with her thumb, lifting her chin so that her eyes were locked onto his. This wasn't working for him. He couldn't do maybes. Or confusion. He was so terrified of doing or saying the wrong thing, of making a wrong move or overstepping boundaries, that he had to get confirmation of what was really going on here.

Before he could stop his gob from seeking this clarification, it went running ahead on its own. 'Look, I think you're incredible. And possibly the most beautiful woman I've ever seen in my life.' That had made her smile, and he'd noticed that her teeth were perfect. Not like the bright white veneers that grinned their way around Brentwood every day. Naturally perfect. White, but not too white. Straight. Natural. 'But I'm not sure what's going on here and I'm not one of those blokes that just assumes stuff.'

For several seconds, while she'd stared at him but said nothing, he'd thought he'd blown it. In fact, he was convinced of it. Until she'd eventually said, 'What do you want to go on here?' Argh, that voice, that accent, it had melted his insides.

His other hand was on her face now too, both of them cupping those gorgeous cheeks, while his soul held up a white flag and surrendered into the pools of her eyes.

'I would really, really like you to stay. I'd like to kiss you on that couch over there for a long, long time. Then I'd like you to come to bed with me and... well, after that, it all goes a bit hazy.' That had made her giggle again. 'But I just want you to know...' He'd kissed her. 'That people have told me...' He'd kissed her again. 'That I have considerable talents...' Another kiss. 'In the area of general spooning.'

Her giggle was as intoxicating as every curve of her rocking body. 'Spooning?' she'd asked, reciprocating the kiss and this time holding on to his bottom lip for a moment with her teeth. Holy hell, this was doing things to him that could possibly lead to permanent damage.

'In fact, some have suggested I could be a world-class spooner. You know, if I set my mind to it.'

'Wow. That's quite a talent you must have there,' she'd grinned, playing the game.

'It is. And it's just as well because I'm crap at everything else, so don't get your hopes up.'

That had made her throw her head back as she giggled again.

'But the thing is,' he'd continued, deciding to just go for it, 'I'm rubbish at reading signs, and fairly shit at interpreting subliminal messages, and as un-sexy as it is, I don't ever want to get it wrong and fuck it up by doing something that isn't welcome. So...'

'So...' she'd echoed, looking at him now in a way that he definitely couldn't read. Why was he so crap at this?

'So I need you to tell me what you want so we're both on the same page. I can make you a coffee. I can call you a cab. Or I can take you to bed, and we can spoon until the sun comes up. But I warn you, I'll ruin you for all future spooners, because I'm the best.'

She was grinning again. 'You might have mentioned that.'

'Did I? I think my mind is slightly hazy tonight. I can't think why.'

There was a pause as she'd weighed up her options, then a wave of crashing disappointment descended when she answered.

'I don't want to spoon.'

Oh. Okay. Just coffee then. Or maybe just a cab.

'But I do want you to take me to bed. I've got a couple of skills of my own that I'd like to get your thoughts on...'

Before his memory could take a single step in the direction of what happened next, he felt a sharp nudge to the ribcage. His eyes flew open and one of his earphones fell out and slid down the side of his seat.

'Sorry!' Bernadette apologised. 'But the meals are here. Would you like chicken, beef or cheesy pasta?'

The question delivered a reality check that suddenly popped into his head. He was travelling thousands of miles to meet a woman he was convinced was his happy ever after. And he had no idea if she'd prefer chicken, beef or cheesy pasta.

2 P.M. – 4 P.M.

13

BERNADETTE

Bernadette was almost relieved when the meal service stopped her conversation with Hayley before it had even started. Not because she didn't want to share the experiences she'd alluded to earlier, although she'd shocked herself when she'd blurted out, 'I used to know someone just like him.' She was always prepared to share her own story if it could help someone and she felt this young woman might benefit from hearing about Bernadette's own experiences, about her marriage and how she'd escaped her own personal hell.

However, she was glad when the meal service got in the way of further discussion, because she wanted to give Hayley time to think about whether she was ready to open up.

But oh, how she recognised Hayley's husband the moment she'd seen the snarl of his top lip. Even though Hayley had been turned the other way when she was speaking to her husband, Bernadette had also recognised every tremble of her voice, and the anxiety and dread that emanated from every pore of her body, even after she'd bravely stood up for herself and then the flight attendant had shunted him back off to business class.

As for travelling separately, how many times had Kenneth done that to her over the years? He used to tell her that he'd been booked in business class by the hospital, or the pharmaceutical company, or whatever big-spending patient was picking up the tab to fly one of the country's top heart surgeons to Dubai, or New York, or Miami, but that he couldn't take advantage of their good nature by booking her a business-class seat too.

'That would just be rude,' he used to say, if she questioned him. No sign of any kind of concern as to whether or not it was rude of him to ditch his wife, despite the fact that they could afford to pay for an upgrade themselves. He was as tight as he was nasty.

It wasn't that she wanted to sit in the posh seats. Truthfully, she couldn't care less. But in the early days, she just wanted to be with her husband, to be enjoying their trip together. Looking back, she wasn't sure that he ever enjoyed a single moment of his time with her. Not really. Not when it was just the two of them and the children weren't involved. Maybe at first. In the early days. Unless she'd been so blinded by her love for him that she'd imagined that too. She'd asked him about it once, years later, between his many dalliances with other women. She'd demanded to know why he'd married her if she was as hopeless, as unattractive, as boring as he told her she was.

'Because you were a safe bet,' he'd told her offhandedly, like he was discussing what to have for dinner. 'I knew you'd be a terrific mother, and you'd support me while I focused on my career. You were the stability I wanted to keep everything steady while I climbed the ladder. And that's what you've been. Just a shame you've let yourself go at the same time.'

Ouch. That one had stung. But only for a moment. Because by then she hated him so much that she didn't give two hoots what he thought.

Over the years, Bernadette had become inured to most of his behaviour, but not all of it. She could tolerate the affairs, the disappearances, the blatant disregard for her feelings. She could put up with the control freakery and the insistence that every single thing he wanted had to be done perfectly. He once wrecked her phone because she hadn't put his breakfast vitamins out in the correct order. While he was berating her, her mobile rang, so he'd picked it up and hurled it at the kitchen wall, smashing it to pieces. She could tolerate the temper and irrational demands, because he never showed any of those things in front of the children and, rightly or wrongly (wrongly now, she knew), she'd lived by the honest belief that keeping their family together was the best thing to do. But what she had never come to terms with was the thing that had made her gasp out loud when Hayley's husband was here earlier: the gaslighting.

Bernadette had heard Hayley's husband saying the same things to Hayley that Kenneth had said to her, in one way or another, a thousand times throughout their marriage.

Hayley's husband's words were replaying in Bernadette's mind. 'What the hell has got into you? You're being totally fucking irrational.'

Gaslighting 101. He acts completely reprehensibly, and when she reacts, he tells her she's crazy. Kenneth had done that to her too many times to mention.

The times when she'd suggested he was having affairs and he'd told her she was imagining it.

The times when she'd challenged him about where he'd been, and he'd said she was neurotic.

The times when she'd expressed doubts over his feelings for her and he'd accused her of being paranoid.

So many times. More than she could count.

And what scared her the most was that on way too many of those occasions, she'd believed him.

It had taken her a lifetime to find her strength and to walk away, and when she did, there had been the predictable rage on his part, the blind fury that she'd gone. Then, more surprisingly, came his remorse, the pleading, the genuine devastation. That led to the casual drop-ins, the fabricated excuses for family get-togethers, the suggestions of things they could all do in the future. That all led up to the biggest shock of all. A couple of years after she'd left him, the great Kenneth Manson, master of the universe, had actually begged her to forgive him and to come back to him.

It was little Casey's fifth birthday, and they'd been at Nina's house for the party in the garden. Stuart was working on a case, so he and Connor couldn't make it, but as always, Bernadette was there early and happy to help. 'You're on bounce patrol, Mum,' Nina had informed her when she'd arrived. She'd gestured to the bouncy castle they'd hired for the occasion. 'You're like the lifeguard at a pool, only it's your job to make sure none of these lovely little buggers bounce right out of this inflatable and do themselves an injury on my whirligig.'

'And what exactly are the requirements for this position?' Bernadette had asked, playing along.

'You sit over there at my new Argos dining set and I'll bring you cold drinks while you keep an eye on them.'

'Throw in some of this carrot cake, and I'm in,' Bernadette had countered, handing over the cake she'd baked that morning.

Nina had laughed as she gratefully accepted it. 'Deal.'

It was the first thing Kenneth had noticed when he'd arrived, all suave smiles and easy charm, as he pulled out a rattan chair and joined her at the table.

'Your home-made carrot cake?' he'd asked, gesturing to the plate in front of her.

'Yes. The diet starts tomorrow. Or maybe next week,' she'd answered lightly, playing her usual glib game of pretending he was a casual acquaintance, not the man who'd made her life hell for years. It seemed ridiculous, but it was the only way she got through their encounters.

Nina was keeping a discreet watch on the interaction between her parents from a distance. Their daughter loved her father, but Bernadette had learned after their split that she also saw his flaws. If there was a side to choose, Nina stuck with her mother, but Bernadette made a point never to put her in that position.

That was the first day that Bernadette had noticed the subtle difference in Kenneth's appearance. He'd always been immaculately groomed, masterful in the organisation of his life, his work and his appearance. To the untrained eye, he would have seemed the same as always, but Bernadette saw something different. The slight shadow on his face that revealed he'd left the house without shaving. The curls of the hair on the back of his collar, unheard of for a man who had a standing fortnightly booking with his barber. The creases on his white linen shirt. The missing belt on the waistband of his chinos. None of that was standard Kenneth, and yes, her first reaction was to have a shallow dig in his direction: clearly whatever thirty-year-old model he was dating now wasn't keeping up with his standards.

There had been quite a few of them since Bernadette had left. Not just the one he was shagging for the last few years of their marriage. That dalliance had fallen apart the night the young woman had shown up at their door and exposed their affair to Bernadette, Nina and Stuart. Kenneth had exploded with fury on their front step that night but Bernadette didn't stick around to watch what happened next. She'd already packed her stuff and was leaving him anyway.

After that, there seemed to be a steady stream of young beautiful women, few of them older than their daughter. Turned out Kenneth had a type. And it was about as far from Bernadette as it was possible to be.

Not that she'd vocalised that thought, of course. She wouldn't give him the satisfaction of thinking she cared enough to notice, and she'd made a promise to herself that she'd always keep things civil, for the kids, the grandkids and for the sake of her own dignity.

'How are you, Bernadette?' he'd asked that day, like she was an old friend and not the woman who'd been his psychological target practice for three decades.

'I'm good. Really good,' she'd answered honestly.

That's when he'd proved that even after knowing him for over thirty years, he could still surprise her.

He'd taken a sip of his coffee, eyes focused on the bouncy castle, not even making eye contact with her when he'd said, 'Bernadette, when are we going to put an end to all this nonsense?'

Bernadette was puzzled. What nonsense? Casey's birthday party? Did Kenneth have something against inflatable play structures?

'Nonsense?' she'd asked, genuinely confused.

'Yes, this... separation. Between us.' He'd made a dismissive gesture with his hand, one she'd seen him make a million times.

Bernadette had felt the hackles on her neck begin to rise and reminded herself to keep it together, keep it amicable. Nina was still glancing over every few minutes, and Bernadette was damned if anything was going to spoil this day for her daughter, her grandson, or the fourteen five-year-olds who were bouncing themselves into a frenzy. 'Separation?' She was staring straight ahead, a fixed smile on her face, her light tone a stark contrast to the words she was actually saying. 'You mean our divorce. The one that came about because you cheated on me throughout our whole marriage, undermined me, betrayed me, bullied me, scared me and made me miserable every day of my life. That separation?'

He acted like she hadn't spoken. 'Bernie...' He never called her that, so it jarred with her. To him, she was always Bernadette. Or bitch. Depending on the day. He turned to face her now, put his coffee down and reached over, putting his hand over hers. 'Bernadette...' he said this time, and for once in his life he seemed to be struggling for the words. 'I'm so sorry. For everything. I know I treated you terribly and it was a mistake, all of it. I see that now, though.'

Bernadette had still stared straight ahead, never straying from her bounce watch duties. Out of the corner of her eye, she could see Nina's jaw drop as she glanced over and spotted the hand hold.

She slowly tried to extricate her hand, but Kenneth just held on to it tighter. 'I've been vile. Inexcusable. I know that, but I also know that we had a wonderful life together and I want that back, Bernadette. I want you back. Nothing makes sense without you. Nothing works. It just all seems so... empty. Like the ground isn't stable any more. Please, Bernadette. Please let me make it up to you. I could cut back on work and we could travel. Take trips. Fly off whenever you wanted. Enjoy our time together.'

Who was this man? Bernadette wanted to check him for signs of a mental aberration. A stroke, maybe. Then it struck her. He was the man she thought she'd married. Somewhere in that, there was a moment of vindication. Looking at him now, or rather, half looking at him, half focusing on some serious bounce action, he was so genuine, so vulnerable, so utterly believable, that it gave her the answer to the question she'd asked herself more than any other in the last few years. How could she have fallen for him? How did she not see that he was a monster? This was why. He was this person too. This loving, sweet, tender man who could win her over with his words. She hadn't been a fool. He'd just been a really good actor. But she was no longer interested in watching the performance.

'Kenneth, move your hand off mine,' she'd said calmly, and only Kenneth was close enough to see that it was through gritted teeth. 'Don't ever touch me again without my permission.'

'Bernadette, come on—'

'Shut. Up. I'm speaking. Let me tell you something in very clear language. I will never come back to you. I will never touch you again. I will never want to be in your company, but I'll do it for the kids and so will you. There is no world in which there will ever be more than necessary civility between us. But if you don't take your fucking hand off mine right now, I will find a way to break it. Do you understand me?'

There was such cool venom in her voice, such absolute conviction, not to mention the completely uncharacteristic profanity, that he'd removed his hand, made an excuse to leave early, and he'd never said any of those things again.

The astonishing realisation that the man who had treated her like mess on the bottom of his shoe had somehow hated living without her, gave Bernadette no satisfaction whatsoever. Rather, it just made her despise him and pity him more. He was a flawed character, Kenneth. A broken person. But one who paraded in a costume of respectability and success. A bit like yer man who'd been sitting in the seat at the end of this row just a few minutes ago.

Watching Hayley deal with her husband had made Bernadette's heart break, just as it had done every single time a victim of domestic violence had come through the doors at A&E. In those cases, the broken bones and scars were visible, but Bernadette also knew that repeated psychological abuse left wounds that cut just as deep. Her scars still ached sometimes, especially when someone reminded her of how she got them.

So yes, Bernadette knew exactly who and what Lucas Ford was. And while she completely understood that – for whatever reason – Hayley hadn't yet found her voice to fight back, Bernadette knew that if he pulled any of that nonsense with his wife again, Bernadette was ready and able to shout loud enough for them both.

14

TADGH

Tadgh was finding it difficult to swallow his food. He'd put his earphones in, and he was blasting some Marvin Gaye into his brain, trying desperately to get back some kind of grip over his thoughts, still unable to accept that the worst could be true. It couldn't. It just couldn't. Not Cheryl. Not Shay.

And not another seven hours stuck in the fecking sky, on the way to his wedding, with his whole life hanging in the balance.

He sighed, gave up on the food, put his blunt knife and mini fork down and tossed his napkin onto the tray. That's when he noticed that the tray on the table next to him was untouched too. He glanced over to his left and saw that Hayley was staring straight ahead, eyes on the mini screen in front of her, watching a bank heist movie that he recognised. He'd watched it with Cheryl just a few weeks ago, one night at his flat, when they were chilling out, wrapped up in each other on the sofa. They'd yet to move in properly together. He'd shared with Shay and Conlan since college and Cheryl had a free room in her sister's house. It had made sense to keep rent costs low while they were saving for the wedding, while Tadgh and the guys were on the road so much and while he still spent a couple of nights a week at his da's place, keeping him company. When Tadgh was at the flat, Cheryl pretty much moved in with him though. After the wedding they were going to rent another apartment in Tadgh's block. At least, that had been the plan when they were happy. Excited about their future. When she wasn't screwing his brother.

He must have sighed really loudly, because Hayley turned to stare at him, and he saw her lips move. He pulled his headphones out of his ears, and she half smiled as she repeated the question. 'Are you okay?'

'Yeah. Yeah, I'm good. Thanks.'

He was about to leave it at that and put his earphones back in, go back to contemplating the shitshow of his life, when she went on.

'Yeah, I can see that you're good. Dandy. When I'm good, I can't eat and I blast Marvin Gaye into my head too. You're giving off all the signs of being good. Great, in fact.'

It was cheeky, intrusive and really, really unwelcome... but there was something about the way she said it, with such complete matter of fact-ness, that made him defrost just a little.

'Sorry. Yeah, I'm not having a great day.'

'Worse than mine? You've met my husband.' There was something so endearing about the fact that she was trying to make conversation, even though they were both very obviously having a shit time.

'Okay, you win. But it's pretty close.' He could feel the gravel in his voice as he spoke. Not enough sleep. Too much Jack Daniel's. One huge big fecking problem.

'Are you going to St Lucia on your own?' she asked, and he recognised something in her expression – she just needed to talk. She just needed to take her mind off whatever she was struggling with right now. And Tadgh's money was on that absolute prick of a husband.

On any other day, he'd have been happy to pass the time with some small talk. Some of his favourite moments had been sitting next to strangers in bars or coffee shops, passing the time with a bit of craic. His mam could talk for hours to a stranger sitting next to her on a bus and he'd inherited the gene. Today, he really couldn't face it, but he didn't have it in him to be rude either. His mother would haunt him if he snubbed anyone. 'Tadgh Donovan, cop onto yerself and treat other people with the kindness you'd be wanting for yerself.' It was her mantra for life. He wondered how she would feel about Shay taking that a few steps too far when it came to his brother's fiancée. He pushed that thought aside, and focused on channelling his mam's elite small talk talents.

'No, my brother and my best mate are back in economy.'

He saw a hint of a frown cross her face and he rushed to explain.

'I didn't ditch them like... you know.' He didn't have to say what he was thinking. He didn't ditch them like her husband had ditched her. 'There was a problem with my seat back there – it had been given to someone else – so they put me here instead. Just one of those lucky breaks.'

Not that he felt very fecking lucky.

'Ah, in that case you're forgiven. What is it, then, lads' holiday?'

'No. I'm going to...' The words got stuck in his throat. 'I'm going to get married. Day after tomorrow.'

Her eyes widened. 'Holy shit, really? Congratulations. That sounds...' A pause. He saw that she was clearly trying to process the mixed signals that he was giving off. Going to get married should evoke giddy glee, yet he knew that he was more on the funereal side of both giddy and glee. '... That sounds, erm, great?' she finished weakly. 'Or it would, if you weren't trying to claim you're having a worse day than me. I feel like you're using some kind of false pretences to get the sympathy vote.' There was a hint of teasing in there. 'Are you having cold feet? Changed your mind? Have you forgotten where you're getting married? Is your fiancée called Euphemia and you're worried about having to say that name for the rest of your life? Or did you sleep with a stripper on your stag night? Only I nearly did that, so I'd understand. Her name was Bubbles. She could do some very interesting tricks.'

That made him chuckle out loud. 'Please tell me you're not making that up?'

'Sorry,' she conceded. 'I was totally making that up. I've had a few Proseccos and I was just trying to build a bit of empathy to make you feel better.'

'I appreciate that.' He realised she was waiting for an answer. 'But no, I didn't sleep with a stripper called Bubbles on my stag night. Or anyone else. And I don't have cold feet. I haven't forgotten where the wedding is – I've already sent the entire contents of my bank account to a place called The Sands to pay for it. And her name is Cheryl, although now I kind of wish it was Euphemia. I'm just... Look, it's complicated. I wouldn't want to bore you with it all.' He wasn't about to unburden himself and share his deepest darkest secrets with someone he'd just met. Conlan had been his best mate for a million years and he hadn't even cracked a light to him. Time to steer the conversation away to safer territory. 'What about you? Why are you having such a bad day if you're flying off for a swanky holiday?' He was tempted to add, 'Apart from the obvious reason that your husband appears to be a complete wanker,' but he didn't.

She let out a sad sigh. 'Because I don't think it's got off to a great start. You know that thing when you're really looking forward to something and then when you get there you realise that there's no way it can match up to the way you thought it was going to be?'

He nodded. She could be describing his forthcoming wedding.

'Well, that. It's just... complicated,' she said, with a sad smile, repeating his conclusion from earlier.

Both complicated. Both messed up. Both sighing a lot.

'Do you want to go back to your Marvin Gaye and ignore the world? I won't be offended.'

'Nah, it's okay. You can get too much of a good thing.' He surprised himself by deciding that was true. Kind of. He could never get too much Marvin, but he didn't want to go back inside his own head. Didn't want to torture himself with ifs and buts and maybes. And talking to this friendly and, now that he was looking at her properly, very lovely face was taking his mind off it all. 'We could rewind off the complicated and go for meaningless trivia?' he suggested.

She seemed to like that idea. 'Like what?'

'Like... what do you do? For a living?'

'I'm a dance and drama teacher in a high school in London.'

'Shit, really?' Dance and drama? He had no idea why, but he hadn't been expecting that. She seemed too... He struggled to pinpoint it. Too straight. Too polished. If he'd had to make a random guess, he'd have said that she was an interior designer, maybe. Or perhaps some kind of doctor.

She was curious. 'Why do you look so surprised?'

He was now on the back foot, trying to make sure he didn't say anything that would offend her. Maybe they should go back to their complicated shit days – it might be less of a minefield. 'I don't know. I guess... I've got a couple of mates who do similar jobs and they're both really... artsy? You know, a bit individual and very obviously creative.'

Damn. That didn't come out right. It sounded like an insult, as opposed to a genuine explanation of his surprise. He really hoped he hadn't offended her, but he didn't have time to suss that out because she came back with...

'What about you? What do you do?'

'I'm a graphic designer.'

'Shit, really?' she countered, replicating his response.

He went along with it. 'Why do you look so surprised?' he asked, joining the repetition game.

'Because,' she said, her smile oozing cheekiness, 'I've got a couple of mates who do similar jobs and they're both really... smart. You know, a bit together.'

'Yeah, I didn't get that memo,' he laughed, with a nod to his attire. 'But in my defence, that's only my side gig to pay the bills. I also play guitar in a band.'

'Really? What are they called? I'm going to be mortified if I've never heard of them.'

'You probably won't have. We've got a bit of a following in Ireland, but nothing major overseas. We're called Home.'

Her reaction was completely unexpected. 'You had a song called "Yesterday".'

He nodded, grinning. 'Yeah. The Beatles probably want a word with us about the title. You've heard it?'

Other than 'Everywhere Without You', the song he'd written for his da about his mam dying, 'Yesterday' was probably his favourite of all their tracks. He'd penned it about a year ago, when all the marriage stuff was just kicking off and he realised he'd never expected to be the kind of guy who had a big flash swanky wedding. It was a song about how people changed, became different from who they thought they'd be. About how life took you in ways you didn't expect. About how it was so easy to lose the person you were. And it also had a killer melody and a hook that got stuck in the brain and didn't shift. It had been their biggest hit so far. Of course, Shay hated it, because he hadn't written it, but his ego put up with it because the fans loved it. Besides, on paper the three of them – Tadgh, Shay and Conlan – had equal writing credits on every song, regardless of who wrote it, so it allowed him to take credit for it even though he hadn't penned a single word.

An incredulous smile. 'I've heard it. Hang on...' She pulled her phone out of her bag and flipped on her iTunes, then showed him her library. 'Yesterday', by Home. There it was. 'I love it. The words, they just speak to me. You know when you hear something, and you just relate? I promise I'm not just saying this, but that's how I felt when I first heard it. One of my students, Aoife, was working on a dance to it for her finals. Sorry if that breaches copyright or something...'

Tadgh shook his head, inwardly chuffed that a teenager in London loved the song so much that it made her want to dance. That's what it had always been about for him. Shay wanted the money, the fame, the adulation from the crowd; Tadgh just wanted the music. 'I hereby give Aoife permission to dance her heart out to it.'

'Thank you. I'll let her know. Oh my God, I'm going to be the coolest teacher who ever lived when I tell her about this. Thank you for raising my street cred.' Her grin was infectious, and Tadgh couldn't help noticing that it completely changed her face, wiping away all the stress and tension that had been there after the visit from her husband. She was lighter. Brighter. And there was no ignoring that she was beautiful.

'Any time.'

'Hang on.' She looked like she was plucking something from her memory and she grinned when she found it. 'Aoife told me she's madly in love with the singer, so that would be...?' The way she was waiting for him to respond, suggested she thought it could be him.

'My brother,' he admitted, making her laugh again and put her face in her hands.

'Noooo, I'm sorry. I'll tell her she should switch her adoration to you. I'm sure you're much nicer.'

Before he could stop himself, he shrugged, 'I hope so.'

Feck. Now he was going to have to explain what he meant by that. Or maybe she hadn't heard him. He caught her quizzical expression. Nope, definitely heard him. Okay, he could just change the subject. Or maybe he should just blurt out the whole sorry fecking story. It wasn't as if he was ever going to see this woman again after they got off the plane. It would give her a great story to take back to her mates. Or her students. Might even sell a few records.

The knot in his stomach was tightening again as the temporary escapism turned to dust and the whole saga reclaimed its place front and centre in his mind.

And she was still waiting for some kind of follow-up to his comment.

A buzz. A vibration. They both flicked their eyes to her phone, but she checked the screen and shrugged.

He reached over and pulled his phone from the pocket in front of him.

New message.

From Cheryl. Nerves tighter than guitar strings, he was immediately snapped back from casual chit chat to the carnage going on in his real life.

He held up the phone, doing that uncomfortable gesturing thing that people do when they need to answer something. 'Sorry. I've been waiting for this message. I'm gonna go stretch my legs while I check it out.'

15

HAYLEY

Hayley watched Tadgh go, blown away by the coincidence. She'd only downloaded that track a couple of months ago, played it dozens of times, and she wasn't making up the stuff about the lyrics speaking to her. It was about who you used to be. And the person she used to be bore no resemblance to the one she was now.

Twisting back to the centre, she saw that, next to her, Dev had finished his meal and was watching something with Liam Hemsworth in it. And costumes. And a whole lot of CGI. One of the Marvel movies, she guessed. Not something she was familiar with. Lucas couldn't bear the comic book adaptations, unless they had Scarlett Johansson in them wearing a catsuit, in which case he was prepared to watch the trailer. The full movie was still a step too far.

Over at the end of the row, Bernadette had finished her meal and her head was resting against the back of her seat, her eyes closed. She was such a lovely lady. Hayley had felt a real connection with her earlier and she hoped they got to have the discussion that Bernadette had mentioned. It was hard to imagine anything terrible happening to someone who seemed so positive and uplifting, so Hayley wanted to hear about the woman's life. She'd always been curious that way. She used to be the person who could walk into a Phuket backpacking hostel and have five new friends before the weekend was done. When they'd been planning their wedding, Lucas had grumbled constantly about the number of guests on her side, all friends that she'd accumulated at school, at college, during her travels. It suddenly struck her that she'd lost touch with almost all of them now. How could so much have changed in ten years? And how could she have lost so many friends and not replaced them? She and Lucas had their 'couple' friends – mostly his mates and their wives, similar people, in similar lines of work, who lived in similar houses, in similar advantaged areas in London and Surrey. The only thing Hayley had in common with them was the Miele coffee machines they all had in their kitchens. Despite Hayley's objection, Lucas had put theirs on their wedding list and to her astonishment one of his wealthy aunts had bought it for them. That's when she truly realised she was entering a different world, one where people paid over a thousand pounds for a coffee machine.

That said, her wedding day had been the best day of her life. They'd held it in a marquee in his parents' garden in the house he'd grown up in in Farnham. It was a far cry from her three-bed semi in Clacton. Property and material things never meant much to her parents. They'd met at college and recognised the other's inner hippy. Her dad had gone on to teach art at a local comprehensive and her mother was a sex therapist, something that Lucas had begged her not to tell his parents until after they were married. It wasn't a tough secret to hide. Hayley had just told them her mum was a wellness therapist and dropped any mention of the orgasmic side of the job. They never heard it from the therapist's mouth either, because the four parents only met twice before the ceremony, and even then, it was at busy events, with too many other people for a cosy chat.

At the time, Hayley hadn't seen the issue with it, too blinded with love for Lucas to seek out any sinister motive in his request. She'd just thought he didn't want to make her embarrassed by discussing her mum's slightly unconventional job. Now she realised he hadn't done it to protect her. He'd done it because he was embarrassed. Embarrassed by her parents, embarrassed about where they were from, just as he was embarrassed now by the fact that her reproductive system didn't bloody work. Back then, she had no idea he could be intolerant.

At the wedding, he'd held her close as they swayed to 'Sitting On The Dock of The Bay', chosen as the song for their first dance because on the night they met, they'd sat on a beach and talked until sunrise. He was so smart, so kind, so interested, that she felt beyond lucky to have met him. They were engaged in six months, married in a year, both of them, she thought, meaning every word of the richer and poorer, sickness and health stuff.

She couldn't believe two people could be so happy. Sure, there were blips. The occasional fight. And yes, he could be jealous and a bit possessive, but that was only because he loved her so much. At least, that's what he told her, and she chose to believe it. Besides, he had so many other qualities that made up for the occasional flash of temper. He worked really hard. He was so charismatic, the kind of guy who commanded every room he was in. He still made her heart pound when he walked in the door at night, although, there was now a thirty-second window of apprehension while she sussed out from his expression and his body language whether he was in a good mood or not.

That aside, she saw now that his strongest quality was his loyalty. Even though she hadn't been able to give him the one thing he wanted most – a family – he'd stayed with her, held her up, stood by her side as they'd tried and failed so many times. He hadn't complained when cycle after cycle of hormone injections had made her emotions fire all over the place, or when she'd become despondent after another failure. Or when she was mentally exhausted by the emotional toll, or physically exhausted by the relentless schedule of consultations, treatments and procedures. Or on the nights that she'd fallen apart, said she couldn't do it any more, only to get up the next morning and find the strength to go again. Fertility treatment was, without contest, the hardest thing she'd ever endured in her life. Actually, that wasn't true. The hardest thing was when it failed. And every time, Lucas had stayed and supported her as they tried again.

That was love. Wasn't it?

She just wished it didn't come with a steady increase in the kind of asshole behaviour he'd shown earlier. If Bernadette hadn't reached over and shown her some kindness, she'd still be sitting there in a maelstrom of anxiety, berating herself and trying to work out what she could have done differently so as not to provoke him.

She blinked back a fresh set of tears that were threatening to fall. No. She wasn't going to let this get her down. For the next... she checked the flight map on the screen in front of her... six and a bit hours, she was going to just block everything out of her mind and enjoy the peace, the movies, and the chat with the new people she'd met.

The conversation with Tadgh had been the loveliest she'd had in ages. She'd just been herself. Just Hayley. Not Mrs Ford. Lucas had done her a favour, because she'd never have struck up a conversation with a stranger if he was with her. He hated small talk. He hated meeting new people. When they went on holiday, he actively avoided anyone who seemed in the least bit chatty. They'd once spent a whole week on a Caribbean cruise ducking into doorways to avoid a boisterous lady from Eastbourne that they'd met at the Captain's Table on the first night and who had a burning desire to talk to Lucas about her daughter's fallopian tubes.

'Excuse me, can I take that tray away for you?' The flight attendant's voice broke into her thoughts. Not Marian. The younger guy with the deep tan and the blonde highlights who served the drinks earlier. Now that he was next to her, Hayley could see on his name badge that his name was Stefan. It suited him. 'Was it awful?' he whispered conspiratorially, in a thick Geordie accent, gesturing to the full meal that was still in front of her, then switching his gaze to the full meal that was still lying on Tadgh's tray too. 'Och, your husband has barely touched his as well. I've got a few bags of pretzels and some Kit Kats that I could bring...'

Hayley was trying to unpack everything that was in that sentence. 'Oh, he's not my husband.'

That clearly confused him, and he flushed a little.

Hayley immediately went for a joke to relieve the awkwardness. 'Unfortunately,' she added with a cheeky smile.

Stefan's shoulders visibly dropped with relief. 'I was thinking the same myself,' he said with a camp wink, and Hayley almost choked on a giggle. She had a feeling that if Marian heard this, she'd headlock Stefan all the way to HR for a lecture on appropriate customer conversations.

'The meal was fine, really. I just wasn't hungry.'

'Well, the offer of the pretzels and Kit Kats stands until we land,' Stefan said warmly, before reaching over for her tray and removing it.

Dev spotted what was happening and he slipped his headphones off and handed his tray over too, before gingerly moving the tray from the table in front of a sleeping Bernadette, taking off the uneaten chocolate pudding and putting that back on her table, before handing the rest of the tray over to Stefan. Row cleared, he moved on to the next one with a cheery wave.

Tadgh still hadn't returned, but Hayley didn't feel like watching a movie. Maybe later. Right now, she wasn't in the right headspace. Perhaps she'd just listen to music for a while and have a nap.

Glancing over at Dev's screen, she saw that the Hemsworth bloke was gone and had been replaced by an old episode of *Friends*. She'd noticed that on the entertainment menu earlier and had made a mental note to watch it. It was the one where…

'Rachel got off the plane,' she murmured, and Dev nodded.

'It's a classic. I must have watched it a hundred times.'

There was a pause as they both stared at the screen, neither of them able to hear the words, but it didn't matter because they both knew it word for word.

'Have you ever been in love like that?' Dev asked, then immediately followed it up with, 'Oh God, I'm so sorry – that was completely inappropriate. It's the journalist in me – makes me ask intrusive questions without thinking. No boundaries.'

How could a guy this cute and this funny not have met someone? How could he possibly have to fly halfway around the world to track down a one-night stand? She understood that the decision was partially fuelled by the need to follow up a wonderful plotline for his novel, but still… It was either the most romantic story ever or a red flag so big it could double as a blanket.

'Yes. I think so,' she answered truthfully. 'When I first met my husband.'

'The bloke who was here earlier?' he asked, and she could see he was trying super hard not to give any hint of cynicism. She didn't blame him. The Lucas that had sat down here earlier wasn't much of a catch.

'Yes.' She wasn't going to try to defend him. Right now, she really didn't give a toss what anyone thought about her husband, and she wanted to talk about him as little as possible.

'And how long was it before you realised you'd fallen in love with him? I'm asking this from a purely professional research point of view and not just being incredibly nosy.' He said it with such sincerity and warmth that Hayley could see he was genuinely interested. However, she was distracted by...

'You really do look like Ryan Reynolds, you know.' It was off the subject, but she couldn't help it. The similarity was impossible to miss.

'I do know. I just wish I had his bank account. And his career. And his wife. Even his wardrobe would do. The only thing I've got in common with him is facial features and a strange affinity for Hugh Jackman. A bit unnerving really.'

'I can see your point,' Hayley nodded, her cheeks beginning to hurt with the effort of keeping her face in a deadpan expression. She could honestly hang out with this guy all day long, just watching great TV and talking nonsense. He couldn't be further away from the man she'd married. 'Let me see...' she pondered, going back to his original question. How long had it been before she'd realised she was in love with Lucas? 'Do you want me to give it to you in hours or days?'

'Both,' he said.

She thought about it again. 'About twelve hours. So half a day.'

His eyes widened with incredulity. 'Seriously? That makes me feel a little less nuts.'

'I don't know if I'd have chased across the world after him the next day though, so you're not entirely off the hook. I definitely wouldn't have splashed out a fortune on a flight. Maybe a bus. A train at a push.'

He didn't mind the teasing. 'You're right. And I'm pretty sure the nice folks at Mastercard will agree with you when the bills come in.'

They watched a few more moments of *Friends*, before he turned to her again.

'Can I ask you something else?'

'Anything. I think.'

'Do you ever regret it? Falling in love that quickly.'

Hayley couldn't speak. Did she? A couple of years ago, she'd have said absolutely not. No regrets.

But now?

She really wasn't sure at all.

16

DEV

Hayley got up to go to the loo, so Dev lifted his earphones to pop them back in his ears, then changed his mind and dug his phone out of the seat-front pocket. There was a notification on the screen telling him that a text had come in from Lizzy just thirty seconds ago. It was spooky how that happened. He would be thinking about calling her and the phone would ring. Or he'd call her, and she'd pick up the phone with a 'Stop freaking me out! I'd just picked up my phone to call you, you scary bastard.' Then she'd laugh and say something about psychic synergies and nuns in a convent all having their periods at the same time.

Hey Romeo, how's it going? Have you changed your mind yet? Or fallen in love at first sight again on the plane? If so, bring her home immediately and save hotel bills. Love ya x

He laughed under his breath as he typed back...

Shut it, Juliet. You're becoming really cynical in your old age. Still following my love at first sight. Also fell in love on plane. Lovely lady called Bernadette. Gutted to say she's not into younger men.

She answered back immediately.

I'm seriously concerned about you. Are you on one of those dodgy teas that enhances your virility?

Dev's fingers flew across the keyboard on the screen.

Yep, Tetley. I'm a sex God in any bingo hall.

He could almost hear her laughing as she read that.

Yeah, that'll be us when we're older. In the bingo hall, I'll be thumping my dabber (not a metaphor) and you'll be on your third divorce. We'll live happily ever after.

He could already picture them. It would be like the Essex version of *Last of The Summer Wine.*

We'd already be living happily ever after if you'd accepted my proposal. And I'd have saved a fortune on air fares.

He threw that one in regularly. It was a standing joke between them because...

You were six. I wasn't sure about your prospects. That hasn't changed.

You might have a point. By the way, there's a guy on this flight that you would love. Just your type.

Photos! I need to see pics.

I can't take a picture of him. He'll think I'm weird.

You're spending your life savings hunting down a woman you shagged once. You are fricking weird.

Fair point. Anyway, I don't need to take a pic. I heard him say he's in a band called HOME.

I'm googling... googling... still googling... HOLY FUCK he is gorgeous!!!!!!!!

How do you know which guy it is – there's more than one of them in the band.

Doesn't matter, cos HOLY FUCK THEY'RE ALL GORGEOUS!!!!! Bring him home for me. Gift wrapped.

He might object. Anyway, think he's on his way to get married. Doesn't look very happy about it though.

THAT'S COS HE'S NOT MARRYING ME!!!!

You're right. That must be it. I'll let him know.

Smashing. I'll find a white frock.

Before you do that, can you check under the couch. Just realised there might still be some mess there from my rapid clear up last weekend.

Yep, Romeo, I'll clear up your mess. Bring this woman back if she likes cleaning. Anyway, need to go, LYLB xxx

Miss ya, LYLB xxx

The acronym LYLB stood for Love Ya Loser, Bye and they'd been signing off their texts to each other like that for a lifetime. Couldn't beat a token word insult to brighten the day.

Okay, what to do now? Another episode of *Friends*? Or another movie where a Hemsworth made him feel like an inadequate member of the male species?

He briefly thought about switching the TV off and using the next few hours to work on his book. He could do background bios for the characters, start on a synopsis, plot out the storyline... Or he could watch a couple of romcoms and call it research.

Yeah, that's what he'd do. A bit of his favourite escapism. Completely unrealistic, but gave him all the feels. Although, as he and Lizzy had discussed countless times, usually over therapeutic hangover-curing Bloody Marys on a Sunday morning, if his life was a romantic comedy, he'd already have married Lizzy, because nine times out of ten, the leading lady always ended up tossing aside the good-looking lust-fest for the quirky best pal, and if Dev was born to be anything, it was the quirky best pal.

However – woe – despite proposing to Lizzy when they were six, and then one of them proposing to the other at least a dozen or so other times over the years (usually due to alcohol, and invariably when one of them was lying on the pieces of their latest broken relationship), the romcom ending had eluded them. They'd even had sex once. Just once. They were eighteen, drunk on cider, and they were in Benidorm on an end-of-school trip with all their mates before they all went their separate ways. Somehow, Lizzy had gone AWOL, and he'd searched the bars for her for hours. When he'd eventually found her, she was dancing the Macarena with three French guys and an Austrian bodybuilder. Yep, it was random, even for her. Anyway, he'd joined in, they'd drank some more, danced some more and then made it back to the apartment, where their mates had already claimed all the beds and the sofas. They'd ended up out on the balcony (thankfully it was a stone one, so anyone walking past wouldn't get flashed if they happened to gaze skywards), two people on a lilo for one. Sometimes, in their nightmares, they could both still hear the squeak of plastic against drunken flesh. The next morning, they'd woken with the sun blinding them on one side, and on the other, at least ten of their mates had their faces pressed up against the door, checking out what was going on. Fortunately, they were both fully clothed and there was absolutely no evidence of the previous night's encounter. Lizzy had given their mates the finger, then rolled over and raised herself up on one elbow, so that her face was only a few inches from his.

'Eh, did we have sex last night?' she'd asked warily.

'We did,' Dev had admitted, then waited as the full ramifications of that set in. 'Oh shit, we did! I... I... I don't know what to say about that.' His head was exploding, and not just because it was already 80 degrees at 7 a.m. and he was so dehydrated he was pretty sure that his kidneys were the size of walnuts. He'd slept with Lizzy. No, not just slept. They'd done that a thousand times. They'd. Had. Sex. Real sex. The kind that they'd always sworn they'd never have because they were too close to mess up their friendship. And now... He'd groaned again. What had they been thinking? And worse, had it even been any good? As far as he could remember, it was great, but he only had a vague memory of it because they'd been way too drunk to make an informed judgement.

Lizzy had sighed, slumped back down, then reached for a packet of Marlboro lights and a lighter that were on the floor where she'd dropped them the night before. She'd lit up a cig – he'd never picked up the habit because he liked his football too much – while he'd tried desperately to rewind the sequence of events in his head.

They'd come back from the club. There were no beds. Alfie, their rugby pal, was on the manky sofa with the wooden arms and snoring like a moose, so they were down to two choices: the bath or the balcony. And they could still hear Alfie snoring from the bath. Balcony it was. They'd come out, spent at least ten hilarious drunken minutes trying to fit both of them on the lilo, then somehow, like some teenage game of drunken Twister, they'd got tangled up in each other and...

'I think you sang the Macarena while we were having sex,' he'd blurted.

Lizzy had stubbed her cigarette out in one of Alfie's Reeboks and groaned as she pulled her knees up to her chest and rested her forehead on them. 'I think I did. I can still hear it now. Oh God, shoot me.'

Even then, as a teenager who'd had sex approximately three and a half times (he wasn't sure if the fourth one counted because it was his first time, it was done standing up and he wasn't convinced all the bits had ended up in the right place), he knew that 'Shoot me now' wasn't the ideal comment to hear from the woman you slept with the night before.

He'd been too busy panicking to even process how he felt about it. He'd slept with Lizzy. His best mate his whole life. On a lilo. And now Lizzy and lilos were probably wrecked for him for eternity.

'Lizzy, I'm sorry...'

'Don't be,' she'd snapped. 'From what I remember, I was the one who thought it would be hilarious to see if sex on a lilo was even possible.'

Now that she'd said that, a little tug of recall backed up her claim. It had taken them several attempts, at her insistence, to get the whole way through it without falling off. All Dev could remember was finding the whole thing absolutely hilarious and when they were done, telling her... telling her... Oh fuck, he'd told her he loved her. Which was nothing completely unusual, because they said they loved each other all the time, but not right after his penis had been doing the Macarena anywhere near her bits. And that one had definitely counted because they'd done it lying down and he was pretty much, 100 per cent certain that everything had ended up in the right place.

'Okay, here's what we're going to do,' Lizzy had said, with such gravity that he'd been half expecting to be left in Benidorm to survive on nothing but cheap beer and chips. 'We're never going to talk about this again. We're just going to pretend it never happened. We're going to forget about it. Deny it until our dying days. That way, it won't be weird or awkward between us because... well, because it never happened. We'll just carry on being best mates and wipe it from our minds. Agreed?'

It was so simple. So brilliant. And it didn't involve being abandoned in a foreign country or losing the person he loved most in the world. Done deal.

'Agreed.'

'Excellent. Now get up, let's go find bacon sandwiches before I faint.'

And that's how it happened. That's how they got over it. Bacon sandwiches, amnesia, and it all stayed completely in the past, unless he saw an inflatable bed or heard the Macarena. It was as good an outcome as he could have hoped for.

And no, it was never repeated, because, well, they both knew that they just weren't a romantic fit. He wasn't her type, and she wasn't his. She liked edgy, cool guys, the kind who were a challenge and who never quite let you know where you stood. Extra points if they liked country music and looked like Tim McGraw. He liked...

he liked... Actually, he'd never really sussed that out. He liked women who made him laugh. Who were funny. Chilled. Happy to just be in the moment and enjoy life.

Christ, he sounded like one of those Instagram banners about living for today and smelling the coffee. Problem was, he just wanted someone to smell the coffee with him.

And Cheryl would smell the coffee. Hadn't she already proved she was a 'live in the moment' kind of girl? Hadn't they had the most incredible night together, with mind-blowing sex and laughs that made his face hurt? And had she requested that he shoot her in the morning? Definitely not. Although, granted, she left before he woke up, but her note had contained no homicidal requests. They were made for each other. She just hadn't realised it yet.

Hayley returned from the bathroom and climbed back into her seat.

'You're smiling,' she teased. 'And the TV is on pause, so I know it's not because you're watching something funny. I meant to ask you – how are you going to find her when you get there?'

Dev's grin got wider. 'She mentioned the name of the resort she's going to. The Sands.'

'Oh. Small world. That's where Tadgh, the bloke on the other side of me, is getting married.'

'Maybe we'll all get an invite,' he joked, thinking that would be highly impressive. Meeting Cheryl again and taking her to a rock band wedding.

'Maybe we will. Don't think my husband will be up for it though. It's hard enough to get him to come to the weddings of people we know.'

'Don't worry – you can come with me and Cheryl. I'm pretty sure she won't mind.'

He was joking. Completely. Just going along with the laugh. But

Hayley suddenly frowned as if he'd said something wrong. Maybe she was touchy about her husband's reluctance to mingle.

'Cheryl? I just remembered you said earlier that was her name.'

'Yes.'

'Oh.'

That now seemed to perplex her. Dev had no idea why. Unless...

'Don't tell me you think you might know her? That would be like the smallest world moment ever.'

Hayley shrugged. 'Erm, no, I don't know her. I definitely don't know her at all.'

4 P.M. – 6 P.M.

17

BERNADETTE

Bernadette woke up from her snooze and wondered what she'd missed. She had a look at her watch: 4.30 p.m. They'd been in the air for close to four hours. Almost halfway then and so far, it had been a terrific flight. The people in her row were lovely and she hadn't felt at all awkward about being on her own. Maybe she should have done this years ago.

She stretched her back up without raising her arms and exhaled. The flight attendant must have removed her tray because she was sure it was there when she nodded off. Now there was just a small square bowl with a chocolate pudding in it.

'Saved it for you,' Dev told her, gesturing at the tub. 'I wasn't sure if you wanted it or not, or if you'd dozed off before you got round to it.'

Bernadette was touched by his thoughtfulness. 'You know, Dev, this girl of yours is a lucky woman. If my Nina wasn't already hitched to a man who's a walking miracle for having her, I'd definitely be taking you home.'

Dev turned to Hayley on the other side of him and laughed.

'The mothers always love me. It's the daughters that don't read the script.'

Bernadette had spent her whole career reading people and watching for subliminal signals and she could see that Hayley had a wee touch of strain across her eyes. Maybe that man of hers had been back again. Bugger. Bernadette should have slept with one eye open.

'Bernadette, fancy a wee stretch of the legs?' Hayley asked her.

Just as she said it, the other lad... Bernadette had to rack her brain for his name. It had been like that since the bloody menopause. Intermittent fog with occasionally stormy outbursts. Tadgh. That was it. He came back to his seat. That lad had barely sat still during the flight. Either he had a very short attention span or he had ants in his pants. Stuart was like that when he was a kid. Never sat in one place for more than two minutes. He hadn't changed much now, and he was twenty-six.

'Sure do. Should probably do a wee circuit of the cabin since I don't have my flight socks on. We can put a man on the moon, but we can't get a woman my age to St Lucia without dressing her up in green stretchy footwear. Have you seen the state of those things? Not even a wee sequin in sight.'

She stretched up and slipped out of the seat, while Hayley squeezed across in front of Dev and joined her in the aisle. They wandered towards the back, stopping next to the galley area that separated premium economy from economy.

Stefan popped his head out of the curtain. 'Can I get you two ladies anything?'

'A coffee would be lovely, if you've got one going.'

'Make that two, please,' Hayley added.

Stefan winked. 'It's like Starbucks behind this curtain. Just a sec...' With that, he disappeared.

Bernadette could see that Hayley was scanning the cabin behind them. 'Looking for someone you know? I always think it would be great if I saw someone I didn't like, and I could give them a wee wave. Sorry, I know that's terrible. It would have to be someone I really, really didn't like. You know. The woman in my street that keeps nicking my wheelie bin. My mother-in-law. Or Satan.'

'Your ex-husband isn't on the list?'

She was right, but Bernadette didn't really want to go into that. In truth, it would be more than a miracle if she met Kenneth Manson up here. Right now, she didn't want to talk about herself though. She hadn't had a chance to talk to Hayley yet, and this might be the only opportunity she had to say something about what she saw earlier. The reality was that it was none of her business. And indeed, back in the day, whenever people had checked in on her after one of Kenneth's outbursts, she'd got embarrassingly defensive and shut down their concern. Hayley was perfectly within her rights to do the same, but Bernadette hoped, for the young woman's sake, that she didn't.

'Och, he'd be there too. Anyway, I hope you don't mind me asking,' Bernadette began softly, 'but are you okay? After, you know, that wee altercation with your man earlier?'

'Here we go, two coffees, cream and sugar on the side.' Stefan chirped as he thrust a little tray through the curtain towards them.

They both reached for the cups, but ignored the cream and sugar. Something else they had in common.

'Thank you, son, you're a gem,' Bernadette told him.

'Ah, they all say that, but they still leave,' Stefan replied in a comical sing-song voice, before disappearing back behind the curtain.

Bernadette waited for Hayley to circle back to the question she'd asked her before the coffees appeared.

'Thanks for asking. I'm fine. Really. He's just... got a lot on his plate at the moment. And sometimes he gets really stressed and it just... makes him not himself.'

Bernadette felt her stomach plummet. It was like a recording of her own words from ten, fifteen, twenty years ago... She didn't say anything until she was sure Hayley had finished speaking. The last thing she wanted to do was cut her off if she was opening up.

'But thank you. You seemed so understanding and I appreciated it. I hate it when he embarrasses me, but I know he doesn't mean it.'

After another pause, Bernadette realised that there was nothing more coming. Hayley was shutting the conversation down. Time for Bernadette to pipe up.

'You know, I meant what I said earlier about knowing a man like that. My ex-husband. Kenneth. Although, God knows I called him a whole lot of different things during our marriage. He was a brilliant man, a surgeon...'

Hayley gasped. 'Lucas is a surgeon too. That's incredible.'

Bernadette nodded her head as another piece of the puzzle dropped into place. Over the years, she'd worked with many brilliant surgeons and 99 per cent of them were good and decent men and women. However, that job called for the best people in the field to have almost messianic confidence in their own abilities, and sometimes, very occasionally, that tipped over into the arrogance and the need for control that she'd witnessed earlier. And that she'd seen every day in Kenneth.

'What field?' Bernadette asked, genuinely interested.

'Gynaecology,' Hayley replied. 'At least, originally. Now he's a partner in a very prestigious fertility clinic in the city.'

Bernadette assumed she was talking about London and if she was, then that explained why she hadn't come across Lucas Ford before. She'd never worked anywhere south of Glasgow.

'Actually, that's why... that's why he's a bit on edge at the moment. We've been trying to get pregnant for a while now and it's not happening. We're really hoping that this holiday will give us a chance to just relax and spend time together, without the pressure we've been under at home.'

Bernadette could feel little pieces of her heart chipping off for this woman. She could only imagine what her situation must feel like. 'I'm so sorry. That must be awful for you.'

'It's been horrendous,' she conceded, relieved at actually being able to say that out loud. At home, only Lucas and their family knew about the IVF, and even when she was speaking to them, Hayley felt an obligation to be strong and positive. 'Lucas has done so much to help get us there and it still hasn't happened, even though there doesn't seem to be any medical issue. That's the most frustrating thing. He can't even fix whatever is wrong because we don't know what it is. And of course, the longer it goes on the more stressed we become, and the more devastated I get because I can't give him what he so badly wants: our own child.'

'Is that what you want too?'

Hayley froze, the question coming like a short, sharp slap. Is that what she wanted too?

'Well, I mean... erm... yes... erm... of course.' The words came out in a stutter, followed by a pause and then a stunned, 'I'm sorry, Bernadette, but you threw me there. I don't think anyone has ever asked me what I want. It was all just taken for granted. I never realised that before.'

Bernadette didn't say anything, just let her mull that over, until she was ready to speak. 'I guess... I've always wanted a family, but I didn't have the same urgency as Lucas. I would happily have waited a couple more years. And if it didn't happen, I'd be open to adoption or fostering kids of any age. In my job, I meet a lot of youngsters that need a good home.'

'So why isn't that the plan?'

'Because Lucas...' She stopped, realised it was a painful truth and it was unnecessary to say any more. It was true. Lucas was the one with the urgency and Hayley was snapping to attention. Christ, she must sound pathetic. That thought made tears pool on her bottom lids. Hayley sniffed, then rubbed them away. 'I'm sorry, you must think I'm such a drama queen. I promise I don't usually spill my personal life to complete strangers. It's just that earlier, it felt like... It felt like you knew. Like you could see me. You were so kind.'

Bernadette reached her arms around the woman and gave her a hug. 'I really don't think you're a drama queen and, lass, you need to stop putting yourself down like that. You don't have to. You're entitled to your feelings and if I seemed to understand, then it's because I had those feelings too. I would never voice an opinion on you, or your husband, or even on the way that he spoke to you today. The boundaries of your relationship are up to you and no one has any right to judge. But let me tell you something about the man I was married to. As I said, Kenneth was a brilliant surgeon, and a brilliant father too, but he was a terrible husband. He was a control freak, a megalomaniac who constructed a world that had to revolve around him. And I let him do that. I also let him bully me and berate me, usually behind closed doors, but sometimes in public too. I lost count of the number of times or number of ways that he humiliated me. I had a choice, of course. I could have left, but I didn't, and I'll always regret that. I thought that staying was the strong thing to do. I'm not judging any other woman here, but for me, it wasn't the right choice, I see that now. I should have left. I should have given myself another chance at happiness with someone who would treat me well. I'm sorry I didn't do that, but I had my reasons. Mostly it was for the kids, but also it was because a part of me believed that he was right. That I was nothing without him. That I would fail if I didn't have him there to support me.'

Bernadette could see that the young woman was hanging on every word of her story, a tale that she'd told over and over again at countless workshops and talks, at counselling services and in the cubicles of the A&E ward that she worked in. She'd once told a woman all of this while she was putting forty-four stitches in a head wound caused by a partner who had cracked her head with a bottle because she hadn't spotted in time that he needed another beer. The woman came back in on numerous other occasions. Many stitches and broken bones later, she left him when she was ready. Bernadette was just overwhelmingly glad that she'd walked away before it was too late to have a choice.

Beside her, Hayley took a sip of her coffee before she spoke. 'He's not... he's not abusive. I don't want you to get the wrong idea.' She paused. 'Actually, that's not true. What I mean is that he's not violent.'

Bernadette recognised that defensive attitude. How many times had she said similar things? 'He doesn't have to be. If he intentionally makes you sad, makes you hurt, makes you feel less than you are, that's enough. The only thing I would say is that there's no excuse. Don't waste your life on a man who doesn't deserve you. I did that and I know it's fashionable for folk to say that they have no regrets, but I have plenty. I'll always be sorry I didn't take the kids and go. For a while, he even managed to convince me that if I did that, he'd get custody of the kids and I'd lose them. He was an impressive man, and I couldn't take a chance on leaving in case he was right. But you don't have that problem yet. I know you're not going to want to think of things this way, but if you don't have kids, you've definitely got more options.'

Hayley fell silent and Bernadette sipped her coffee, resisting the urge to fill the gap in the conversation. This wasn't about her and there was no point pushing because, as she'd seen time and time again, people had to process things at their own speed and make their own decisions.

There was a sad smile playing on Hayley's lips. 'This is the most bizarre conversation ever to be having with a stranger on a plane. I can't quite believe I'm talking about this. I haven't even told my closest friends about how things are.'

'Sometimes it's much easier to talk to a stranger. To my friends and family, I defended Kenneth right up until the day I left him. I made excuses for his rudeness, his arrogance, his disdain for anyone who didn't matter to him.'

'That sounds so familiar to me.'

'Then, lovely,' Bernadette reached over and put her hand on Hayley's arm, 'all I would say, and I mean this from a place of care and concern, is think really hard whether you want to look in the mirror in twenty years' time and see me.'

18

TADGH

This whole journey would be so much more bearable if he could just go to sleep like the majority of the other passengers on the plane, but unless someone took a mallet to his head, the chances of him sleeping were zero.

Besides, he'd probably have to get up in a minute to let Hayley back into her seat. She was pretty cool. If he had to be stuck next to anyone today, then he'd probably opt for her. Only, that is, if Cheryl was unavailable, because right now he could definitely do with being sat next to his girlfriend, so they could get to the bottom of whatever the hell was going on.

Cheryl's reply to his text hadn't given him any real answers.

Looking forward to seeing you too, babe. Can't wait till you get here. Cxoxo

Part of him just wanted to ask her outright, but the truth was, he didn't have the bottle. And the other truth was, he didn't want to accuse her of something if he was completely wrong about the whole thing. She'd be totally within her rights to tell him to piss off and cancel the wedding on the grounds that her fiancé was a para-noid dickhead. No, he had to wait until he got there and could look her in the eye. He would know then. He was sure of it.

He was about to put his earphones back in and stick on a bit of Jackson Browne this time when he felt a tap on the shoulder and looked up. Conlan. His mate crouched down at the side of the row. 'Save me. Your brother is doing my head in. Either I come talk to you or I'm opening a door and going for it.'

'Hitting on the cute flight attendant?'

'It's like you're psychic,' Conlan replied, rolling his eyes. 'I wouldn't mind, but he smells like the floor at The Sub Club and he's still managing to pick up the most gorgeous chick on the flight. It should be illegal.'

Tadgh felt his knuckles tighten, and pushed himself out of his seat, beckoning to Conlan to follow him back to the space just in front of the toilets. On the other side of the plane, he could see that Bernadette and Hayley had the same idea and he gave them a nod and a smile. In another world, one where he wasn't getting married in two days' time, and one where Hayley wasn't already married to a prize arse, she would definitely have been the woman he was asking out at the club. Now that she'd pulled her hair out of the ponytail, it was falling in some crazy dark wavy action past her shoulders. She didn't have the thick eyebrows and the long fake lashes that Cheryl and all her mates wore either. She looked like she could handle a surfboard or chill in a beach bar in Koh Samui. He loved that vibe. These days, Cheryl preferred the more upmarket resorts, with the spas and the cocktail menus – thus the swanky wedding venue – but Tadgh would always choose a beer and a beach, preferably with his girl and his guitar for company. He'd thought that girl would always be Cheryl, now he wasn't so sure.

'Christ, I feel rough,' Conlan sighed, running both his hands through his hair. Unlike Shay and Tadgh, Conlan's hair was relatively short because he hated tying it up and he got pissed off with it falling in his face when he was working. He was one of the best tattoo artists in Dublin. In all of Ireland, maybe. Every piece of ink on Tadgh's body had been put there by Conlan, and he loved every curve and line of it, even the really shit musical notes that Conlan had put on the inside of his bicep when they were about fourteen. His mother's rampage could be heard three towns away when she saw it. As always though, his da just shook his head, kept that knowing smile on his face.

His da was one of five brothers, so there was pretty much nothing he or his siblings hadn't seen or got up to. Although, as far as Tadgh knew, none of the brothers had ever been caught shagging another one's fiancée. That's probably why they all still managed to work together and be part of each other's daily lives. They had a haulage company that covered the country and beyond and it was his da's other love. His family and his trucks. He'd made no secret that he wanted Shay and Tadgh to join the firm, just as a whole load of their cousins had done, but he respected that it wasn't for them. Tadgh had always loved graphic design and Shay was bone idle. It was pretty obvious they would never draw a wage from the family business.

Conlan was staring at the ceiling now, his whole body slumped against the partition between the two cabins.

Tadgh's eyes narrowed. 'What is it?' He knew his pal too well. Conlan could barely make eye contact with him and that was always a sure-fire sign that something was going on and he didn't know how to tell Tadgh. It was the same when Shay changed the name of the band to The Smokers, in tribute to a weekend he'd spent in Wicklow with a bag of weed that he said was the finest mind-bender he'd ever experienced. Conlan had found out about it first, but it took about an hour of avoidance tactics before he'd eventually blurted it out to Tadgh, who had then, predictably, lost his shit at Shay and changed the name back before it went on the publicity posters for the next gig. The time Shay lost the band's van in a poker tournament with a bunch of fiddlers from Kildare was up there too.

'Look, bro, I don't know where to start with this, but there's some weird shit going on and I just want to get it out there, because if it all blows up, I want no part of it.'

Tadgh exhaled as every cell in his body tensed into fight mode. So this was how he was going to find out. From his mate, on a plane, in the middle of the fucking sky, where he couldn't even punch out his brother because it would terrify every other passenger on the flight. 'Go on.'

Conlan sighed now too, ran his fingers through his hair again. His mate wasn't a grass, or the kind of guy who got up in other people's business, but unlike Shay, he had a pretty strong sense of what was right and wrong, and if he thought something was shit, he'd call it out. 'I think Shay's crossing lines and messing around where he has no business being.'

Tadgh felt his hands tighten into fists again. 'Where's that then?'

'Couple of weeks ago, I was dropping off your Fender at Cheryl's place for you, remember?'

Tadgh did. His favourite guitar had been in for repairs at a guitar store right next to Conlan's tattoo studio. His mate had done him a favour, picked it up for him and dropped it off at the flat Cheryl shared with her sister and brother-in-law, because Tadgh was going there when he got back from his da's house.

'Yeah, well when I got there, Shay was coming out the front door.'

Tadgh tried to rewind the time in his head. Couple of weeks ago. That made it a week before Cheryl and the girls had left for St Lucia. They'd been like ships in the night that week, because he'd been staying with his da a couple of nights, and on the other nights she'd had a crazy schedule of hair stuff, dress stuff, packing stuff, Shay stuff... He added that last one on, but it was beginning to look more probable by the second.

'Anyway, he saw me coming, jumped the fence and bailed. I think he thought I hadn't seen him, but he was hard to fecking miss. He looked like he'd just tanned the place and was doing a runner. Surprised neighbourhood watch haven't got him on CCTV.'

Conlan's mum and Shay's mum had been best friends, so they'd all been brought up together as cousins, and Conlan had known Shay for as long as Tadgh. If he said Shay was acting shifty, then Tadgh knew that it was almost definitely true.

'I chinned him about it the next day because it was bugging me. The whole pole-vaulting, doing a runner thing...'

'What did he say?' Tadgh asked through gritted teeth. He felt sick. And the anger was rising in his throat like bile.

'Went completely fecking mental and started shouting about how it was a free fecking world. You know what he's like.'

'I know what he's like,' Tadgh agreed, dreading what was about to come. If Shay went on the offensive, it was because he was cornered. Every. Single. Time. It was only a few hours ago he'd done the very same thing to Tadgh.

His head was starting to hurt again. How did he even begin to deal with this? He was going to have to speak to his dad. Jack Donovan was the person Tadgh turned to first in any crisis and this was definitely a fecking crisis.

'But I kept pressing and eventually he just lost his shit and admitted that he's screwing around with—'

Tadgh blurted 'Cheryl', at the very same moment as Conlan said, 'Cindy.'

Hang on, what? Tadgh tried to replay the last ten seconds. Cindy? Cindy O'Rourke was Cheryl's sister. Cheryl's very married sister. After a brief teenage romance with Conlan, Cindy had eventually married Jay, one of their closest mates and the roadie for the band since they were in high school. Shay was having an affair with Cindy? Behind Jay's back? That was pretty fecking low, even by his brother's standards. What the hell was wrong with the guy? And no, right now it wasn't much of a consolation that Cheryl wasn't involved here. Actually, that wasn't true. It was a massive consolation. Thank God, he hadn't asked her outright, because that kind of accusation would have been a deal-breaker with Cheryl. He should have known better. Not once in all the years they'd been together had she ever given him reason to doubt her. Being together that long, the truth of it was that he'd slept with one woman and she'd slept with one man. Another reason he was pretty much the worst rock star ever.

'Can I get you gents anything?' The air steward popped his head through the curtain beside them and just about scared the crap out of Tadgh.

A beer. He really needed a beer. Conlan asked for the same, and the head disappeared, then reappeared with two small cans of Bud.

'Not exactly enough to have you swinging from the overhead bins, but at least it's something.'

Tadgh grinned, his first genuine smile since he'd picked up Shay's phone that morning.

Cxoxo

Cindy. She must sign off her texts the same way. That's who it was from. And her need to tell 'him' must be Jay. Poor git. Tadgh made an immediate plan to go see him as soon as they landed and check he was okay. He wasn't going to be the one to blow the affair into the open, but he was going to make sure Jay was taken care of. Feck, he still had the urge to punch some sense into his brother.

Conlan had been quiet for a few moments, as both of their hangovers reacted to the incoming nectar of two cold beers.

'Wait a minute,' Conlan said, frowning. 'Did you just say Cheryl?'

'No, I—' Tadgh couldn't answer, too stunned to absorb all this.

'Mate, you did. You said Cheryl. Are you insane? Why the feck would you think he was messing around with your missus?'

'I didn't... I just... Look, it's a long story, but I saw a message on Shay's phone and got the wrong end of the stick. I thought it was from Cheryl. Must have been from Cindy.'

Conlan thought about that in silence for a few seconds, then lifted his gaze to the back of the cabin, where Shay was still deep in flirtation with the young flight attendant.

'Yeah, it must have been.' Conlan whistled. 'Unless he was lying through his teeth.'

19

HAYLEY

Hayley rested her head against the bulkhead wall behind her. Why didn't she have a Bernadette in her life at home? It was such a weight off her shoulders to speak with someone who wasn't judging, who wouldn't hold anything she said against her, or worse, against Lucas. She could have talked to her mum, but she'd never tried, because she knew that her mother would look at Lucas in a whole new light. She'd also bully Hayley into leaving him, and that wasn't something she'd ever seriously considered. Well, maybe once or twice in her head, in her darkest moments, but she'd never vocalised it. Mostly, all she'd thought about until now was making things right. Listening to Bernadette, maybe what she'd actually been doing was making things wrong.

One way or another, oh God, it felt so good to talk to someone about it. Every single thing that Bernadette had said had meant something, eased the pain a little, like picking thorns out of a wound, one by one. 'Can I ask you some questions now?'

Bernadette nodded. 'Of course you can. As long as you don't mind me looking like a prize numpty while we speak. I just need to keep doing these calf raises, or I'll spend the next four hours sitting

in that chair, racked with guilt, convinced that I'll need to be evacu-
ated as a medical emergency at any moment. I know I should be
less dramatic than this, but it's been a highly emotional day.'

'You and me both,' Hayley agreed, going up on to her tiptoes, just to
add a bit of moral support. 'What happened when you left him? Your
husband. Did he rage?' The very thought of pushing back in any way
against Lucas filled her with outright terror. The truth was, she didn't
want to. In an ideal world, she'd get pregnant, his stress would evapo-
rate, and they'd live happily ever after. For the last year or two, that had
been the only scenario in her mind, the only possible outcome that
would make her happy. But today, and all the other days over the last
few months, when she'd had to deal with his temper and his cruelty...
maybe, just maybe there was another outcome to be considered.

Bernadette paused, mid-raise. 'There's the thing. Sure, at first,
he did. Oh, he wasn't happy. Called me every name under the sun,
told me I'd burn in hell for leaving him, that I couldn't live without
him.' Hayley saw a flash of sadness cross the other woman's face,
before something else kicked in. Defiance. Bravery. 'All fairly
pathetic, really. But then, the strangest thing. He started calling.
Started being nice to me when we were around family. I noticed
differences in him. Small things. He was a bit less in control, unrav-
elling a little. That's when I realised we'd both been wrong. You see,
he'd said I would crumble without him. And I thought he'd go on
and live his best life now that his wife was out of the way. Truth was,
I survived, and he fell apart without me. We both realised it.'

Hayley couldn't ever imagine Lucas falling apart, but she was
desperate to know what happened next. 'Did you ever think about
going back to him?'

'No. Not even once. The only thing that changed after I left was
that I hated him a little less with each passing year, until he meant
nothing. Not a thing. No fear, no hatred, no regret. Just nothing.'

Hayley felt a sharp pain and realised she was chewing her bottom lip.

Bernadette noticed her flinch. 'Lass, you know I'm not telling you what you should do here. I'm just sharing what happened to me. No judgement. I just hope our chat today has helped you think about things.'

'It has. Thank you. It's so bizarre. Like I said before, if you'd told me this morning that I'd be sharing all this with someone I met on the plane, I'd never have believed you.' Yet, she was so, so grateful that their paths had crossed, even if their discussions were adding to her confusion about her relationship. Meeting Bernadette had added another perspective to her situation. The parallels were uncanny.

'And if you'd told me this morning that my friend Sarah would call off and I'd still come on this trip on my own, I'd never have believed you either. I honestly think sometimes, people are just put in the right place at the right time and there's no way to explain it. I'm glad I met you. Where are you staying in St Lucia?'

'At the Sugar Beach.'

Bernadette let out a low laugh when she said that. 'Same as me. I promise I'm not stalking you. Kenneth picked it.'

'Kenneth? Your ex-husband?' Hayley was confused again. How could he pick Bernadette's holiday and why would she allow him to tell her where to go?

'It was somewhere he'd always wanted to go.'

'And that's why you're going now?' Hayley was going to need Botox soon if she kept frowning in puzzlement like this. Lucas had bought her a voucher for it years ago, before they'd started trying to get pregnant. She'd asked the clinic for a refund and bought a new wetsuit instead. He'd been livid.

'No. Kind of. It's a whole other story. I think we're going to have to extend the flight for that one.' Bernadette shook her head and let out a chuckle.

Just at that, Stefan popped his head out of the curtain again. 'Right, ladies, I don't want to be a bad influence, but we've got a couple of bottles of wine left over from the meal service and I've just checked – they've got your names on them.'

'Son, before we leave this flight, I'm going to write a note to your mother and tell her you're a bloomin' treasure.'

'Excellent. That lovely offer just got you a tube of Pringles thrown in too.'

Two bottles of Prosecco, complete with straws, and a tub of crisps materialised from the galley. 'If my boss spots you, I'm going to claim you stole them,' Stefan warned with another cheeky wink. 'But don't worry, I used to go out with a good lawyer. If he hasn't blocked me on Insta, I'll give you his number.'

Hayley had a sudden thought that she wished these were her holiday partners for the next two weeks. Stefan would make her laugh all day. Bernadette would be a fountain of wisdom and great chat. And the guys sitting in her row would be invited too. Tadgh, well, let's face it, he was easy on the eye and seemed like a very genuine soul. And Dev would make her giggle every day with his antics and keep things interesting with a romantic situation that had disaster written all over it. After the stresses of the last couple of years, that was the kind of fun, easy, holiday she could do with right now. And she wouldn't have to worry for a second about having a glass of wine, or upsetting Lucas, or whether or not she was ever, ever going to match up to his expectations.

The thought almost stunned her into silence as the other side of her brain stormed in with some objections. She loved her husband. Always had. She just wasn't sure any more if she was in love with the man that she thought he was rather than the man that he'd turned out to be.

'Tiptoes, lovely. Up on the tiptoes,' Bernadette chided her play-fully, clutching the two mini bottles of Prosecco while gesturing to her to carry on with her calf raises. 'The worry will slay me if I don't do them. Are you okay? You looked deep in thought there.'

Hayley stretched up as commanded. 'Yeah, I was just...' She paused, deciding she couldn't go on talking about Lucas. She still couldn't believe that she'd said anything at all. Offloading to strangers was definitely not her style. If Lucas hadn't pulled that aggressive stunt earlier and shown a mortifying snapshot of their lives to the people around them, chances were she'd have spent the whole journey making small talk with the hot guy on her right, the funny guy on her left and the kind lady at the end of the row. The one who was waiting for an answer to her question. She bluffed it out by changing the subject to something that was niggling at the back of her mind. '... Just thinking about something a bit strange that came up earlier.'

'It's been a whole day of strange, my dear, so you're going to have to narrow it down. Pringle?'

Hayley took a crisp, wondering if Lucas would have a problem with that too. Was there a salty snack ban?

'It was something Dev said. Actually, something Tadgh said too.'

Bernadette looked a little puzzled. 'Dev is the one sitting next to me, and Tadgh is the Irish lad on the other end? Have I got that the right way around? Honestly. The way Mother Nature treats women my age is shocking. The memory goes, the ankles ache... Wouldn't the aging process be grand if it reversed after the menopause and your boobs went back up and you could find your waist again without a map?'

'Whoever designed the process was definitely male,' Hayley said, loving this lady's quirky humour.

'That's what I'm thinking,' Bernadette replied. 'Okay then, hit me with whatever is puzzling you about the lads' chat.'

'Just something coincidental that they both said. I'm sure it's nothing... I mean the chances are pretty slim... Miniscule. But it's niggling at the corner of my mind, all the same.'

'Go on...'

'Well, Tadgh was saying that he's on his way to get married at a place called The Sands, and that his fiancée has been over there for a week preparing for the wedding.'

Bernadette sucked on her straw as she pondered that. 'Makes sense. It's a good idea to milk it for a wee holiday beforehand.'

'Yes, but... Well, the girl that Dev met a week ago, the one that is the reason he's here – he said he met her because she was flying out to St Lucia for a wedding that was taking place this weekend. At The Sands.'

Bernadette gasped as she joined the dots. 'So you think it's someone from Tadgh's bridal party? Och, what a coincidence that would be.'

'Maybe more than a coincidence. Tadgh's fiancée is called Cheryl.'

Another dot of realisation joined, another gasp. 'And that's the name of the lass Dev is chasing too! Aw, no. Surely not. It can't be.' Bernadette reached over and knocked on the partition at the side of the galley curtain. 'Stefan, son, we're going to need another couple of bottles of that Prosecco.'

'I think one will be enough,' a voice from behind Hayley interjected. Male. Firm. Sounded agitated. She didn't even have to turn around. 'Darling,' her husband went on, his voice tight. 'Can I have a word?'

20

DEV

Dev was beginning to wonder if it was something he'd said. Or maybe his aftershave. He'd started the flight with a full row of new acquaintances, and now he was the only one left. He stretched around to see where they'd gone and spotted Tadgh at the gap in front of the toilets on the left-hand side of the plane, in deep conversation with a tattooed guy who obviously shopped in the same rock band outerwear store as Tadgh – black T-shirt, beat-up jeans, lots of piercings and rings. He couldn't see the guy's feet, but he'd bet his last piece of cheesy pasta that there were black boots on them.

He stretched around the other way and saw Bernadette talking to Hayley on the other side of the cabin, just outside the entrance to the galley.

The cabin lights had been dimmed, so most of the other passengers were sleeping, or huddled under blankets, watching movies, earphones in. He got a bizarre rush of incredulity. What the hell was he doing here? Followed by a rush of excitement. How freaking amazing could this be? Followed by a swift boot in the reality check bollocks. How could he even think that this was, in any way, shape or form, a good idea?

Then he remembered that Richard Gere picked up a hooker and climbed up a fire escape in *Pretty Woman*, yet even that had a happy ending. It could happen in the real world too, couldn't it? There had to be more to life than writing about the scores at the football every week, speculating over the transfer window and reporting on the latest drink driving arrest of an overpaid, over-entitled Premier League star?

He waited for a feeling of regret to kick in, but it didn't. Even if he landed on his arse in this whole mad romance thing, skint and humiliated, he'd always be glad he did it, because he'd remember the excitement and the sheer thrill of it for the rest of his life. And every single plucked heartstring of this mad plan was going into this book to make it next-level real and authentic.

Inspired by the thought, he pulled out his laptop. He'd been reluctant to work on the novel while he had people sitting directly on either side of him, too self-conscious in case they had a sneaky swatch at what he was typing and came to the conclusion that it was shit.

Now though, he had a window of solitude, and he wanted to use it, so he flicked the laptop on and navigated to his continuity page. It was a tip he'd seen in an interview with another writer – always keep a continuity file open while you're writing, so that you can constantly update it with character details, plot twists and ideas for future chapters.

He scrolled down to the section of the document that covered characters and made some notes about his newly imagined secondary characters.

Bernadette – a Glaswegian nurse, middle-aged, sweet, the kind of person that makes you feel better just because she is in the room. Red hair. Bright cheeks. Freckles. Chatty.

Hayley – a smart, gorgeous London teacher, has loads of great stories about how she travelled when she was younger, skiing and surfing. Somehow, she's ended up married to a flash douchebag.

Tadgh – plays in a band, looks like he just walked off stage at Glastonbury, bit broody, not a barrel of laughs, doesn't even seem to clock the fact that the two women in the next row follow him with their eyes wherever he goes.

Yep, that just about summed them up. This journey would be so much less interesting if he'd been stuck in the middle of a family of three who spent the whole journey ignoring each other. A similar thing had happened to him and Lizzy in Nice once. They'd joined a boat tour that they'd heard was a rowdy booze cruise and instead had got stuck with a family of eight from Dudley, who'd pretty much stared at their phones and bickered with each other all day. He and Lizzy had headed straight to a bar at the end of it and had saved their day by singing karaoke until 4 a.m. with a lovely bunch of Ukrainian hockey players. Now that he thought about it, that was another one of those nights that should definitely be in the book. It didn't matter if Cheryl didn't like karaoke in real life, her fictional character was going to be a blast at 'The Shoop Shoop Song'. He typed a note about that on the continuity sheet so he didn't forget, then decided to bang out a brief intro to the book, one that he could share with publishers or perhaps even the readers who might one day pick it up if it ever got published. Something like the voiceover at the start of *Love Actually*. A narrative that sets up the story, that makes the readers connect to the tale that's about to be told.

He thought for a moment, sorting his ideas in his head. Keep it real. Authentic. Just speak from the heart. How to start it though? Once upon a time? Foreword from the author? Or should he just title it, 'Introduction'? Almost autonomously, his fingers started typing the answer.

Dear You,

I had no idea that this book even existed until a week ago. Don't get me wrong, I've been planning to write it for years. Had a few false starts too. Somehow, though, I could just never find the right story, the ultimate romance, the one that I haven't read before, or watched on a Sunday afternoon on the couch, while administering Pickled Onion Monster Munch to treat a hangover. You can tell I'm a real suave guy. It's probably why I'm still single at thirty. Thing is, I'm the guy that women see as the brother-substitute. The friend zone. They'll put that on my gravestone. 'Here lies Dev. Wrote a bit, had some great mates, not bad at football, shite at basketball, invented the friend zone.'

I'm not the guy to take chances. I don't do wild and crazy shit. I'm not the 'treat them mean, keep them keen' kind of dude. I'm more the one who shows up the morning after a date with a cream bun and a coffee, and then has to hang about while the girl gives him the 'it's not you, it's me' speech. Incidentally, single blokes out there, don't go the cream bun route. It's a minefield. Last lady I did that to stormed off in a huff. Turns out she'd told me the night before that she was lactose-intolerant, but in my defence, it was in among a dozen other likes, dislikes and ailments, so I'd missed it.

My last partner, I'm not naming her here because she's now seeing a bloke from HR and I want to keep my job, dumped me after she had sex in the cleaning cupboard of a Basildon night-club with the Robbie Williams impersonator in a tribute band called Fake Twat. That might not be the actual name of the band, but in my head, it fits better than any other moniker they could come up with. After I found out, I thought about giving her another chance, but what was the point? It was done. I didn't see the need to back up and reverse the truck over my pathetic heart. And besides, every time I see her now, I think of cleaning materials and I get a faint whiff of pine fresh antibacterial spray.

The demise of that relationship pretty much sums up where I am now: relationship disaster, with a side dish of misplaced trust.

However, Dear You, that was before I met her.

The One.

She fell into my life last weekend and for the first time, I knew that love at first sight really existed.

There was just one catch. Like so many of the great love stories of our time, it started out with two people being in the right place at the wrong time. She was just passing through. Only there for one night. Had a plane to catch in the morning. Tragically, when I woke up, she was gone, and I haven't stopped thinking about her since.

She was… she is… my person. I can feel it. I know it. Because already she's changed my life. Did I mention where I'm writing this?

Dear You, I'm on a plane, 38,000 feet in the air, crossing oceans and continents to track her down, to get to where she is right now. Yep, me. The one who never takes chances. The one who always does the 'what will be, will be,' stuff is a changed man. Sod all that fate and destiny nonsense. This time, I'm not waiting around and hoping for the best, I'm putting myself out there with my heart on my sleeve and hoping she'll take it.

That's why I'm on my way to St Lucia, to tell her how I feel. A million things could go wrong. I feel like we're at that bit near the end of every romcom where the obstacles get in the way, the spanner drops into the engine, and you think that you've just wasted two hours of your life and a family pack of Monster Munch because love isn't going to beat the odds after all.

That's where I am right now.

I'm about to find out if love at first sight beats those odds.

If it does? Well, the ending to this story will be written, and I'll finally have my first, completed manuscript on my hands. That means you just might read about this one day. The story of Dev and Cheryl could be a book, a play, or a movie that comes to a multiplex near you. With Ryan Reynolds in the leading role, of course.

You know I'm joking, right? The chances of me actually getting published are even slimmer than finding that Cheryl has been sitting on the beach for the last week, watching the waves while pining for me with a broken heart. Unlikely. Incidentally, if she has been sitting there waiting for me all week, then I can only hope that she found a shop in St Lucia that sells medicinal pickled onion snacks. And I'm pretty sure Mr Reynolds is fully booked.

However, even if this story never sees the light of a book-shelf, all that matters is that there's a happy ending for us. If I write it, and Cheryl reads it, that will do for me.

Because at the heart of this story is love. Crazy, difficult, unpredictable, wonderful, hopeful, foolish, earth-shattering, heart-warming, impossible, irresistible love.

I think I've found it. And by the time you turn the last page on this story, you'll know if I was right.

Dear You, wish me luck.

With all my optimistic heart,

Me. xx

Dev put his head back against the seat and sighed. It summed up where he was so far, but he had no idea if it was good enough or if it needed work.

One way to find out...

He went back to the document, clicked 'share', typed in Lizzy's email address, then connected the plane's wi-fi. Send.

It had just whooshed off into cyberspace when Bernadette slid back into the seat beside him and thrust a tube in his direction. 'Pringles?'

He closed his laptop and accepted them gratefully, his stomach beginning to growl. The cheesy pasta hadn't been enough to sustain him for this long.

'I was just thinking, this lass of yours,' Bernadette said with cheery curiosity, 'the one you're going to find.'

'Cheryl,' he added without thinking.

'Yes, Cheryl,' she nodded. 'Is she by any chance Irish?'

Dev chomped on a Pringle. 'She is. How did you know?'

6 P.M. – 8 P.M.

21

BERNADETTE

Oh dear. Bernadette had a sinking feeling that there was a chance this lovely bloke next to her was about to land in a whole world of pain and disappointment. Not to mention debt, if this trip had gone on a credit card.

Sure, there might be more than one Irish lass called Cheryl in St Lucia, but what were the odds of them both flying out there for a wedding last week? Still, it could happen. There could even be more than one lass with the same name in that one wedding party. Yes, that must be it. Coincidences like that happened all the time. There had been four girls called Kylie in her Nina's primary school class, but, right enough, that was not long after that nice Kylie lassie from *Neighbours* had a hit with the 'Locomotion'.

Dev's expectant expression reminded her he was waiting for an answer to her question. She brushed it off with a casual... 'Och, I was just wondering. I thought I'd heard you say that she was Irish earlier. I love it there. I try to get over every year.' She wasn't wondering and she hadn't heard him say that, but he didn't seem suspicious, especially as she'd thrown in her genuine love of Ireland and regular visits there to make the whole conversation seem innocuous and chatty. She decided to change the subject and avoid detonating a potentially explosive situation that was probably best avoided while they were thousands of feet in the air. 'You didn't tell me where you were staying in St Lucia though.' Hayley had told her, but she just wanted to check, in the hope that it was a misunderstanding and he was actually staying somewhere far from Tadgh's Cheryl and their wedding.

Dev's face lit up with a very gorgeous smile. She had no idea why this lovely man hadn't been snapped up yet. 'The Sands. I managed to get a room at the last minute. It's where Cheryl said she was staying and I really hope that doesn't make you think I'm definitely a stalker.'

Bernadette could see his point but... 'No, I don't think that. I think it's sweet, actually. Like an old-fashioned romance.' That was true. Kind of. It was exactly how she'd felt until she'd realised there could be a conflict of interest sitting at the end of their row on this flight. 'The only thing is though, and I'm sorry if this isn't what you want to hear, but what will you do if she doesn't feel the same way? I mean, you know nothing about this lady, really. Sorry if that sounds harsh, son.'

'No, no, you're right. Actually, I was just thinking about that because I was writing an introduction to my book. I know it could all be over before it starts, but if that's the case I'll be okay with that because I tried and because, no matter what, I'll never forget this week. For years I've just been coasting along, waiting for life to happen, but this is the first time I've actually put myself out there for something spectacular. I've felt more buzzed up this week than I've ever felt. And that can only mean this is one of those life experiences I was meant to have. And if it all goes wrong, well...' He paused, shrugged, then gave Bernadette a cheeky smile. 'I'll just write a misery memoir instead. It's a win-win.'

'Good plan,' Bernadette agreed, laughing, feeling slightly better that he seemed to be equipped for all possible outcomes here. It was impossible not to hope for the best for him though. She'd long since stopped believing in that kind of passionate, romantic love, so this was a lovely reminder that it still existed. Maybe not for her, but at least it was out there.

'What about you? Where are you staying?' he asked, cutting through her thoughts, his wide grin absolutely infectious. 'And before you answer, I promise I'm not going to turn up there tomorrow morning, pledge undying love and beg you to marry me. It's not something I do to every single woman I meet.'

Bernadette feigned outrage. 'I don't know whether to feel relieved or offended about that, to be honest. I was already preparing my acceptance speech and getting ready to declare that I'd love you until the end of time. Except on Thursday nights, because I've got my Over-Fifty Pilates and if I don't go, my hips seize up.'

'That's okay. I play basketball on a Thursday night. I think we can make it work.'

'Excellent,' Bernadette beamed. 'I'm glad we got that sorted. I'm staying at The Sugar Beach.'

'Ouch. I clearly can't afford you. That place is pretty flash and hugely expensive.'

Bernadette could see the slight surprise on his face, and she wasn't offended. She'd been pretty surprised too. 'I know. In fairness, it's not my type of place. I usually go for something a bit more... low-key.'

'So why are you staying there then?' She could see he was understandably curious.

'My ex-husband chose it.'

'For the two of you?'

'Yes. Although we were already divorced at the time and I knew nothing about it,' Bernadette nodded, dreading where this was going, but failing to come up with any plan to stop it. Bugger.

'So then he changed his mind about coming and you decided to come anyway?'

'No.' Again, bugger. There was no way around this, so she was as well just going right through it. 'He didn't change his mind. The bugger died.'

Deep exhalation. There it was. He died. Kenneth Manson, the indestructible master of the universe, an esteemed cardiac surgeon and one of the pioneers in his field, had dropped dead. Of a heart attack.

And by the look of the open-mouthed shock on the young lad next to her, he was about to have a heart blip of his own. After a few stunned, astonished seconds, he found the words first.

'Shit. I thought I was going to have the most surprising story on this flight. I think you just gazumped me. Can I ask what happened? Of course I can't. No, I'm not asking, that would be rude. I can't. Although, you did kind of set me up there. You know, throw the ball up in the air and then hit it out of the park before I had a chance to catch it. I'm sorry. I use sporting analogies when I'm lost for words. It's an occupational hazard.'

Bernadette put her hand on his arm to stop him before he talked himself into a faint and she had to summon Stefan the air steward for some smelling salts. 'You can ask what happened,' Bernadette conceded. What's the worst that could happen? She'd never see this lad again, and if he did end up writing a misery memoir, at least he'd have some extra material because this wasn't hearts and romance love. This was twisted love. The dark stuff. The stuff that put people off relationships for life. And death. 'I'm a nurse and I've told this story to many women at work, but never to a stranger I just met on a plane, so jump in if I don't explain it all.'

Dev was turned fully round in his seat now, facing her. 'Okay, will do. But if it's uncomfortable, you really don't have to...'

'That's okay. You can always use it for another chapter in your book. You know, after you've turned up at my hotel tomorrow to tell me you love me.' Again, she could see he found the teasing funny. In her experience, that was a rare quality in a man. And that summed up the problem with her experiences. 'My husband was a brilliant man, but not a good one. I won't go into all the details, but he was a control freak who cheated on me and treated me like I didn't matter throughout our whole marriage. My bad, as the young ones say. I should have left him decades ago, but I didn't. I stayed until my children were adults because I thought that was for the best. By that time, he wanted me back. Begged me. Tried all sorts of gestures to persuade me to reconcile. I had no intention of going back there, didn't want to speak his name or have anything to do with him ever again. Then he did the one thing that would force me to get involved in his life again. The bugger died and left me everything.'

Bernadette saw that she could chuck a Pringle in Dev's direction and it would fly right into his open gob. No wonder. She'd been shocked by the whole bloody thing too. Not for a single moment did she ever think that Kenneth Manson would keep her in his will after their divorce. More than that, at some point he'd actually made a specific change, cutting out everyone else, including the kids, and putting all his worldly goods in her name. She could only suspect that it was a ploy he was going to use to try to win her back. Just as arranging the holiday must have been too. One that back-fired dramatically, because he died before she'd even found out that he'd done it.

It was Nina who had found the tickets after her dad had died. The lawyers had already informed Bernadette that the house, the cars, everything was hers, and the kids had offered to help her clear out his possessions so they could put the house on the market. Of course, she'd had no intentions of keeping any of it. She was going to sell the lot and split the proceeds between Nina and Stuart, as should have happened in the first place. In some way, this was so typical of her ex-husband, trying to control the narrative, trying to pressure her to accept his wishes, even after he was gone, and Bernadette had no intention of playing that game.

She'd delayed dealing with it all for months after he'd passed away in the bed of a thirty-year-old nurse in his practice. Only a few weeks ago, she'd finally buckled, under pressure from Nina and Stuart, to get it over with and gone with them to the house for the first time since she'd packed her things and left. She still found it surprising that he'd stayed there and not moved to some swish bachelor pad, but their house had been a lovely piece of architecture in arguably the most prestigious area in the city and he'd loved it since the day they'd moved in there. Bernadette had been happy to move out, to a rented place at first, and then to her lovely wee cottage with the stream at the end of the garden.

They'd only been at the former family home for a couple of hours when Nina had hollered, 'Mum! Come into Dad's office and look at this.'

Bernadette had hesitated, preferring to stay in the sanctuary of her old kitchen, the one room in their former family home that had been her domain.

'Mum!' Nina had beckoned her again.

It was no use. Bernadette had surrendered to the inevitable. Walking into the office, she'd felt her hands start to shake. His office had always been out of bounds to her. Yep, even then she couldn't quite believe that there was a room in her own house that she'd actually been banned from. It had been Kenneth's den, the place where he'd spent almost every moment. She'd only ever gone in there to vacuum, and then on the day she was leaving him, to access some financial stuff on his computer.

Sitting behind his desk, Nina was holding up a folder of documents. 'Erm, something you want to tell us, Mum? You kept this quiet.' There was a hint of teasing in her daughter's voice that Bernadette didn't quite understand.

'Kept what quiet?'

'A week in St Lucia. With Dad. Leaving in six weeks' time. Flash, swanky hotel as well.'

'I have no idea what you're talking about,' Bernadette had replied, astonished.

Nina had adopted her very best Chicago PD cop-like voice. 'Well, there appears to be hard evidence.' She went on to read out all the details. Flying Glasgow to London, then on to St Lucia. One week at the Sugar Beach resort. For Mr and Mrs Kenneth Manson.

'I swear he never told me. I mean, he said he wanted us to get back together at Casey's birthday party and that we could have this wonderful life of travel and excitement, but I told him he was being ridiculous. I guess he didn't want to take no for an answer.'

'What are you going to do about this now then? Look, Mum, it's paid for and it says...' Nina had scanned the invoice. 'Non-refundable if cancelled within eight weeks of travel. You can't even cancel it now or you'll lose the money. And it'll be worth thousands.'

Bernadette had sighed. The bloody audacity of that man. The arrogance. He was so sure that she would agree, that he hadn't even bought a flexible trip. She hated to speak ill of the dead, but urgh, he was a complete bastard. 'You take it, my darling. Swap it into yours and Gerry's names. I'll watch the kids for you.'

'Tempting, Mum, but no. Absolutely not. We're already away next month to Disneyland and there's no way Gerry will get more time off work.'

Bernadette was already backing out of the room. It gave her the creeps just to be there. 'See if Stuart and Connor can take it then. I'm not going.'

Back in the kitchen, she'd put the kettle on and made a cup of tea. How dare he? Psychology wasn't her specialist field, but she was pretty sure she could build a case to prove that Kenneth Manson was a narcissistic sociopath. Yet, she'd married him. What did that make her? Foolish, blinded by love and too young to know better.

Emptying the kitchen cupboards kept her busy for the next couple of hours, so it was lunchtime when Nina and Stuart appeared in the kitchen doorway.

Stuart had kicked off the discussion. 'Nina says I've to tell you this because I'm your favourite and you're more likely to take it from me.'

Bernadette's gaze went first to Nina. 'Number one, your brother is not my favourite. You've been pulling that card out since you were seven and it's time to stop.'

Nina had cackled with amusement. God, Bernadette loved the actual bones of her feisty, funny, good-hearted daughter. Just as much as she loved the bones of her kind, funny, soft-hearted son. No matter what years had been wasted with Kenneth, she wouldn't change a thing about these two amazing adults in front of her.

'Number two, I don't like the sound of this, so get it over quickly.'

Stuart had inhaled like his life depended on it. 'Okay, Connor and I can't use this trip because we've both got work commitments that we can't move, so we called the tour operator and explained that Dad died, but it's a whole palaver involving travel insurance to claim back the costs and it seems Dad didn't have travel insurance because he thought he was indestructible...' The oxygen for his unpunctuated outburst had run out and he'd gasped for breath before continuing. '... So the best suggestion that they had was that because you are a named passenger on the trip, you can still go and they'll allow you to change the name of the other passenger for a fee, so we called Aunt Sarah and she says she'll go with you, so you're almost all sorted.'

Bernadette had been horrified. 'Wait a minute. I'm not going on a holiday that was paid for by your late father behind my back. No way. It's ridiculous.'

'Why?' Nina had shot back.

'Because... because...' Bernadette had realised she had nothing. No reasonable argument came to mind. Now, sitting on a plane telling this stranger all about it, she could see he agreed.

'I totally agree with your family,' Dev spluttered. 'It would have been a shocking waste, not just of the money, but of the experience too.'

'I came around to that way of looking at it, although I did think Kenneth might have got the last laugh when Sarah cancelled this morning. I'd have hated to give him the satisfaction, so that's why I'm still here and I'm glad. My only stipulation was that I wasn't travelling first class, because every moment would have reminded me of a hundred horrible journeys with him. So we downgraded to premium economy, and the tour operator reorganised it so we could stay for two weeks all-inclusive instead of one week room only.'

'I thought my story was going to be the most dramatic one on the plane today,' Dev answered, shaking his head. 'Bernadette, I'm sorry about the horrible husband, but I think the universe has found a way to repay you in some small way for the heartache, because you're on your way to paradise...'

Bernadette hadn't thought about it like that, but she liked the sound of it.

He went on, 'And I know I might be getting carried away with the whole spontaneous romance thing, but maybe the universe has got some more surprises in store for you. Maybe this trip is where you're going to fall madly in love with some amazing man too.'

The very thought made Bernadette laugh, with just a little bit of reality thrown in there. 'Och, son, at my age I'd settle for a good cup of tea and a foot rub. Now, let's talk about the stuff that really matters. Have you been rotating yer ankles?'

22

TADGH

'Christ, I need another drink,' Tadgh sighed. Seconds after he said it, a bottle of beer came straight through the curtain from the galley, making him and Conlan crease over.

'I need Shakira in a bikini singing "Hips Don't Lie",' Conlan said hopefully.

Stefan popped his head out the curtain. 'I can't do the bikini, but if you two start whistling the tune, I can probably rustle up a passable version of the first verse and the chorus.'

Despite a head that was on the verge of combusting with unanswered questions, Tadgh couldn't help but laugh.

The air steward then emerged from the galley, pushing a trolley. 'There's another beer in it if you buy all the duty free on this trolley, so I don't have to pretend I enjoy the cheery sales pitches.'

'Och, you enjoy it really,' Tadgh joked, thinking he wasn't even sure who he should buy some duty free perfume for. Unless there was one called 'Infidelity'.

As Stefan laughed and pushed the trolley towards the front of the cabin, Tadgh handed his beer over to Conlan, concerned that if he had one too many drinks, then he might say or do something that he would regret, and this wasn't the time or place.

Jesus, his mam would be going nuts if she could see this. As far as he could work out, Shay, his dearly beloved brother, was either messing around with Cheryl, Tadgh's soon-to-be wife, or with Cindy, her sister, who also happened to be very married to their tour manager.

How could his own brother have turned into such a complete dickhead? Their mam was the most moral, honest, trustworthy person that ever walked the face of this earth. And their dad had exactly the same values: family came first, his word was everything, and as much as he loved a party and a good time, he only ever wanted to go home with his wife at the end of every night. They'd adored each other, his parents, and to them, their marriage was something that they'd both honoured. Sometimes Tadgh had wondered if that's why he'd agreed to get married in the first place. It had seemed like the next step, Cheryl was pushing for it and his mam was like a woman possessed the first time around, booking churches, organising the reception, planning buffets. She'd spent every Saturday in Brown Thomas, the upmarket department store in Grafton Street, for months, trying on outfits and shoes and hats for the occasion. She'd adored every second of it and when she'd died so unexpectedly, just a week before the big day, they'd all been crushed. Going ahead with the wedding wasn't even an option.

It had taken months before he could even contemplate being happy or celebrating anything again. It was his da who had finally put him right. One Saturday afternoon, they'd all been at his da's for dinner, and Cheryl had tentatively brought up rescheduling the wedding. Tadgh had shut it down immediately, saying there was no rush, it was just a bit of paper. He'd meant it. He adored Cheryl, but the only reason he'd been going with the big wedding was for the fun and the family memories. Now that his mam was gone, the only memory would be that she wasn't there.

Later, after Cheryl had gone back to her flat, Tadgh had been sitting on the front step with his dad, drinks in hand – a whisky for his dad, a Jack Daniel's for him – when Jack had said, 'You know, son, yer ma would be gutted to know that her passing had cancelled your wedding. You know how much she was looking forward to it.'

Tadgh had taken a sip of his JD. 'I know. I think that's why it doesn't matter any more.'

'But it matters to Cheryl. And she's the one you need to think about now, son. Don't mess that up. Yer mam wouldn't want that and if she's up there watching, she'll be mighty displeased that you're stalling it in her name.'

Jack Donovan was a man of few words, but every one of those made Tadgh think. He was being unfair. He could see that now. That night, he'd called Cheryl and agreed to book a new wedding. His only stipulation was that it wasn't at home in Dublin. That would sting too much. Cheryl had taken on the challenge and before he knew it, he was getting married in St Lucia. In Tadgh's mind, it had gone from being a wedding to being something he was doing to honour his mum, not even giving a second thought to whether or not it was still what he really wanted.

Tadgh dipped back into the conversation, realised that Conlan was chattering away about some new amplifier and bailed back out to his thoughts again, catching up with where he'd been and castigating himself. What the hell was he thinking? Of course he wanted to marry Cheryl. She had been at his side since they were fourteen years old and he couldn't imagine his life any other way.

Conlan caught his attention again. 'By the way, what we were talking about earlier, you won't tell Shay, will ya? I can't be doing with the drama.'

'No, mate, yer fine, don't worry.'

'Won't tell Shay what?' Neither of them had even noticed his brother approaching from the other side of the partition wall.

Tadgh snapped straight in to cover-up mode. 'That he's a shite singer and we'd be far better off if we could find someone who could hold a tune,' Tadgh quipped, getting the reaction of utter disdain that he expected.

'Fuck off. I've been carrying you lot for years. If it was down to you two, you'd still be playing in Da's garage and Mam would be the only one dancing.'

That threw up another memory. The boys, fifteen and sixteen, playing in their dad's huge haulage garage, in the corner that their da had blocked off for their rehearsals. Their mam bringing them ham sandwiches and crisps for dinner, then staying to have a wee dance with their da to the next few songs in their set. How had they gone from that tight, unbreakable family to this?

Tadgh knew Shay was way too paranoid to settle for the jokey answer, so he came back with something a bit more believable. 'Okay, so we were saying that we reckon we could do a song at the wedding. We just didn't want to say anything until we got there and checked out if it was going to work with the hotel.'

'Yeah, that would be pretty cool. We could do "Locked In",' Shay offered, naming his favourite song in their set, mostly because he'd written it.

'There's the thing – we were thinking "Yesterday".' Tadgh couldn't help himself. 'Cheryl loves that song. It's always the one that she asks for at gigs.'

'Look, whatever,' Shay answered, and Tadgh could see he was trying to go along with it but not quite getting there. 'Whatever Cheryl wants, Cheryl gets.'

There was something in the way he said it that made the hairs on the back of Tadgh's neck stand up. A hint of goading that he couldn't leave unchecked.

'You okay, bro. I don't know, you seem a bit... off. Something on your mind?'

Shay shook his head, and as he did, Tadgh could smell the alcohol on his breath. Shit. How much had he been drinking on the flight? His bloodstream must have started the day pretty much 90 per cent Jack Daniel's from last night, and he'd obviously been topping it up. This wasn't a good sign. Sober Shay was great company, a born entertainer who was a bit of an egotistical dick, but still the kind of good time that everyone wanted to be around. Drunk Shay went one of two ways – either life and soul of the party, or an arrogant tosser who wanted to antagonise the world. Tadgh wasn't sure which one he was getting, and going by Conlan's wary expression, he should probably fear the worst.

'You want to know the truth?' Shay was blatantly goading him now, and it was a fight Tadgh was ready to take on.

'Yeah, sure,' he shrugged, keeping it low-key. He didn't need to puff up his chest and raise his voice to get a point over. That had never been his way. His da was the same. In all his years, Tadgh couldn't remember his da ever raising his voice, even when he was pushed to distraction by their antics. His ma had berated Shay loud enough for the whole street to hear when he'd 'borrowed' his da's car at sixteen to go pick up a girl from Blackrock, and then crashed it into the front window of the kebab shop on the high street on the way back. Not his da. He just took the keys and walked away, but he'd been so pissed off it had been weeks before he could look Shay in the eye again. It wasn't too different from how Tadgh felt right now.

'I just don't know why you're getting married. I mean, what's the point? It's not as if she's going anywhere, know what I mean? And what, you're seriously telling me that you're going to go through your whole life and only be with one woman? Give me a fucking break.'

The fact that Cheryl was the only woman he'd ever slept with had always been a source of piss-taking from his brother. Tadgh honestly didn't care – he didn't need to play Shay's game and shag someone new every weekend. Truth was, he couldn't think of anything worse. 'Worked okay for Mam and Da,' Tadgh countered calmly.

'That's my point. It's not nineteen fucking sixty-five. Things have changed. You've got the whole fecking world out there, so why tie yourself down to one person?'

Tadgh shook his head. 'You just don't get the whole love thing, do you?'

'Oh, I get the whole love thing. I just don't think it needs a contract.'

They'd had this discussion, in one way or another, so many times over the years, but never so directly aimed at Tadgh, and never two days before his fecking wedding. He couldn't stop himself from prodding the bear just a bit more.

'So what are you saying? That I shouldn't marry Cheryl?'

'I just don't think you need to put your whole life in the hands of one person. What if it goes tits up somewhere down the line? Won't you regret wasting all these years of your life when you could have been out having yourself a real good time?'

On the inside, Tadgh knew he had a point, and he'd have been stupid not to have thought that one through himself. The reality was that there was no way round it. If he wanted to go out and live life as a single guy, he'd lose the only woman he'd ever loved. It was a price he wasn't willing to pay. Simple as that.

He steeled himself. It was excruciating playing this cool. All he wanted to do was poke his brother in the chest, ask him what was going on, point out that he was playing with fire if he was messing with Cheryl's married sister. And he was playing with something far more explosive if he'd lied to Conlan and he was actually messing with Cheryl. Tadgh felt his teeth clench. He just couldn't contemplate the fallout from that situation. It would destroy them all.

'Why would my marriage to Cheryl go tits up, Shay?' That came out just a bit more confrontational than Tadgh had intended and he could see that Conlan was starting to look a bit nervous. It wasn't like any of them could leave the room to cool down.

Shay put his hands up. 'Hey, I'm just saying it could happen. Maybe somewhere down the line she'll decide that she doesn't want to go through her whole life and be with only one guy.'

Conlan closed his eyes, doing the out-of-body thing that he'd been trying to master in times of conflict since they were all about twelve. A fight had once broken out at one of their gigs, and Conlan had done the last four songs and the encore with his eyes tight shut.

Tadgh had listened to enough of this. He still couldn't bring himself to accuse Shay of anything outright. Not when they were on a plane and couldn't get away from each other. This was the kind of stuff that could end relationships and do damage that couldn't be fixed. With every passing mile and minute though, he was getting closer and closer to asking the question he really wanted an answer to.

For now though, he settled for, 'Why would you think that, Shay? Is there something you're not telling me? Something I should know about the woman I'm about to marry?' Tadgh's gaze was piercing, and he refused to break eye contact until the plane juddered and forced the issue. Shay swayed to one side, the alcohol kicking the ankles out from his balance.

The seatbelt sign came back on and Stefan trundled back with the trolley. 'Sorry, gents, need to break up the party.'

Tadgh turned and walked back to his seat. This was the second time that turbulence had saved his brother's skin. And he still wasn't sure that his relationship with his brother wasn't about to hit a very painful crash landing.

23

HAYLEY

It had been less than an hour since Lucas had interrupted them and Bernadette had gone back to her seat, but it felt like a whole lot longer. When Bernadette had excused herself, it was all Hayley could do not to grab her hand and beg her to stay. Not because she was afraid, because she wasn't. She'd never feared Lucas. Dreaded him, maybe, but never feared him.

Predictably, though, after the initial dig about the wine, and his frosty request to have a word, he'd adopted an attitude of complete innocence.

'How's your flight going?'

Just like that. Like he hadn't been an aggressive dick to her just a couple of hours before, like he hadn't embarrassed her, tried to intimidate her, been rude to the passengers sitting near her on the plane. As always, she'd plastered on a smile and gone along with the act. And the Oscar for Best Imitation of A Happily Married Wife Goes To...

'Fine.'

He'd run his fingers through his hair, the way he always did when he was antagonised or had something on his mind. Usually, she'd jump in to fill the space and to smooth the issue over before he even had to explain it. Not today.

'Look, I'm sorry, darling. For earlier. That was... unacceptable. I was just tired. And irritated. And I guess I haven't decompressed yet from everything back home.'

'I get it,' she'd lied with a shrug. She didn't get it. Why was she the metaphorical punching bag for every bad day he ever had? And shouldn't today be a great day? First day of their holiday, off to the sun, just the two of them... in different cabins because he saw the opportunity to boost his own ego while trashing hers. None of which she said aloud. That's when it had occurred to her that she spent a lot of her time not saying what she thought aloud.

'And when I saw you drinking alcohol again, it just tipped me over the edge. You know you shouldn't.'

It would have been easier not to argue, but she'd been done with internalising every thought. 'I know I shouldn't get plastered and I know that I shouldn't drink more than a few units a week. I'm on a break from the fertility drugs, so, strictly speaking, the alcohol ban isn't in play. Lucas, I'm not going to keep arguing with you about this. I'm a grown woman and this is my body.'

'One that's supposed to be carrying my child,' he'd spat back sharply.

'Your child? Not ours?' she'd challenged him.

He'd paused, hands on hips like a petulant child before exhaling. 'Jesus Christ, Hayley.'

She'd wondered what he would do if she were simply to walk away from him right then, to go back down to her seat, and just get on with the important business of enjoying her flight. Sure, he earned far more than her, but she contributed a fair salary to their joint income, so this was as much her holiday as his. She'd earned it. She was coming off another year of teaching kids who had their challenging moments, while filling herself with fertility drugs and going through a punishing regime of fitness and sacrifice. Surely, she was entitled to one day off from his bullshit rules?

Perhaps it was Bernadette's story and her strength. Perhaps it was exhaustion. Or maybe it was just time that was giving Hayley an irresistible urge to stop holding back, to fight for herself, to stand up to him and use her voice.

'Lucas, why do you want this?' Her voice had been calm.

'Want what?' He'd regarded her with absolute puzzlement, those piercing brown eyes burning right into her soul. She used to stare into them for hours. One seductive glance and she'd be reduced to mush, desperate for him, needing him more than she'd ever needed anyone.

'Me. Us. A family.'

That had seemed to take the wind out of his sails, and he'd leaned against the partition wall, then reached over and took her hand, turning it over, his thumb tracing the lines across her palm. 'I don't know how you can even ask me that. It's because I love you. You know I do. I want...' He'd searched for the words. 'I want everything with you. I want us, I want our family and I know sometimes I let the stress of that get to me, but it's only because I want it so badly. I don't know why you can't see that.'

This was the moment that the discussion would normally end, when she would assure him that she did see it, say she was sorry for doubting him and promise him that everything would be better. And he would tell her he loved her and say sorry again and then they'd maybe go to bed and make love until she repaired that connection, reminded herself why they were together, how much she loved him, how much he loved her. They would fuse themselves together again, and it would be great... until the next outburst. And then it would start the cycle all over again. But not today.

'Maybe because you don't show it.'

His eyes had narrowed. 'Is this because I upgraded to business class?'

Hayley had almost laughed, but she'd stopped herself because she knew that would send him into orbit. 'No. It's because I just don't understand. You say you love me, then you speak to me like you don't. You say I'm everything, then you treat me like I'm nothing. You say you want me to be the mother of your children, then you act like I'm not good enough. I don't understand, Lucas.' Her voice was beginning to tremble, but she'd stuck with it despite the shock on his face. 'Explain it to me. Tell me how that works.'

For a moment she'd thought he was going to open up, and perhaps right there, in the most bizarre of places, they were finally going to have a real conversation that would help them reach a new level of understanding and consideration. She should have known better.

He'd dropped her hand like a stone. 'What the hell are you talking about? Seriously. Who the fuck have you been talking to that's put this crap into your head?'

'No one, I—'

'I mean, what the hell is wrong with you, Hayley? Why do you feel the need to conjure up issues where there are none? The only problem we have is that you can't get pregnant, and if we can get that sorted, then we'll be fine.'

'And if I can't? What happens if I never get pregnant, Lucas?' Her voice had cracked at the very suggestion of that.

His face darkened at the suggestion, and she knew why. Lucas Ford didn't do failure. He never had. Everything he'd ever done, as his mother had been so fond of telling her, had been a roaring success. Top in every class. Captain of the rugby team all through school. Straight A grades in every subject. Accepted to do medicine at his first choice of university. Graduated top of his year. Got the most coveted placement in the best hospital. Damn, he'd made partner in a top Harley Street practice by the time he was thirty. The hard, devastating reality was that their inability to conceive was his first failure. Moments had passed. Many of them. His silence so long she had to clench her jaw to stop herself jumping in to fill it.

That's where they were right now. Him silent. Staring at the wall. Her deflating, breath by breath, second by second.

Eventually, he spoke.

'You can,' he answered simply, refusing to accept the alternative.

'But what if I can't. What do we do then? Adopt? Use a surrogate?' He'd always refused to discuss either option because, well, that would be to contemplate the failure of his chosen plan. Hayley had thought this through time and time again, but she'd always come to the conclusion that she had to trust it would be okay, had to go along with his absolute positivity that they would get the outcome they wanted. But what if they didn't? Maybe it was time to face the answers to that question. In her head, she'd repeatedly denied confronting the uncomfortable truths, hanging every shred of hope she had left on this holiday. For months, it had been the mantra in the house. 'We just need a break. Some relaxation. Let's worry about that after St Lucia.'

There had been countless variations of those words since the last round of IVF failed.

There it was again. Failure. Hers. No wonder he was losing his temper, being impatient, treating her like she didn't deserve him. To him, she was his failure.

Another realisation dawned.

If he called time on their marriage, he'd view that as a failure too. One of the first things he'd ever said to her was that his parents had been married for thirty-five years, and for him, divorce would never, ever be an option. At the time, she'd thought it was wonderful, a sign of true commitment. Now she saw it as a challenge. The answer to a question that she didn't want to ask.

If he was faced with the failure to have a family or the failure of his marriage, which would he choose?

He could only pick one option. Live a life without children or divorce and marry someone who could give him the family he wanted.

Like a mist clearing to reveal a bloody great big flashing sign, it came to her – either way, he would view whatever choice he made as a failure. That's why he was unbearable. That's why he was so angry with her. That's why his behaviour towards her had become utterly disparaging. She was his failure.

Flash those words out in bright blue neon.

Hayley Ford was his failure.

Her mind had gone off so far on the tangent of realisation that she almost forgot she'd asked him if they would try other pregnancy options.

'No,' he said simply.

'That's it? If I don't get pregnant naturally, it's just a "no" on any other options.'

'We keep trying,' he said, with gut-wrenching finality.

'Wow. We keep trying. Do I have a say in this?' Bernadette's comments from earlier came rushing back. What about her? What did she really want? 'What if I don't want to keep trying? What if I want to take a break from this for a while?'

'Don't be so fucking ridiculous. Of course you want to keep trying. Why the hell would you want a break when our chances are diminishing with every month that passes?' His exasperation boiled over and she flinched as he took a step towards her, his beautiful, man at GQ face flushing with anger. 'What the hell has got into you? Why are we having this discussion now?'

This was yet another point when she'd usually back down but his utter disregard for her feelings, layered over a blanket of confidence from her conversations with Bernadette, emboldened her.

'Because I think that I'm realising that maybe this isn't about love any more. Maybe it's about achievement. Not once have you asked me what I want to do.'

He lowered his voice and leaned right into her ear, so no one else could hear. 'You ungrateful bitch.'

The words were more brutal than a slap across her face. And he wasn't finished.

'I have done everything for you. Everything. You've had thousands of pounds worth of treatments, every new innovation at your service and I have tolerated it because it was what we wanted. How the fuck do you think this looks for me? How can I tell my patients there is hope when I can't even get my own fucking wife pregnant?'

She pulled her head back, gasping for breath. There was the reality. There was the truth. For months, they'd danced around the subject with no conclusive answers, just a husband who was getting angrier by the day.

When the plane lurched, and the fasten seatbelt sign lit up, she saw the cabin crew on the other side of the aisle pushing their trolley back to the galley, the young blonde guy gesturing to her to return to her seat. She didn't need to be asked twice. She turned and walked away without saying a word.

Two weeks in St Lucia. One more chance to turn this round.

But she was beginning to doubt that chance was worth taking.

24

DEV

The cabin crew had passed along the aisle with drinks and duty-free when a thought had struck Dev: should he have something to take to Cheryl? A gift, some token of his love? Maybe a bottle of perfume with a tenner off high-street prices?

Only, this seat had cost him the last of his savings and he didn't get paid for another week, so unless he was going to load it onto his credit card – already circling his limit after the night out with Lizzy and their mates last weekend, and shaking at the thought of the forthcoming hotel bill – then it wasn't going to happen.

He leaned over to his left, where Bernadette was reading a book on her Kindle called *The Solo Traveller's Guide to St Lucia*. 'How is it?' he asked, gesturing to the words on the page of the e-reader.

'There's a lot of sand. And a lot of looking at things. I feel I'm just going to find a sun lounger and plonk myself down and stay there for fourteen days. I'll stick a note to my back asking the hotel staff to roll me over every two hours and spray me with sun cream, and to run a drip of pina coladas into my arm. What do you think?'

'I don't see the problem. Sounds like pretty much every holiday I've ever been on.'

If Dev had to choose a travel buddy for this flight, a middle-aged nurse, flying solo on her dead ex-husband's dime would not have been on his top passenger bingo card, yet here he was, already hoping that she'd agree to keep in touch because she was a fricking delight. He hadn't laughed this much since his last all-day sesh with Lizzy. Or that time they'd rented a canal boat and got stuck at a lock in Chelmsford. Or the time they did the inflatable assault course for charity and Lizzy got stuck at the top of a five-metre high bubble replica of London Bridge.

Now that he thought about it, what if Cheryl and Lizzy didn't like each other? Oh crap, that would be an issue. Come to think of it, none of his girlfriends had ever really gelled with Lizzy and one of them was her second cousin. In fact, Poppy had used Lizzy as an excuse for shagging Robbie Williams – said she'd been fairly sure Dev was sleeping with Lizzy behind her back, so she just thought, fuck it, and did the same. In what world did that logic even begin to make sense?

Lizzy always said it was insecurity and she was undoubtedly right. Some people just didn't get the whole 'platonic best friend with a member of the opposite sex thing' and he understood that. He'd had the occasional grit of the teeth when Lizzy had brought home her latest bloke and Dev didn't think he was good enough. He sometimes wondered if anyone ever would be.

'Can I ask your advice?'

Bernadette turned slowly to face him. 'Is it about an unfortunate rash that may or may not have a dodgy origin?'

By some fluke of rubbish timing, Dev had just swigged back a mouthful of water, which, after Bernadette's comment, he now had to struggle not to spray across the wall in front of them.

'Nooooooo! Why would you think that?' he asked, horrified.

Bernadette shrugged, but he could see she was amused by his reaction. 'I'm an A&E nurse. That's the kind of stuff people ask me about all the time. Honestly, you wouldn't believe it. I once had a teacher at Nina's school parents' night ask me if I could have a wee look at her piles in the gym store. A very posh gentlemen once stripped off his sock and asked me to confirm his athlete's foot diagnosis on a train to Penrith. This job is a minefield. What's the strangest thing you've ever reported on?'

Dev thought about that for a minute. 'Alien impregnation.'

'Really? I think I helped birth a child who was conceived in similar circumstances. When the mother filled out the religion section of the patient form, she wrote Jedi.'

'I thought I would be the person with the strangest story. You know – the whole following a one-night stand across the world.'

Bernadette shook her head. 'Not even close. Unless you've also got a dodgy rash.'

If this lady was twenty years younger, Dev would be in love by now, he decided.

'So what did you want to ask me?'

Dev had almost forgotten his dilemma. 'I'm wondering if I should take her a present.'

'Who?'

'Cheryl. Like, a bottle of perfume from the duty-free. Or would that be too much? Too pushy?'

'Did you miss the part where you spent a fortune flying here to meet her after you'd known her for one night? Please don't think I'm insulting you, because I think you're marvellous, but you've already got "pushy" covered.'

'I'll take that as a "no" to the perfume then,' he concluded with mock gravity.

'A definite no to the perfume.'

Before they could discuss it further, the seatbelt sign pinged on, and the cabin crew appeared at the front of the cabin and started working their way back, row by row. As some point, they must have passed Tadgh and Hayley, because they both reappeared, one on each side of the cabin. Tadgh slid into his seat and Hayley climbed over Bernadette and Dev, into the seat next to him. Bernadette. Dev. Hayley. Tadgh. Throw in a couple of blonde wigs and some more singing talent (Tadgh already had that covered) and Dev was pretty sure they could form a decent Abba tribute band.

Dev took in both their expressions. Tadgh's face was like thunder – he definitely didn't do sweetness and light, that guy. If that was the rock star life, he could keep it. Hayley didn't seem very happy either. Her lips were tight and her eyes were red. Dev had noticed when Bernadette returned to her seat that she'd been replaced up at the back by Hayley's husband. It wasn't a massive leap to suspect that the guy had said or done something to upset her, just as he'd done when he'd come to talk to Hayley earlier in the flight. Dev hated to judge, but as Lizzy would no doubt say, the guy had come across as a mighty cock.

Dev decided to give her some space – or as much as possible when their hips were strapped to seats only inches apart – before asking if she was okay.

In the meantime, he decided to check if Lizzy had responded to the email he'd sent her with his book introduction, so he flipped open his laptop and refreshed his email.

One new message.

Dear You,

You're an idiot.

Seriously.

But I'm even more of an idiot because the introduction to your book made my heart hurt. That's why I'm starting this off by reminding you that I love you. Even though you're an idiot.

Let me begin by addressing some of your comments. How about we start with the absolute cracker: 'Here lies Dev. Wrote a bit, had some great mates, not bad at football, shite at basketball, invented the friend zone.'

First of all, you're equally shite at both football and basketball.

More importantly, you did not invent the friend zone. You lived in it, but you did not invent it. It was your choice, every time, to put yourself in that place. Remember Joanie from school? She was madly in love with you, but you had no idea. Even when we told you, you didn't listen. Instead, you just acted like a lovely but romantically disinterested friend, until she got fed up waiting for you to realise how she felt, and she copped off with that bloke from chemistry who set the lab on fire with a Bunsen burner.

And Virginia from college. The one who went through a rebellious feminist phase and changed her name to Vagina for a month and a half? She was crazy about you too. I think you actually spent the night with her, messed around in her Virginia, and then didn't call her afterwards because you convinced yourself that she wasn't interested. Newsflash – she was.

I could go on, but I'll spare you the background stories and just say that Carol from the Spotted Duck, Kelly from the sports centre and Donna, the interior designer I worked with on the Guild Hall project, were all fairly besotted with you too. And Tim, the plumber who fitted my new bathroom, was ever hopeful that you'd swing the other way. You just couldn't see how people felt about you. And even when we told you, again, you didn't believe us.

Which brings me to Poppy. She didn't sleep with Fake Twat because you weren't good enough to keep her interested. It was because at her core, she was deeply insecure and a fickle eejit who always felt she wasn't good enough for such an honest, decent, funny bloke as you. She was right.

Oh, and the one with the cream bun? I'll give you that. It was a mistake. But next time, please detour with said cream bun to a best friend who would appreciate it. Because sometimes, you might want to question whether you're sharing your buns with the wrong person. You idiot.

So yes, Dear You, the friend zone has been a familiar destination for you, but only because you chose to be there. I know a young woman who once slept on a lilo with you, who will back that up that conclusion.

I have more to say, but I'd like you to think about my aforementioned comments before I go on. Stay tuned.

With all my platonic heart,

Me xx

8 P.M. – 10 P.M.

25

BERNADETTE

'Ladies and Gentlemen, we will shortly be coming through the cabin with a light snack. We would ask at this time that you remain seated, with your seatbelt fastened, as there is a possibility of further turbulence up ahead. We hope you are enjoying your flight with us, and should you need anything at all, please do not hesitate to call a member of our cabin crew.'

That Stefan had a gorgeous Geordie accent. Bernadette could listen to him all day, she decided as she stretched up, rotated her head and commented to no one in particular, 'I need a cup of tea and a shoulder massage. I don't think that's part of the service.'

The little plane on the interactive map on her TV screen was telling Bernadette that it was now less than two hours until they landed. The trip had definitely been full of surprises so far. She'd expected nine hours of solitude, with a bit of awkward embarrassment thrown in, but the reality couldn't have been further from that, partly due to the lovely guy sitting next to her.

'If you can get the tea from the scary cabin crew lady, I'll volunteer to do the shoulder massage, but I warn you, last time I tried to massage my pal, Lizzy, she asked me if I was wearing oven gloves because I was resoundingly rubbish at it.'

'I like the sound of your friend, Lizzy.'

Dev nodded thoughtfully and Bernadette could see that there was something on his mind.

'You know, you remind me of my boy, Stuart. Can't keep anything to himself because every single thought is always written right over his face. To be honest, between you and me, I don't think it's the best quality for someone who has just qualified as a lawyer. He's going to have to work on his poker face. Tell me, then, what's bothering you?'

Bernadette could see that his first reaction was going to be to brush it off, and act like all was fine, but then his body language changed and there was a shade of resignation. 'Can I show you something on my computer?'

'Is it porn? Or one of those dodgy websites that steals your identity? Only, they can have mine. I'd like Julia Roberts' identity instead.'

Oh God, she was chattering like a budgie. She always did this when she was tired. By the time she got to the last couple of hours of a night shift, she'd usually had a conversation with every single person in A&E. She'd spent twenty minutes the other night dissecting the greatest hits of Tom Jones with an elderly head wound patient who swore she'd had a fling with him back in the day. Bernadette really hoped it was true. That was going to be the hardest thing about spending the next two weeks alone – no daft, frivolous chat to make her laugh and pass the time. Too much time to think. Bernadette wasn't sure she was ready for that.

'I promise it's definitely nothing racy. I'd just like your opinion on this.'

Bernadette laughed. 'As my children will tell you, you never have to ask me twice to give my opinion.'

Dev opened his laptop back up, clicked a whole load of buttons, then turned the screen so that she could read what was there. It looked like some kind of letter.

'It's the introduction to my book,' he explained. 'At least, I think it is. Maybe it's just a blueprint for the letter I'll send to publishers and agents. Or the extract that the magazines will run when it's a bestseller,' he joked. 'I wrote it earlier while you were off wandering with Hayley. Would you tell me what you think? If it's terrible, please just say, I can take it. I've already had some feedback that I don't really understand, so I need a second opinion.'

A very unexpected lump formed in Bernadette's throat. This young man really was so like her Stuart. A good person, with a big heart, who just hadn't figured the world out yet. It had taken Stuart a while too. Just a few years ago, he was studying medicine to please his father, and living a double life that he was too afraid to share. Eventually, he decided to live in his truth, to be authentic, out and proud. He'd switched to law and announced to his father that his flatmate, Connor, was actually his boyfriend. Bernadette and Nina had been delighted for him, but it had taken Kenneth a long time to get on board, not with the relationship, but with the change in his son's career. She would always be proud of Stuart for deciding what made him happy. She got the feeling that Dev hadn't quite sussed that out yet.

As she began to read, the lump just got bigger, as he cut his heart open and let it bleed all over the page. Just a few lines in and she was gripped. His openness. His vulnerability. His humour. Everything she'd thought about him since their first conversation was right there on the page. When she got to the final paragraph, the lump in her throat fragmented into thousands of little nuggets of hope. This lad deserved love. If he didn't find it with this lass he was chasing, then Bernadette was going to make it her life mission to help him look elsewhere. She was already preparing a mental checklist of all the young single woman she worked with. Some of them were so raucous, they'd eat him alive – a busy A&E ward in a Glasgow city centre hospital was not for the faint-hearted – but she could think of at least a couple of her friends at work that would be a lovely match for him.

'What do you think? Too sappy? Is it pathetic?'

'No!' Bernadette blurted, with complete honesty. 'I'd read that book in a heartbeat, I really would. It's the perfect introduction. Honest. Raw. It had me completely hooked.' She saw the confused expression on his face.

'You don't think I'm an idiot?'

'What? No. Don't be ridiculous. Of course not. I think you're incredibly brave to put yourself out there.'

'Okay, so would it be a newsflash if I told you I don't understand women sometimes?'

That made Bernadette giggle. 'Nope, not at all. No offence, son, but I got that from you about six hours ago.'

'Okay, so will you read this then and tell me what you think? Because I'm reading it one way, and I'm pretty sure that I have to be reading it wrong.'

Bernadette glanced down at the new letter on the screen.

'It's from my flatmate, Lizzy. She's also been my best mate since we were kids. I sent her the introduction, and this is what she sent back. Apparently, I'm an idiot.'

Bernadette frowned, her inherent maternal protectiveness rising on Dev's behalf. How dare this woman speak about him like that. Wasn't she supposed to be his friend?

A few lines in, her opinion pivoted in a whole new direction. By the time she got to the end, the smile on her face was as wide as her jaw would allow.

'Dev, have you and Lizzy ever been more than friends?'

He flushed slightly. 'Only once. A million years ago. That's where the comment about the girl on the lilo comes from. That girl was Lizzy. It was just a one-night stand and she made it clear that it wasn't to be repeated.'

'And did you make it clear what you wanted?'

The poor guy looked horrified. 'No. I just went along with what she said, because I didn't... well, I guess I didn't want to upset her. She's my best mate. Always has been. What? Why are you shaking your head?'

'Because I'm no expert, but what I get from this letter is that this lass is in love with you.'

'I know she loves me.'

'Nope, *in* love with you. It's a whole different—'

'Ball game? I'm good with sporting analogies.'

'In that case, yes. I think what she's trying to say here is you've been booting the ball in the wrong direction all along. Granted, it's not 100per cent certain, because she doesn't come right out and say it, but it's pretty heavy on the hints.'

'See!' he replied, exasperated. 'This is where I don't get it. Why wouldn't she just say?'

Bernadette shrugged helplessly. 'Because maybe she doesn't want to hurt your friendship. Maybe she's scared of saying or doing the wrong thing.'

'Nope,' he answered, with not even a glimpse of uncertainty. 'That's my schtick. I do terror and indecision. They're right up there with romantic hopelessness and an inability to decipher subliminal messages. Lizzy is fearless. She's the one who knows exactly what she wants, and she goes for it. 100 per cent. Straight to the target. Right over the finish line. Sorry, I'm doing the sporting references again. It's a nervous affliction.'

Bernadette wanted to hug him. 'Maybe she was just waiting for you to catch up.'

That made him pause. 'You really think so?'

'I'm not sure,' Bernadette said honestly. 'But you might have to consider the possibility that your best friend of... how many years?'

'We lived next door to each other all our lives and since we left college, we've shared a flat. So, forever.'

'Okay, well, your best friend of forever is definitely trying to tell you something in this letter. And I'm no expert – I've had one relationship in my life and it was tragic, to be honest, but I think that it's saying that she wants more than just friendship. How would you feel about that?'

His face was set in a perplexed frown and Bernadette realised she was rooting for him to say he felt the same way. She was gutted when he didn't.

'I'd say that I'd need to think about that. I don't know. I just can't get my head around it. What if you're wrong?'

'But what if I'm right?'

'Then our timing is crap and I'm probably headed on a plane in the wrong direction. It's too late. I've met Cheryl. And the way I feel about her... That's never happened to me before. I can't turn back on a maybe. Not when I'm this close. Lizzy and I have had thirty years to work something out and we didn't. I think that says something.'

'It might just say you're not great at seeing what's right in front of you.'

'Or that she's not in that kind of love with me at all,' he countered.

Bernadette couldn't argue on that one. She didn't know this Lizzy, but from everything he'd said, and the letter she'd just read, she definitely seemed like the kind of woman Bernadette would like to meet. Cheryl, not so much. The very thought that she could be the same woman Tadgh was about to marry was still giving her anxiety.

Before he could go on, they were interrupted. 'Here you go, my lovely. Slightly chewy sandwich with an indescribable filling. Tea with that?' Stefan asked with a cheery smile.

'Why, yes indeed,' Bernadette responded, leaning back so that the tray could be placed on her table.

Dev got the same, and the two of them ate their chewy sandwiches in silence for a few moments.

'You know, Dev, your romantic life is the most excitement I've had in months.'

He seemed rightly proud of that, but still he was bashful as he answered, 'Which is ironic, because I'm pretty sure that until twenty-four hours ago, I had the most tedious romantic record in the history of mankind. Or maybe Lizzy was right, and I just couldn't see what was in front of me. Maybe I need to change how I look at things.' He nudged her shoulder. 'Maybe we both do, Bernadette.'

Bernadette took a sip of her tea, thinking about what he had just said.

Since the day that she'd left Kenneth, she'd been completely locked down and disinterested in the prospect of another relationship. But something about Dev's optimism, his excitement, made her remember that it wasn't all pain and heartache. There was joy in there. Hope. The prospect of creating true happiness with someone new.

'Maybe you're right, Dev. Maybe I do.'

26

TADGH

The exhaustion was like something Tadgh had never felt before, an absolute bone weariness in his body, combined with a brain that was racing on overtime. What the feck was he doing?

From the minute he'd returned to his seat, he'd had his eyes closed, but his jaw was beginning to ache from the pain of clenching it. Less than two hours until landing. Adding on the time to get through the airport, travel to the hotel... That meant that it was only going to be a few hours until he discovered the truth. Or the lies.

The time difference in St Lucia put them five hours behind, so although it was evening in the air, it was only late afternoon down below. He wondered what Cheryl was doing now. Lying by the pool? Chilling out, waiting for her fiancé to come and marry her? Or pacing the floor of the hotel room, trying to find a way to tell him that she didn't want this any more?

He pulled out his phone and sent a text.

Landing in a couple of hours. Are you coming to the airport, or will I just come find you at the hotel?

...

Three dots again.

Just twinkling.

Moving from side to side.

Then... nothing.

What was that about? It was so unlike her. Cheryl was an 'answer back straight away, don't give it a second thought' kind of girl. Always had been. It was one of the things he'd always loved about her – she didn't play games or keep him guessing. It was ridiculous to think that had suddenly changed in the week since he'd kissed her goodbye at Dublin airport, waved her off as she flew to London with her girlfriends for a hen party in the city, then their flight out to St Lucia the next day. Had something happened before she left? Or after? Or was he reading too much into this as well? Maybe there was just a delay in the signal. Slow Wi-Fi here on the plane or at the hotel... Or maybe it wasn't.

For obvious reasons, in some ways he wanted to buy the story that Shay was actually seeing Cheryl's sister, Cindy. It left his relationship with Cheryl protected. Kept them together. Salvaged their wedding and their future.

But it wasn't a perfect solution, because if Shay was seeing Cindy, well, that was their mate, Jay's wife. And Tadgh didn't know if he could keep his mouth shut about that.

'Sandwich? Tea or coffee?'

'Coffee, please,' he murmured. No food. He couldn't face it.

A voice beside him said, 'Same, please,' and he turned to see Hayley giving Marian, the cabin crew manager, a grateful smile.

As Marian moved on to the next row, Hayley turned to him. 'You know, I'm just thinking that 99 per cent of the people on this plane will be so excited right now, and we seem to be the only two people who are letting the side down.'

Tadgh ran his finger around the rim of the plastic coffee cup. 'You could be right about that. How are you doing? I saw you speaking with yer man back there. If you're still in the Downer Club with me, I'm guessing that it didn't go well.'

Hayley shook her head, let it fall to one side so that she was facing him, her whole body half turned so that her back was to that bloke, Dev, on the other side. Not that he noticed – he and Bernadette seemed engrossed in something he was showing her on his laptop.

'Okay, so we've got under two hours left. We could do that thing…' she suggested. Without even realising it, Tadgh mirrored Hayley's body language, turning towards her, their faces maybe half a metre apart now.

Curiosity made the corners of his mouth turn up. 'What thing is that, now?'

'You know,' she said. 'What's said on a plane stays on a plane.'

There was a split-second delay in his response because he was thinking how beautiful she was. It wasn't just her face, although that was undeniably pretty. There was something else: the kind of hypnotic, bright light in her eyes, that people wrote songs about. The crazy thing was, he wasn't even convinced that she realised that.

His grin came easy. 'I think you might be making that up.'

'No, really, it's a thing!' she argued, pulling her blanket around her. 'Okay, so maybe Bernadette along at the end invented it with me a couple of hours ago, but that still means it exists. I'm making it official.'

'Fair play,' he went along with it. What else was he going to do for the next couple of hours? Stare at the wall. Or at something on a TV screen that he wasn't even absorbing? Or put the music on and get back inside his own head? He'd had enough of hanging out there for today. The novelty had definitely worn off. 'I can say anything, then?' he asked, 'And it never leaves this...' He struggled for the word.

'Bubble,' she finished the sentence, drawing an invisible line in a circle around them. 'This is our bubble. It's sacred. What's said here stays here. Okay, you go first.'

Tadgh wasn't sure what he was supposed to say. Unburdening his soul didn't come easy to him. His mam could always get the truth out of him. He could walk into a room and she'd do that thing. 'Right, what's going on? I can see it in yer face,' she'd start.

'Nothing, Mam, everything is cool.'

'Tadgh Eamon Donovan, don't you dare lie to yer mother. Now what's going on? And don't be giving me that "cool" nonsense. If you keep stuff in, it's bad for your digestion.'

Or 'it'll give you piles.'

Or 'yer hair will be grey before the year is out.'

Or whatever other medical scenario she could come up with, all of which were based on no actual science other than the theories developed at the Jean Donovan School of Tactical Interrogation.

He didn't believe a word of it, but it would be enough to make him laugh, and shake his head, and spill out every detail of whatever was on his mind. After she died, he missed that. When something was troubling him, he'd write songs instead. The ache of watching his da trying to live without his mam, and the loss Tadgh felt every day without her too, was where 'Everywhere Without You' came from. 'Yesterday' too. Just a feeling, a pain that he wanted to release.

Back in the day, he would share everything with Cheryl too, but she'd been so busy lately with the wedding that their moments of conversational intimacy had tailed off. At least, he'd thought that was the reason. Maybe he'd called that one wrong too.

Christ, when did life become so complicated? He was a pretty simple guy. All he wanted to do was work, play music, love someone, be loved back. That was enough for him. Why wasn't it enough for everyone else?

'I think the woman I'm about to marry might be having an affair with my brother.'

There it was. He'd said it aloud. And the woman beside him was now choking on her coffee.

'You what?' she spluttered when she eventually caught her breath. Dev, on the other side of her, began thumping her back, while saying, 'Bernadette, we might need the Heimlich here,' to their fourth row-mate.

Shit, this had suddenly become a spectacle. Not what he had intended at all.

Hayley took charge, defusing it all. 'No, really, I'm fine. Just some coffee went down the wrong way. Totally fine now,' she assured the other two, before coming back to their bubble, eyes wider now, brow frowning. 'I'm so sorry,' her voice was low, almost a whisper, so that they couldn't be overheard. 'Why would you think that?'

Weariness made his sigh catch in his throat. 'This morning, before we got on the flight, I saw a text on my brother's phone from her. At least, I think it was from her. It might have been her sister. Sorry, I know this is confusing...'

'Keep going, I'll catch up,' she said, and he could hear the genuine concern in her voice.

'I thought it was from her. From Cheryl. But I was talking to my mate back there and...'

He carried on with the story, leaving out no details. He told her about his conversation with Conlan, about the story Shay gave Conlan about seeing Cheryl's married sister, about the potential consequences of that for their family, their band, their future.

'And you know what bothers me most?' he said, half an hour later, when he'd told her the whole sorry tale from start to finish.

'Tell me,' she said softly.

'Even if he's done something awful, I still feel like I want to defend him. He's my brother. I mean, I want to kill him, but I want to defend him too. What the feck is that about?'

'I think it's about how much you love your brother. I get it. Sometimes I feel exactly the same way about my husband. It's because there's love there, and care, and it's almost like you want to save them from themselves, because no matter how low they go, it's hard to let them drown.'

'It's not just for my sake. This will kill ma da' too and I don't want to hurt him. He's a good man. He lost my mam a couple of years ago. I don't want him to lose Shay too and I'm not sure he'd be able to forgive him. I don't want to be responsible for that.'

A single curl had escaped from the knot as the back of her head, and she pushed it back. 'You're not responsible for that. It's on them. It's their relationship to work out.'

Tadgh nodded, appreciating the perspective she was giving him.

'But I think that what you need first, more than anything, is the truth. Do you really think your fiancée would do that to you?'

'If you'd asked me before this morning, I'd have said no. You know, me and Cheryl...'

He saw her flinch when he said that and wondered if she was about to have another choking fit, but it passed.

'We've just been together forever. It's the way it's always been. I'm marrying her because I've loved her all our lives and because she wanted to do this. Why would she push for it if she was capable of doing something like this with Shay?'

'Maybe she isn't. Don't give up on trusting her, because maybe this is all an innocent misunderstanding.'

'I get that. And it scares me that I can even doubt her, because surely there should be no question in my head over whether or not this is even possible.'

'Don't do that. Don't beat yourself up for questioning what you saw. You're only human. Could you forgive her?'

Tadgh shook his head. 'I don't think so. I think I'd never understand it so couldn't forgive it. I'd ask myself every day how it happened. How could someone do that to the person they love?'

'Because sometimes we think we want something, and we're so focused on making that happen that we lose sight of what's best for us. Maybe she's changed. Maybe she's realised that she wants something else. Or maybe she just made a mistake.'

'You sound like you've got some experience in this.'

The sadness on her face when she nodded made something in his gut ache with sorrow for her. What the feck was going on here? This woman was clearly having a shit time and he was banging on about himself.

'Can you do me a favour?' he asked. 'Any chance we could stop talking about me, and shift our bubble over to you?'

27

HAYLEY

Hayley had been so immersed in Tadgh's story that it had given her some sweet relief from thinking about her own. His bravery inspired her. Here was a guy who was confronting what could potentially be the worst kind of betrayal, but still thinking about the repercussions for others. His father. His bandmates. Even his fiancée and his brother, and if the worst was true, Hayley had already decided that Cheryl and Shay deserved each other. Or Cindy and Shay, if that's what was going on here.

She couldn't help contrast Tadgh's compassion for others against the sorry reality that Lucas only saw the world from his own point of view. Not once had she seen him bend, seen him take other people into account. He was laser-focused on himself, on success, on his own targets in life.

The overwhelming truth of that realisation repulsed her, and she knew: right there and then, she knew. And she couldn't stop herself from blurting it out. 'I think I want to leave my husband.'

Tadgh's response oozed nothing but concern. 'Wow. That's a big decision.'

Hayley nodded, not quite able to absorb what she'd just said, but with the absolute conviction that she meant it. The blinds on the cabin windows were still mostly down, yet – not to get too spiritual about it all – she felt like she was seeing the light clearly for the first time in years. 'We used to be so happy. He was everything, or, at least, I thought he was. But I guess, in hindsight, I can see that I always felt that I didn't quite match up to his standards. I always thought that was down to my own issues, but there's no doubt he helped them along, made it worse. My husband is a doctor, a fertility specialist. He's regarded as one of the best in his field. A few years ago, we started trying to have a family and...' She paused. 'Am I really discussing my reproductive system with you?'

Tadgh found this amusing. 'As long as there are no diagrams or photographs, I should be fine.'

'Aw, that's a shame. I always keep my photo album handy for showing graphic images to strangers.'

She decided there must be some kind of weird oxygen in this bubble because they were pouring out their very own heartbreaks to each other and yet there were these moments of levity that came out of nowhere. She carried on, never more willing or more comfortable in sharing a piece of her soul.

'The infertility journey put so much more strain on our relationship. I get it. In his mind, it was so much bigger than his wife's inability to get pregnant. I see now that it was all tied up with his career. He saw it as being a personal attack on the thing that meant the most to him: his professional reputation.'

'Jesus, that's about as twisted as it gets,' Tadgh sighed. 'Just so you know, I really want to tell you that he's a prick, but I'm trying to be the silent, supportive, bubble listener here.'

Hayley smiled gratefully. 'Noted.'

'But you know he's a prick, right? The way he behaved here earlier—'

'Yeah, I'm sorry about that.'

'Don't apologise. It's not your place to be sorry. It's his.'

'I've realised I need to work on that. Actually, Bernadette helped me see a lot of things in a new light today.'

'Did you know her before you got on this plane?'

Hayley shook her head. 'No. That's the crazy thing. I feel like something put us in the same place so we would meet today. It's like she saw straight away who I was and who he was. She was married to a very similar man, and she stayed with him for a long time to protect her family, but now she feels she should have left before she did. I'd never thought things through from that perspective. If I stay with Lucas and we do manage to have a family, what will that look like? Will he go back to being the man that I married, or is this who he really is? I don't think I want to take the chance on finding out.'

She watched as he pondered that thought. He didn't tell her she was wrong. Or right. Or give his opinion. He didn't tell her she was being ridiculous, or stupid or rash. He just listened without judgement. When was the last time her husband had done that?

When Tadgh spoke, it was only to ask, 'What's next then? Have you got a plan?'

'Not really. I think I need to talk to him tonight while I'm feeling brave enough.'

The buzz of an incoming text interrupted the conversation and he retrieved his phone from the seat pocket.

'Cheryl?' Hayley asked, feeling strangely protective of this man she didn't know.

He read the words on the screen. 'Yep. She says she's on the way to the airport. She wants to meet me there.'

Hayley felt a twinge of anxiety. Cheryl would be at the airport. Tadgh would be there. Shay would be there. That situation already had an explosive potential for disaster. Add in Dev and – if by any chance her suspicions were right and he was crossing the globe to track down the same Cheryl – then they'd be as well all diving for cover. Surely she couldn't be having an affair with his brother and picking up one-night stands too? Or maybe she could.

Hayley felt she needed to get ahead of the situation. 'There's something I want to ask you. Is there anyone else in your bridal party with the same name as your fiancée?'

'No, why?'

Disappointment and dread made Hayley's shoulders slump. Damn. 'Oh, it's nothing. I heard someone else on the flight say something about meeting someone on the island with that name.' More than anything, she wanted to tell him, but she couldn't bring herself to say it. The thought of putting more worry in his mind made her shiver. It couldn't be the same woman. Surely the universe wouldn't do that to someone as sweet as him? *Come on, karma, do your stuff. Sort it out and take the pressure off this guy – he has enough to deal with.*

The voice of the cabin crew manager, Marian, took very definite charge as it came over the airwaves. 'Ladies and gentlemen, we are now beginning our approach to Hewanorra International Airport, St Lucia. We'd ask at this time that you fasten your seatbelts, close your tables and put your seat back in an upright position. Our flight attendants will be coming through the cabin to collect any items you may have for disposal. Thank you for flying with us today. We hope you've had an enjoyable flight and we look forward to seeing you again in the future.'

Hayley carried out all the instructions, then sat back and exhaled, her hands on the armrests, thinking about the announcement that had just been made. Something about travelling again in the future. 'You know what's crazy?' she pondered aloud in Tadgh's direction. 'I've got no idea what the future is going to hold. I don't even know what's going to happen in the next few hours, but for the first time, I've got a feeling that's okay. Maybe that's the way it'll be for you too. Maybe you'll both come to the same decision at the same time, or maybe you'll see each other and realise that all this stuff that's happened in the last twenty-four hours is nothing to do with you both and it's just there to throw in a curveball and test your relationship. Do I sound really wise? I'm feeling like I sounded a bit Oprah there.'

'Definitely Oprah. Couldn't agree more.'

The noise of the landing gear coming down almost drowned out Tadgh's words. But not quite.

'I hope you're right about the test thing. Just hope we pass it.'

Hayley reached into the pocket in front of her for a bottle of water she'd put there earlier, aware that even talking about this was making her throat tighten and her mouth dry up. Was she losing her mind? Was Lucas actually right when he said that she was crazy? Who got on a plane, married and trying to have a family, and then, nine hours later, got off the flight having decided to leave their husband?

She took another sip of water and her swallow reflex threatened to go on strike through sheer fear at the prospect of how Lucas would react. That said it all. Why was his reaction the thing that was worrying her most?

Tadgh leaned towards her. 'Okay, I have a suggestion. Hear me out here. Could you stay and make one last go of it this holiday? I'm not saying for a second that you should. Like I said, the guy didn't impress me, but you must have had something once. Maybe it's not too late to get back to that place.'

'This from the guy who is considering bailing on his wedding,' she teased him, and he shrugged, acknowledging her point.

'You're right. You see, this is why you're Oprah, and I'll just always be a guy in a band.'

Hayley didn't want to admit that she'd thought about the plan that he'd suggested. If she was being brutally honest with herself, it had been sitting there, in the corner of her reasoning, since this holiday was booked. But now she saw that there was one huge, potentially catastrophic consequence of doing that – what if it worked? What if she got pregnant? Wasn't Bernadette the cautionary tale of why that wasn't a great idea? Hadn't she ended up tied to a man of cruelty for half her lifetime?

Tadgh was still considering all her options. 'What will you do if he refuses to accept your decision?'

'I'm not sure. Leave anyway, I guess. I can't see any scenario that would make me want to stay now. Urgh, the thought of all of this is making my stomach churn. I'm not even 100 per cent sure that I'll have the guts to do it. At least Bernadette is staying at the same resort as us, and it kind of makes me feel better to know that I have someone else there that isn't a complete stranger. I think that going by our newly established boundaries, nine hours on a plane makes us practically family.'

'Okay, I hereby nominate her to be an honorary member of our bubble, should you require to add to the group.'

'Excellent,' she agreed. 'And we'll let Dev in too because he looks so much like Ryan Reynolds that he'll get us great tables in restaurants.'

'Did I hear my name being mentioned there?' Dev asked, leaning forward so that he could see into their bubble.

'Yes. We'd like you to hang out with us because you look like you're famous.'

Dev nodded. 'My services can be bought. Throw in some chicken wings and a few beers and I'm yours. Just as long as I can bring Cheryl. Assuming she hasn't had me arrested by then.'

Hayley held her breath. She saw that Bernadette's eyes had widened too and as their gazes locked, she sent up a silent prayer.

Dear Universe, just on the highly bolloxed off chance that both of these men are on their way to meet the same woman, please don't let

Tadgh have heard that last comment. Thank you and sending love, Hayley and Bernadette.

She slowly, painstakingly turned her head to her right, expecting to see Tadgh in a full state of shock, on the cusp of throwing out furious questions and demanding answers. Instead, she saw that Stefan was standing at the end of the row, distracting Tadgh by clearing a tube of Pringles and several bottles of beer off Tadgh's tray, while attempting to tie down an audition for the band.

Panic averted.

But for how much longer?

28

DEV

The plane's descent was making Dev's ears pop and, like the perfectly prepared mother, Bernadette handed him a couple of huge mints to suck on to make it better.

Dev wondered if he could persuade Bernadette to come home with him and live with him forever. Given the erratic nature of his current adventure, he might have to explain it wasn't a hostage-type situation. He was just enjoying every minute of her company and he was fairly certain that Lizzy would love her just as much as he did. Unless, of course, Cheryl had other plans for their romcom ending.

He realised that he hadn't given a single thought to what happened next. Definitely a flaw in the plan, but one that he wasn't going to worry about right now because he could see the potential issues. She lived in Ireland. He had no idea where. Should probably have asked that. He was fairly sure she told him what she did for work, but that information had been wiped by too many beers. Anyway, those were all technicalities. Small details. No one ever wrote about what happened after the final romcom moment. They didn't worry about where to live or how they were going to split the electricity bill, or whose family they were going to go to on Christmas Day. The only thing that would matter was that Lizzy and Cheryl had to like each other because that was non-negotiable.

Thinking of Lizzy took his mind back to the email she'd sent him earlier. He was sure that Bernadette had interpreted it wrong, not understanding the nuances of their relationship. Lizzy loved him. He loved her. That was true. But she couldn't possibly be 'in love' with him. There was no way on this earth that Lizzy Walsh would have kept that to herself.

In fact... his mind drifted back to another moment that could have opened that box. His twenty-fifth birthday. They were in Amsterdam with a few blokes from the *Tribune* and they'd ended up in a snooker bar that sold very dodgy mooncakes. Lizzy had got completely wasted on a blueberry hash muffin, and Dev was a good bucket of beer or two in. They'd hustled a couple of German blokes for fifty euros on the snooker table, the naïve tourists not realising that Dev and Lizzy had spent most of their teenage years bunking off school and hanging out in the snooker hall behind their local Asda. Even with Lizzy, as she put it, 'off her tits on sponge cake', they'd delivered a conclusive win. It hadn't hindered their case that Lizzy was wearing ripped-up hipster jeans and a white T-shirt, her blonde corkscrew curls the size of a small bush, and was easily, without a doubt, the most attractive woman in the bar. And the whole street. Maybe even the city.

Fifty 'extorted from the Germans' euros in hand, Lizzy had swayed slightly as she'd asked, 'What should we bet this on?'

Dev had chugged back some beer before he answered. 'Nothing. We should buy some more alcohol and a few more of those muffins for you. And maybe find a kebab shop on the way back to the hotel.'

'No, no, no,' Lizzy had crooned. 'I bet you, Dev Erasmus Robbins...'

Dev had closed his eyes as he'd tried not to laugh. She always threw out his mildly embarrassing middle name when she was drunk or, on this occasion, stoned.

'... that one day, you are going to wake up and realise that you are madly in love with me.'

The moping Germans at the bar may have thought Dev's laughter was directed at them, because they responded with angry glares.

He'd bought into the hypothetical joke, 'And what would you say if I did declare my undying devotion, Elizabeth Enid Walsh?'

'Ouch!' she'd exclaimed, feigning a bullet to the chest. 'My granny will haunt you if you take her name in vain. Anyway, what would I say?'

'Yep.'

'I would tell you that I loved you back.'

That had stunned him, and it must have shown because he'd frozen, and within seconds, her cheeky, teasing smile had switched to horror.

'I'm kidding! I'd tell you to stop being ridiculous because, clearly, I'm a catch and I'm going to marry Tom Cruise. He seems like a nice normal guy.'

Dev had swiftly recovered, and they'd sang 'You've Lost That Loving Feeling' all the way to the kebab shop.

Didn't that prove that what they had was the perfect platonic love? Surely if she'd actually had those kinds of feelings for him, she'd have taken his first answer and they'd have staggered off happily into the sunset because... there was definitely some truth in his reply. He'd been a little bit in love with Lizzy Enid Walsh his whole life, but it was like his childhood dream of being a footie star – it was an unrealistic ambition that he never allowed to become all-consuming because he was fairly sure he didn't have the skills for the job. He definitely didn't have the suave, bad-boy, self-assured skills to be the kind of man Lizzy wanted for her happy ever after.

The little email icon flashed up on the laptop he was balancing on his knees. One new email. From Lizzy Walsh.

'Can you close the laptop, please?' Scary Marian warned him, one eyebrow of intimidation raised in his direction as she passed by the end of his row.

'Certainly. Sorry,' he fumbled as he tucked it into the seat pocket and pulled out his phone instead. He checked the screen. Yep, the email was there too, so he clicked to open it.

Dear You,

You're still an idiot. I just wanted to get that out of the way, because I'm about to share some stuff that will reinforce that conclusion.

Okay, I'm doing this. I'm taking a deep breath right now because I am, quite frankly, bricking it. I'm also going to S-P-E-L-L it out, because I know what you're like and I'm 100 per cent sure that you probably didn't get the message I was trying to convey in my last email. Am I right?

Dev realised he was nodding in agreement. It didn't take a genius to work out that when it came to emotional stuff, he wasn't great with subtlety.

He carried on reading...

Okay, here goes...

Dev, do you remember we once snogged after a party in your garden? Granted, we were twelve, and you'd just won the huge tub of sherbet dib-dabs in pass the parcel, but the reason I kissed you is because, even then... I L-O-V-E-D you.

When we were fifteen, and bunked off school, and we had to hide in the estate agents' doorway because we spotted Mr Edwards, the maths teacher, approaching, I kissed you. Not because I was trying to hide our faces (I still can't believe you bought that), but because... I L-O-V-E-D you.

The mistletoe every single year at my front door? Bought with my pocket money and put there so I could snog you because... I L-O-V-E-D you.

That morning we woke up in bed together after the school disco. We were about sixteen and I only had a bra and my Atomic Kitten flared jeans on… I hadn't, in fact, taken my T-shirt off because I'd spilled Diamond White cider on it, I'd taken it off, hoping you'd get the fricking hint because… I L-O-V-E-D you.

Benidorm. Oh, dear God, don't get me started. We finally slept together, on a fricking lilo, and it was drunken, and daft, and fantastic, and just so utterly us, and perfect because… I L-O-V-E-D you.

And the next morning, I pretended it was a drunken mistake because you looked so shocked and horrified and I didn't want you to feel bad about it, because… I L-O-V-E-D you.

And Amsterdam. I mean, seriously. Idiot. I practically confessed that I wanted to spend the rest of my life with you, then retracted it pronto because you didn't buy into it, and then I pretended the whole thing was just a big laugh because… I L-O-V-E-D you.

In the years since then, I've watched you date women who weren't right for you, some who didn't deserve you and a couple that were downright mingers. And I didn't criticise (okay, I did, I'm only human) because… I L-O-V-E-D you.

And I waited for you to see it. Waited for you to feel the same way. And yes, I may have amused myself with some very cool distractions along the way, but that didn't mean my feelings had changed. In case you still haven't picked up the message, I L-O-V-E-D you.

Which brings us to now. This trip you're going on to prove the whole 'love at first sight thing'. Sure, she is a goddess. And I've no idea if she feels the same way as you. Knowing my luck, she probably will, and you'll sail off into the sunset together. Hang on, I need to get a gin and tonic to get me past that scenario…

Okay, I'm back. All I'm saying is, I really, really don't want you to go with the love at first sight, because love that lasts a lifetime is so much cooler.

I love you, Dev Erasmus Robbins. I always have. Even your hopeless bits and your flaws and the things other people don't get. I do. I get you. You get me. We're meant to be. And I hope beyond all kind of words that when you read this, you'll realise that you've always loved me too. If you do… if you do… I'm trying to find something poignant and romantic to finish off this sentence, but I can't, so I'm just going to go with…

If you do in fact realise you love me… then sack off the goddess with the forty-inch legs and pert boobs and come back to me.

Because I love you.

Love, Me xx

Dev's cardiovascular system shut down and he felt his lungs shrivel as they lost the ability to breathe. He almost dropped the phone, catching it just as it threatened to slip from his grasp. 'Oh shit. Shit. Oh shit, shit. Bernadette, I think you were right.'

He turned the phone so that she could read the screen, then watched her face as her eyes scanned the words, and she gasped, kept reading, her hand over her mouth, and then, to his surprise, tears popped up on her bottom lids.

'Oh, my goodness, Dev, that's the most gorgeous letter I've ever read. She loves you. She actually loves you.'

'That's what I thought she meant.'

Bernadette threw up her hands. 'What you *thought*? Dev, it's there in black and white. It couldn't be more definite if she wrote it on a banner and had a plane fly it past that window. She loves you. Question is, given that you're, you know, currently on your way to tell someone else you love them…'

'I can see the issue that you're highlighting here…' he agreed, his shoulders sagging.

Bernadette carried on with her train of thought. 'What are you going to do about it, then?'

Dev's head jolted back as the plane's wheels hit the ground and a round of applause burst out in the cabin. Bollocks. Landed. He was here. Bernadette's question stood, but he needed more time to think about it. What was he going to do about this?

'I really don't know. I need some time. Do you think we can ask the pilot to go back up and do another couple of circles?'

Bernadette laughed as she shook her head. 'I don't think so, son. This is it. And your gut should tell you what to do. So what is it? Go chase the love at first sight? Or go back to the one that's been there all along? No pressure. But it might just be the most important decision you ever make.'

5 P.M. – 7 P.M. ST LUCIA TIME

(WHICH IS 10 P.M. – MIDNIGHT UK TIME, SO THEY'RE ALL GETTING A BIT KNACKERED)

29

BERNADETTE

'Ladies and gentlemen, welcome to St Lucia, where the local time is 5.07 p.m. Please stay seated while we taxi to our gate, and we will get you disembarked as soon as possible.'

Bernadette exhaled and gave her ankles another wee rotation, just to kick-start them back into action. She'd made it. She was here. And somewhere over the last nine and a bit hours on this plane, her perspective on this holiday had completely changed. When she'd arrived at the departure gate at Gatwick, she'd been a definite 50/50 on whether to get on the flight, and definitely less than 50/50 as to whether or not there was even a possibility that she would have a good time on her own. This flight had given her confidence that it was going to be fine. If this was a taste of how the rest of the holiday was going to be, then she was going to meet lovely people, have a right few laughs and be able to help a couple of souls who needed it.

'You okay there, Bernadette?' Hayley was leaning forward, so they could lock eyes around Dev. There were lines of exhaustion around the younger woman's eyes, and a weariness, maybe sadness in her shoulders, but there was also a calmness that hadn't been there earlier. Bernadette wondered if that was anything to do with being deep in conversation with Tadgh for the last couple of hours. Bernadette had seen them in her peripheral vision, huddled down close together as they spoke. That was the crazy thing. If she was a stranger walking past them, she'd have thought they were a couple and a lovely one at that.

It had also had another effect on her thinking, she realised. The whole time Hayley and Tadgh had been in conversation, Bernadette had a nagging sense of unease, and she hadn't been able to pinpoint the cause. Worry for Sarah and her daughter, Eliza, over in Crete? Anxiety about being far from Nina and the kids in case they missed her or needed her? Dread that something could happen on this holiday – an accident or illness, maybe – and she would have no one here to turn to? Eventually she worked out that it was none of the above. It was a dread that Hayley's husband would come back and see her talking so closely to Tadgh, because that was the kind of trepidation Bernadette had lived with her whole marriage.

The irony still turned her stomach. Kenneth was the one who'd had affairs throughout their entire time together, yet if he so much as saw her talking to another man, his rage would be deathly. Not at the time, of course. In public, he'd presented such a dashing, amenable persona. But as soon as they got home, he'd accuse her of flirting, of humiliating him, of acting like a slut, a whore, an unfit mother.

She had absolutely no idea if Lucas followed the same pattern, and she truly hoped for Hayley's sake that he did not. That didn't stop Bernadette feeling anxious about it though, and she was just glad that she was staying at the same resort, as she had a real sense that Hayley was going to have a bumpy fortnight. That man of hers was a nasty piece of work who reminded her so much of Kenneth. All that easy charm and charisma, the façade of respectability and decency, and a trained surgeon too. What were the chances? Bernadette had always wondered how much of his shit Kenneth would have got away with if he'd had a run-of-the-mill job that didn't come with the illusion of importance and brilliance.

'I'm fine, thanks, Hayley,' she answered the question with a warm smile. 'How about you two down there?' she gestured to Hayley and Tadgh.

'Och, just sorting out the world,' Tadgh replied, with that slow, easy grin that she'd seen flashes of when he wasn't doing the whole stormy, brooding thing. He seemed a bit lighter though. Or maybe that was just because they were back on solid ground.

'Do you think they'll sort out my world?' Dev murmured beside her.

Bernadette wondered if it would be deeply inappropriate to reach over and hug this young man. Oh, that letter. It was so loving, so moving, Bernadette had almost wanted to marry that girl herself.

'No further forward on what you think you want to do?' she asked him quietly.

He shook his head. 'It's just... it's just... it's Lizzy. She's honestly the person I love most in the world, always has been. I just don't know how to... process this. The inside of my head feels like a tumble dryer right now and I don't know how to make it stop. Do you think she means it?'

Bernadette rolled her eyes in exasperation. 'In the name of God, what would it take?'

'I know, I know, I'm sorry,' he blurted. 'But it's just... it's Lizzy. We've shared a flat for a decade. You'd think she might have dropped a hint.'

'Sounds like there's been plenty of hints and you've just been too daft – no offence – to take them.'

'Do you think Scary Marian would shout at me if I put my tray table down? Only, I think I need to bang my head on it a few times.'

'I think she'd have you in a headlock within seconds.'

'Okay, I'll just go back to staring hopelessly into space waiting for all this to process.'

'Good plan. I'm here if you need me though.'

Bernadette patted his arm and then returned to her own thoughts, another niggle prodding at the back of her mind. The conversation she'd had earlier with Dev, and Hayley's comment about Tadgh's fiancée having the same name. Both Irish. Both flew out to St Lucia last weekend. It was exceptionally coincidental.

It really wasn't in Bernadette's nature to meddle. It truly wasn't. Unless, that was, she really felt she could solve a problem or make a difference. Even then, any interference would be highly reluctant. But she'd grown to like this young man over the last few hours, and she couldn't bear the thought of him being humiliated if, by some incredible twist of fate, the one-night stand had been with Tadgh's fiancée. And she also couldn't bear to see Tadgh mortified by that scenario either.

No, she chided herself. *It's none of your business. Keep your mouth shut. Say nothing. Back off.*

There was a strong argument for letting it be, and just allowing fate to run its course, but maybe, well, maybe it would give Dev his answer. Maybe he'd realise that this had all been folly, and he could high-tail it back to the angel who had written him that letter.

'Dev, forgive me for what I'm about to do,' she whispered to him. 'I promise you, I've got yer best interests at heart, son.'

'Tell me it doesn't involve nudity or a whip-round for cash,' he fired back, making her snort out a strangled giggle.

'Dear God, your mind works in mysterious ways. I don't even want to know where that came from, but no.'

They jolted slightly as the plane went over a bump and began a wide turn. It propelled her forward enough to get a clear view of both Hayley and Tadgh.

'Tadgh, can I ask you something?' she said, loudly enough for her words to reach Tadgh, but trying to keep it as light as possible. She caught Hayley's gaze and a subliminal message passed between them, making Hayley's eyes widen with the knowledge of what was about to come. 'The lass you're about to marry. What's her name?'

'Cheryl,' he answered casually, probably thinking it was a completely innocent question.

Bernadette's stomach was churning at the prospect of the havoc she may be about to unleash.

Beside her, Dev's head swung first to her, then to Tadgh, then back to her, like he was watching the worst tennis match in the history of mankind.

'And she's Irish, isn't she?'

Tadgh's amenable nod gave away just a hint of confusion. 'Of course. Born and bred. From Dublin, like myself.'

Bernadette waited for Dev to jump in with a frantic question, but he appeared to be entering some kind of weird catatonic state between shock, dread and avoidance. So it was up to her.

'And did you say that she flew out from Gatwick last weekend?'

She prayed he'd say no, that there would be a newly discovered fact that cancelled out any possibility of these two girls being the same woman. Anything...

'Yeah, last Saturday. Think they went out on the town in London the night before. They were all rough as anything when I spoke to Cheryl after they landed here the next day. Makes me feel a bit better about getting plastered last night.'

It was official. Bernadette hated herself for doing this, for sticking her nose into this situation.

Hayley still hadn't spoken, transfixed by every word that was being exchanged.

'It couldn't be. Just couldn't.' Dev was murmuring now, still in utter shock.

She backed up, so she could whisper in Dev's ear. 'I've got you, son,' she said, before leaning forward again.

Bernadette wasn't ready to tell Tadgh what was going on. No point in traumatising them both. Better to establish the facts first. She had no idea how Tadgh would react if he were to find out that the guy sitting two seats along from him for the last ten hours or so may have been intimate with his future wife, knowingly or not. She was not going to be responsible for the potential scenario of Dev leaving this plane with two black eyes and Tadgh leaving it in handcuffs.

'Och, yer only young once,' she responded to Tadgh. 'You're quite right to have a blow-out before you get hitched.'

She thought through her next move and decided to go for it, reminding herself that no matter how underhand this felt, she was doing this for their own good. At least Dev would have full disclosure and wouldn't go rushing up to her at the airport, just as Tadgh wandered over to have a happy reunion with his soon-to-be wife. This way, Dev would know if it was her. He could avoid confrontation. Backtrack. Maybe it would give him clarity to make what was, let's face it, the far more sensible decision to go back and give things a try with Lizzy. 'Have you got a photo? I'd love to see her.'

'I think I'm going to have a stroke,' Dev muttered, so only she could hear.

'Yeah, sure.' Tadgh pulled out his phone and scrolled through a couple of images, before turning it so Bernadette, and by default, Dev, could see it.

'Oh, she's stunning,' Bernadette said, truthfully. The lass was gorgeous, with her long, waist-length caramel waves, cheekbones that belonged in a magazine and sparkling green eyes.

Dev was still staring straight ahead so Bernadette nudged him to spur him on. This couldn't be avoided. It had to be faced.

'Ladies and gentlemen, you are now welcome to disembark this aircraft. Please check that you have all personal belongings and be careful opening the overhead lockers because some items may have moved and could cause injury. Thank you again for flying with us today and have a wonderful holiday.'

The volume of the announcement covered Bernadette's insistent whisper. 'Dev, you have to look at it. Do it now. Do. It. Now.'

Reluctantly, as if his head was an oil tanker and it was being pulled in a long slow circle by a tugboat, Dev turned to the right, peered at the picture, then gasped.

'It's her!'

30

TADGH

Tadgh didn't understand what was going on here.

'It's who?' he asked, puzzled, just as Hayley murmured, 'Oh Jesus,' under her breath.

What was he missing? Hayley was giving off some seriously strange vibes, Bernadette looked crushed all of a sudden, and Dev was staring at Tadgh's phone, nodding his head, repeating, 'Yes, that's her!'

'Who?' Tadgh asked again.

Hayley finally re-entered the world of the living, putting her hand on Tadgh's arm. 'The thing is, Tadgh, we think that—'

'Yeah, that was the woman who was having her hen party last weekend,' Dev interjected, cutting Hayley off.

Tadgh noticed that Bernadette and Hayley swung their heads to face Dev.

'Having her hen party?' he heard Hayley say. 'Not—'

Dev cut her off again with a very definite, 'No! That's the woman who was having the hen party,' he repeated. 'I didn't realise her name was Cheryl too. What a coincidence. The Cheryl I met was definitely with them.'

Tadgh still didn't understand. Obviously, the effects of last night's alcohol were making a comeback because he could not for the life of him work out what the hell was going on. It was like they were all having a conversation in code that he wasn't following. But he had picked up the bit where Dev recognised Cheryl from her hen party last weekend.

'You met her? You met Cheryl?'

Dev shook his head. 'No, not that Cheryl. The woman I met was called Cheryl too.'

Tadgh was even more confused now. And not just by the fact that Dev seemed to be sagging with relief. What the hell was going on here?

'Another woman with them? Called Cheryl. Are you sure? And it definitely wasn't this one. I mean, I know it couldn't have been—'

'It definitely wasn't this lady. I'm as positive as it's possible to be. This lady was there though. It was her party and she was wearing a tiara and singing to Shania Twain about things not impressing her,' Dev told him.

'Yeah, that sounds like Cheryl,' Tadgh conceded. That was always her first choice of karaoke song. Something still didn't make sense about all this though. There was only one Cheryl in his fiancée's wedding group, and that was the woman he was marrying. Hang on...

Tadgh's mind started working on a hypothetical scenario. Dev was on his way to find a woman he'd had a one-night stand with. Imagine if that had been his Cheryl. He shrugged the thought off as ridiculous, but then... was it? Was it really that crazy?

He chided himself. Yes, it was. Cheryl wouldn't betray him. This whole day had been an absolute aberration. What had he been thinking? Cheryl wouldn't sleep with someone else, and definitely not this bloke, Dev, and absolutely not Shay. How could he even have thought that? It had to be a mix-up. Had to be. And the fact that he even doubted her... That had to be some kind of weird cold-feet shit. It was his mind searching for excuses or reasons to back out, because getting married – even to someone you'd been with for almost fifteen years – was scary stuff. Well, no more. It was time to stop being an arse and get on with it. He was going to marry Cheryl the day after tomorrow. It was all going to be fine. And actually, maybe he'd invite everyone here, because he'd really enjoyed his time with them... especially Hayley. She was special. He'd never met someone that he'd connected with like that, so hopefully they could stay in touch. Although, her psycho husband might think differently. Still, maybe if he wasn't around... She was thinking about leaving him, and from where Tadgh stood, that seemed like the best plan she could have.

'Well, look, if she was with Cheryl's wedding party, then Cheryl must know her. Cheryl's here at the airport to meet me, so come hang with us and we'll see if we can suss out who it was.'

'Yeah, I... Definitely. Good idea. It's just that...'

Again, Tadgh had no idea what was going on. This guy had been talking all flight about finding the love of his life and now he was acting all reticent. Must be the day for cold feet all round.

Everyone around them was standing up now, and the usual landing scramble for bags was beginning. Tadgh stood up and moved into the aisle, followed by Hayley, who opened the overhead bin above them. Tadgh reached in and pulled out his backpack and the white bag next to it.

'Thank you,' Hayley said, blushing a little. He got that. It almost felt like a 'morning after an intimate night with a stranger' kind of scenario. Only, unlike Dev, they weren't about to go firing around the world looking for each other. They'd definitely shared something though. A moment. An intimacy for sure, just not a sexual one.

On the spur of the moment, he said, 'Look, I'm easy to find. If you feel like it, drop me a line on Instagram. I could send some new tracks over to Aoife for her dance. Get you some cool teacher points.'

For a second, he thought she was going to brush him off, then she blurted, 'Give me your phone.'

He handed it over, and she punched her name and number into it, then returned it to him. 'That's how you can find me, if you ever need to jump back into the bubble for a chat. It was good to meet you, Tadgh Donovan. And I hope you and Cheryl are... you know, that she didn't... Argh, I'm hopeless at this. Oprah would be much better. What I mean is that I hope you're good, I hope the wedding is fantastic and I hope you live happily ever after.'

He nodded, surprising himself when a twinge of sadness kicked in. 'And I hope you work it out for the best too... Whatever that is. And same goes about the bubble... Any time you need a chat, I'll be there. Except the day after tomorrow, because I think I've got something on that day.'

He noticed that her eyes were glistening and the sadness he was feeling turned to sympathy. She had a shit time ahead of her and he just wished he could help. He knew that he couldn't overstep though – he wasn't about to get involved in her business and make things worse for her. Her husband didn't strike him as the kind of guy who would be up for double dates or for his wife having male friends. Best to back off. She knew where to find him. Tadgh just hoped that at some point she would come looking.

There was a queue beginning to form in the aisle behind them, so Tadgh reached over and shook Dev's hand. 'Good meeting you. Come find me in the baggage claim and I'll take you to meet my Cheryl. Hopefully she can help with your search.'

'Eh, yeah, I will do, thanks,' Dev blustered, and Tadgh thought again that he'd definitely lost his bottle. That was the reaction of an indecisive man if ever he met one. Probably not a bad thing. Sure, the thought of someone travelling halfway around the world to find a stranger seemed like a romantic idea, but in reality, it was more likely to have him up on charges of stalking. The guy would be better to just have a week in the sun, then trot off home and meet someone the normal way.

Tadgh stretched into the space in the front of their row, so that he could reach out and hug Bernadette. He hadn't had much of an opportunity to talk to her on the flight, but she seemed lovely and Hayley said she'd been great. 'We didn't get a chance to talk much, but I hope you have a cool holiday. We're getting married at The Sands, day after tomorrow at noon – you're all very welcome.' His gaze went to all three of them, but he had a feeling that Bernadette was the most likely to come.

'Ooh, I might just take you up on that. I do love a wedding.'

'My mam was exactly the same,' Tadgh said, laughing. 'Sometimes on a Saturday afternoon she'd disappear, and we'd find out later she'd slipped into a church or chapel, and sat up the back to watch a wedding. She even had a special hat for it.' Until that moment, he'd completely forgotten that. Just another one of his mam's hilarious, but undeniably eccentric, qualities. She was one in a million and he felt an intense pang of longing for her to be here with them now. She'd be loving every second of the wedding prep, she'd be immersed in all the dramas and she'd be working out a plan to help everyone get sorted. That's who she was. Bernadette reminded him of her fearless, caring, fiercely loyal personality. Although, his mam would also be freaking out that his wedding suit was in his suitcase and it could have gone missing at any point in the journey.

There was a waft of warm air as the door not far in front of them opened and they began to shuffle forward. So today had turned out wildly unexpected. Time to put an end to all the nonsense and get back to reality. And reality was him, Cheryl and the wedding with all their family and friends. That had to be the way this ended. He had to believe that Conlan's version of events was true. His Cheryl would never betray him, never sleep with someone else, let alone his own brother. He was building his conviction with every word. Shay wasn't seeing Cheryl. He was messing around with Cheryl's sister. And it was none of his business if they were getting up to no good behind closed doors because what Shay and Cindy did was up to them.

When the others began moving, he slipped back into their row and let them all go, waiting for Shay and Conlan to work their way forward towards him. He assumed that by now, Hayley would have caught up with her husband, and Bernadette and Dev would be on their way to the baggage claim, and to his surprise he felt a twinge of something sad. He wasn't sure if it was saying goodbye to them, or the thought of leaving their bubble and facing reality. Or both.

When they reached him, his first thought was that Shay looked like shit. He wasn't sure if his brother had tanked some more booze and was now seriously inebriated, or if he'd stopped drinking and this was the hangover starting to catch up with him. His eyes were bloodshot, his hair was chaotic, and his unshaven face pale. If his adoring fans could see him now, they wouldn't recognise him.

The three of them walked in pretty much silence to the baggage reclaim. There, he spotted Hayley and her husband, unspeaking, over at the other side of the hall. For a second, their eyes locked and he winked and smiled, which was about the uncoolest thing he'd ever done. He definitely wasn't a winker. He'd just wanted to send some subliminal messages of moral support. Dev and Bernadette were down at the end of the baggage reclaim, so he gave them a wave too, then gestured to Dev that he'd wait outside for him. He was genuinely interested in whether Cheryl knew his mystery woman and he wanted to help the lad if he could.

Shay and Conlan's bags were the first to appear on the belt, with his right behind them. That must be an omen. Their bags had never come off first on any flight ever. They dragged them off the conveyor and pulled them behind them as they walked to the exit. He was experiencing a strange feeling, and it took him a few seconds to put his finger on it: he was nervous. What the feck was that about? He never got nervous. He could be in front of five thousand fans at a festival and he'd still be perfectly calm. But that was when he hadn't had a whole day of worry that his world was about to implode. He summoned his convictions again.

Sod it. He dismissed the doubts with an internal monologue pointing out that he was one of the luckiest guys ever. He was happy. Nothing to be nervous about. He was grand. Solid. It was all going to be great.

The doors from the baggage claim to the terminal building whooshed open, and as soon as they got through, he spotted some familiar faces. The first one was his da. Of course. He should have known that his father would be there to pick them up. Hadn't he been doing that their whole lives? And didn't they adore him for it? The next recognisable face was Cheryl's sister, Cindy. That didn't surprise him either. The two of them were joined at the hip. And the next face was... His eyes did a more thorough search of the people waiting there. It took him a moment and when he eventually spotted her, he was taken aback.

Cheryl. His Cheryl. Yet, it wasn't. There were bags under her eyes, her shoulders were slumped and her hair was pulled back in a lifeless ponytail.

Either she had a chronic hangover, or... or...

They got closer. Closer... His stare was locked on hers, and with every passing step the tornado in his stomach twisted more of his guts, knocking holes in his newly built wall of conviction that everything was going to be ok. Hangover. Maybe food poisoning.

Maybe even last-minute nerves. It had to be any of those things, because the alternative was...

They got to two metres away from her, and her gaze darted to Shay, then back to Tadgh, then...

'Tadgh, Shay and I have something to tell you. And I'm sorry, but this is killing me and I can't live with it for a single second longer. Shay?'

Tornado spinning, Tadgh watched as her gaze went pointedly to Shay, who paled even more and suddenly felt the need to stare at his shoes. This seemed to irk Cheryl even more.

'You have got to be kidding me...' she blurted weakly, in Shay's direction. Then back to Tadgh. 'Okay, if your brother won't be honest with you, I will. Tadgh, I'm so sorry, but Shay and I, we've been... well, you can probably guess the rest. Forgive me, Tadgh, please – but I can't marry you.'

31

HAYLEY

Lucas hadn't spoken a word to her since they got off the plane. Not a word. Now they were at the baggage reclaim, he was on his phone, scrolling through, answering emails, immersed in the world of being Dr Lucas Bloody Ford. She was back to being the invisible Mrs Ford. Ignored. Controlled. Tolerated. The bastard hadn't even apologised for the way he'd treated her. Why? Because she didn't matter. She was just the wife. The womb. The one with the reproductive system that didn't even bloody work.

Hayley couldn't help thinking how different the last ten hours of her life had been since she left Lucas at the departure gate. Other than his brief visits, she'd felt free. Noticed. Valued. She'd made Dev laugh. She'd felt seen, really seen for who she was, by Tadgh. And she'd felt the empathy of Bernadette, a woman who had been somewhere pretty close to where she was now.

And that was somewhere she couldn't bear to be. Not now. Not tonight. Not tomorrow.

'Lucas, I don't want to go to the hotel with you.'

'What?' He didn't look up.

'I said... Look at me when I'm talking to you,' she demanded fiercely.

That got his attention. His head shot up like it had been dealt an uppercut to the chin. Almost instantly, the familiar snarl started to form on his top lip. Hayley cut it right off.

'Don't even think about saying one nasty word to me. What I said before was that I don't want to go to the hotel with you. And there's more, so now is probably the time to get that out too. I don't want to be on holiday with you. I don't want to be married to you. And I definitely, absolutely, don't want to have children with you. I don't want to be anywhere near you. I'm done with all of it. With the abuse, the pressure, the negativity, the criticism. With you, Lucas. I'm done with you.'

His voice was like a low, thundering train. 'What the fuck are you talking about? Are you drunk?'

She threw her hands up and her voice became slightly elevated, loud enough for the people around them to hear. Hayley didn't care. He'd mortified and embarrassed her in public way too many times. Let him see how it felt this time. 'No, I am not drunk, Lucas. But I tell you what I definitely am: I'm pissed off, I'm exhausted, I'm disgusted with the way that you treat me, I'm sad that I've let myself put up with this for so long, and I am absolutely gutted that I've not done this before now.'

He took a step towards her, but Hayley refused to flinch. Okay, so she flinched a tiny bit, but hopefully it was too subtle for him to notice. 'Stop being so fucking ridiculous. You're just tired. Hormonal. We're going to get these cases and we're going to go to the hotel and we'll talk about it in the morning when you've calmed down.'

She had never wanted to punch his patronising, condescending, smug, controlling face more, but she didn't get a chance because their cases had trundled around the conveyor and were in front of them now.

He leaned over and pulled his off. Usually, he'd get Hayley's too, but she didn't give him the satisfaction. She reached down and pulled hers off herself, holding on to it tightly.

'Let's go,' he growled, taking a step forward.

He'd only gone a metre when he realised she wasn't following him. The people around them had mostly dispersed, either because they'd claimed their luggage or because they wanted to be nowhere near an escalating domestic.

'Hayley,' he barked at her, and a couple of people on the opposite side of the belt glanced over.

She stepped towards him, and for a second, he seemed to think she was falling into line. She wasn't. She just didn't want to shout.

'Lucas, I've told you already. I'm not coming with you. So the way I see it is that you've got two choices. You can either forcibly drag me out of here, in which case I'm fairly sure the St Lucian authorities would be delighted to have a bloke in custody who could afford to pay big money to get himself bailed out tomorrow morning. Or you can walk away now, go to the hotel and get on with your life and I'll go somewhere else and get on with mine.'

'I fucking knew it.'

Hayley closed her eyes, depressingly aware of what was about to come next.

'This is about that guy on the plane, the one you were all cosied up with. Fucking admit it. You were coming on to him and what... did you let him screw you on the plane? Is that what happened? Did you whore it into the mile-high club with him, Hayley?'

Her face was burning with rage but she wasn't going with her temper because if she did that he'd win. 'I hate to deliver a newsflash at such a critical time, Lucas, but I joined the mile-high club long before I met you and I enjoyed every minute of it.'

Okay, so it was a low blow, but she just couldn't contain it any more. And by the look of him, neither could he. His face was turning more purple by the second and he'd taken in so much air with his gasp of fury that his chest was double the size. She feared he could combust at any second.

'Exhale, Lucas. You're going to do yourself an injury and it won't change anything. I'm not coming with you, so please go.'

He snorted as if it was the most ridiculous thing he'd ever heard. 'And where are you going to go, exactly? Are you going to him? That's it, isn't it. You're fucking off with him.'

'No, she's fucking off with me, son.'

In the eye of the storm, Hayley hadn't even noticed Bernadette coming up behind them, but Lucas sure had noticed her now. He was like a guppy fish, fighting to take in air.

'What? I don't... what?'

'You seem confused, so I'll help you out,' Bernadette said calmly, but with a 'don't mess with me' tone that Hayley would never have believed could come out of that tiny, sweet, warm, self-effacing Scottish woman. 'First, don't think I'm fighting that lass's battles for her, because I'm not. She doesn't need me to because she's got this all by herself. You're the one that seems to have a problem listening to what she's saying. I'd see a doctor about your hearing. Oh, wait, you are one. My husband was too. He was also a controlling, abusive arse just like you, but that didn't work out too well for him either because he died and I'm here, so that tells you everything you need to know about who won that war.'

'With all due respect, this has got nothing to do with you, so butt out.'

'Ah, but it has, because what I was about to say is that Hayley is coming with me and she's going to stay with me for as long as she wants. And you're not going to contact her, or harass her, or try to make her change her mind, because if you do, I'll call the police so fast you'll have handcuffs on before you've hung up the phone. That's it. Simple. Those are your options. Now on you go and let this lass call her own shots.'

'Hayley, what the fuck—'

Right then, a security guard who had been wandering around the baggage hall stopped beside them. 'Is everything okay here?'

'I'm not sure, officer,' Bernadette replied with sunny innocence before switching her death stare to Lucas. 'Is everything okay with you, doctor?'

'It is. I was… just leaving.' He grabbed his bag and marched out of the reclaim area. The security guard strolled behind him, perhaps ensuring he'd actually left, and as she watched them, Hayley felt wave after wave of relief soak through every pore of her skin. She didn't know whether to laugh, to cry, to scream or to punch the air. He was gone. She had absolutely no illusion that he was gone forever. Lucas Ford would never tolerate that kind of defeat, but for now he was gone and she felt the tension ooze from her body and soul. And she had the woman standing next to her to thank for it.

She threw her arms around Bernadette and squeezed her. 'Thank you, thank you so, so much, Bernadette. I'm so grateful.'

'You did it by yourself, lovely. I just speeded up the process.'

Hayley squeezed her again, feeling hot tears drop down her cheeks. She'd no idea why she was crying, but she didn't care. These were tears of relief and she'd earned them.

She pulled back so that she was eye to eye with her newest and fiercest friend. 'Can I ask you something, though?'

'Anything.'

'That thing you said about the hotel – did you mean it? Because otherwise, I'm going to have to find a comfy chair here.'

Bernadette cackled with laughter, the two of them getting slightly high on relief and delight that they'd overcome the demon.

'Of course I meant it. I'm booked into a suite with two bedrooms and you're very welcome to one of them and half the minibar. I'd quite like to get started on that, though, so should we go?'

Hayley hugged her again, feeling such gratitude, the tears were beginning to well up again. She forced them back down. 'We should. Let's go.'

Bernadette gestured behind her, and Hayley saw that Dev was still standing there, with an expression on his handsome face that was somewhere between panic and terror.

'Great,' Bernadette replied. 'Because Deadpool over there is having a tumultuous time of it. Right, Dev, let's go,' she shouted over to him, and then when they got nearer, she added, 'Have you decided yet? Are we going forward or backwards?'

Hayley had no idea what they were talking about, but it sounded like a dilemma, and after the day she'd had, she was up for taking her mind off her troubles by watching someone else's drama unfold.

32

DEV

Dev needed as few options as possible because his brain was still in a state of shock and refusing to co-operate. Lizzy loved him. Was actually in love with him. And she couldn't have broken the news last night when they were on the sofa watching *Chicago Fire* and dipping into a large tub of popcorn. Oh no. She announced it when he was halfway around the world and on the cusp of finding out if love at first sight truly existed – and if it was reciprocated.

What was he supposed to do with that right now?

He was just grateful he'd met Bernadette and Hayley. If he wasn't with them, there was a possibility that his brain would go into total meltdown and he'd just end up like a malfunctioning robot, walking in circles, unable to process his next move.

Right now, he was standing in the baggage reclaim area with Bernadette, despite the fact that he had no suitcase to claim, because he needed more time to think this all through. He'd narrowed it down to two options. He could go out into the arrivals area and find Tadgh, be introduced formally to Tadgh's fiancée, Cheryl, and hope that she could solve the mystery of the other

Cheryl that he'd hooked up with that night. Or he could go out into the arrivals area, bypass the introductions and any chat that could lead him to 'his' Cheryl, and then book the next flight home to Lizzy.

He tried desperately to re-establish the links between his emotions and his logical brain, blown to smithereens by Lizzy's letter. How did he feel about her? Easy. He loved her. Adored her. She was the most important non-mother woman in his life and had been since the beginning of time.

But was he 'in' love with her, like she now claimed to be with him? And how did he know that this wasn't a phase? This was the woman who went vegan at least once a year, but never lasted longer than the next 4 a.m. visit to a kebab shop after a night at a club.

And then there was his Cheryl. His love at first sight. That had been a whole new feeling for him, and he'd been so sure that it was the start of an amazing new chapter in his life. But maybe that was all it was meant to be. A fictional chapter. Maybe the whole thing was down to his resounding feeling that he was in a rut in his life: a job that bored him, an unfulfilled ambition to write a novel, not forgetting Poppy, the ex-fiancée who'd ceremoniously dumped him by shagging Robbie Williams from Fake Twat. It was probably the lowest point in his life and maybe he just got carried away with all this because he needed something to dig him out of that huge hole of a heartbreak.

So. back to Lizzy, or forwards to the woman he'd met for the first time last weekend?

Both paths were possible, but there were two major problems with deciding which road to take.

Problem number one was that he didn't trust himself enough to decide what he wanted. To know what was right. Because, let's face it, he'd pretty much stuffed up the whole 'winning at life' thing so far.

Problem number two was that there was only one person he trusted enough to talk this over with, the one who would listen, and then give her opinion, and it would be the right one, even if it was delivered with a significant amount of mocking and a side order of derision. But that person was the one that had just written him a letter and was currently one side of the problem.

'Are you okay if I give Hayley the bullet points of this?' Bernadette asked, as they walked towards the doors that led out of the baggage claim and into arrivals.

'Yeah, sure,' Dev responded, then tuned out because he went back to his complex deliberations while Bernadette shared the details.

Twenty metres. That's how far away the doors were. That's how long he had to decide what to do. Of course, the other option was to find Cheryl, see how that went, discover if his feelings were reciprocated and then make an informed decision. That would probably be the most logical plan of action. However... that just didn't feel right. That felt like he was hedging his bets, especially if it all went wrong with Cheryl and then he hotfooted it back to Lizzy. What if she one day found out that she was his second choice? His back-up plan after love at first sight turned out to be a big fat dud.

No, he couldn't do that to her. Not in that way. If he was going to choose Lizzy, then it was because she was his first choice, the one he wanted with every bit of his heart.

And if he was going to stick with Cheryl, then he had to go all in, and if it didn't work out, then he'd take the consequences, because at least he'd have tried. He'd have no regrets about letting go of something that could have been amazing.

Ten metres.

'Dev, are you okay?' Hayley asked him, voice oozing concern. 'Only, you're really flushed. Do you need some water?'

'No, I'm fine, I'm just... I don't know what I am. I don't suppose that you have any pearls of wisdom in the love department.'

Hayley shook her head. 'Did you see who I married? I'm clearly no expert.'

'I take your point.'

The doors opened in front of him, and after he'd established that his heart hadn't burst like a blown-out tyre from the sheer stress of it all, he scanned the room and... there she was.

Cheryl. His Cheryl.

The one with whom he'd had one of the most amazing encounters of his life – if you didn't count that night on a lilo on a Benidorm balcony.'

The one he'd had the most instant connection with – if you didn't count the bond that had formed when a shy five-year-old kid met a bolshy girl next door and they decided to be pals forever.

The one who'd made his heart thud like no other – if you didn't count the million times that he'd watched his best mate walk towards him with that mischievous grin on her face that announced they were about to have a great night out.

Yet there was Cheryl. Over there, standing with Tadgh and a few other guys, and the Cheryl that Tadgh was engaged to. So they must know each other after all. Two Cheryls. What were the chances?

'There she is.' He wasn't sure at first if he'd said it aloud, but he must have, because Bernadette and Hayley stopped in their tracks.

'Where? Who?' Bernadette spluttered, her eyes going from side to side like a submarine periscope searching for an enemy aircraft carrier.

'That's Cheryl. Over there. The woman standing off to the side, next to Tadgh.'

His two trusty advisors stared over. 'Wow. I see what you mean. I think I just fell in love with her myself,' Bernadette said, deadpan.

'That's not helpful,' Dev countered, heart still racing. She was every bit as spectacular as he remembered. What should he do? Should he go over there? How would she react when she saw him? What if she'd been waiting here, hoping he'd somehow show up and find her?

What if she was it? His person?

What if...

'I don't want to go over there.' It was out before he could stop it.

Bernadette nodded sagely. 'Okay, but can I ask why? Is it because there's a whole cold-feet thing going on? Are you apprehensive about how she's going to react when she sees you?'

'No, I'm...' He stopped, hoping the words would come to articulate what he was thinking. 'I'm not apprehensive at all. I just don't want to go over there because it doesn't matter. Shit, that sounded like a dickhead thing to say. It's not that she doesn't matter. It's that... I'm making such a crap job of explaining it. Nothing matters. There, that's it. Nothing matters... except Lizzy. I just want to go book the next flight back. I want to see her and tell her that I want to be with her. I think I always did.'

'Oh, thank the lords,' Bernadette interjected. 'I didn't want to say anything because you had to make the decision on your own, but honestly, you made me nervous. For a minute there, I thought I was going to have to stage an intervention and talk some sense into you. The letter that lass wrote to you – that was love. Real love.'

'I know!' The relief and sheer joy of that realisation brought on a grin so wide his jaw ached. 'It's crazy. I've come all this way, and now I have absolutely no reason to be here. I just want to go home. Hang on...' He clicked the airline app on his phone and scrolled. 'There's a flight tomorrow, so I'll book on that.' It would have been perfect if there was one leaving that night, but in truth, he probably needed some sleep and a shower. 'What do you reckon, ladies? Taxi for three?'

Hayley nodded. 'Taxi for three sounds pretty perfect to me.'

'Why don't you come stay at our hotel tonight, Dev? I've got a swanky big suite and there's a sofa bed in the lounge. We could go there, raid the minibar, order some room service...' Bernadette suggested.

'Maybe watch an old romcom? Only, I've ended up with a shite ending for the one I was writing, so I'm going to have to scrap it and start again. In no movie I've ever seen does the hero change his mind and bugger off home.' Even as he was saying it, he knew he didn't care that he was blowing the ending. He'd made the right decision. He knew it.

'Yep, it's a bit of a flaw, I'll give you that. And we don't need a taxi because there is a car booked to collect us.'

'Of course there is.' Dev laughed, looking around. There was a row of chauffeurs in suits holding up signs, so he scanned the hall from right to left to... 'I'm hallucinating.'

Bernadette stared up at him quizzically. 'What do you mean, you're hallucinating?'

'I am 100 per cent imagining that Lizzy is coming out of those doors from the baggage area. And now she's looking straight at me, and walking towards me, and...'

'Dev?' his best friend said, with a very uncharacteristically nervous smile.

'Lizzy? What are you doing here? I don't understand.'

'I guess I didn't trust you to make the right decision all by yourself,' she teased. 'So I got a last minute ticket – I was up the back the whole time.

Beside him, he could hear Bernadette whisper to Hayley, 'Oh, this is lovely. I'm filling up.'

There was a voice in his head. His favourite TV romcom scene of all time. Friends. Ross. Rachel. Just a bit different.

'So... you got on the plane?'

Lizzy laughed, that raucous, crazy, beautiful, life-affirming laugh of hers.

'Yes, you gorgeous big idiot. I got on the plane.'

And that was the last thing she said before he kissed her.

AFTER 7 P.M. – ST LUCIA TIME

(WHICH IS AFTER MIDNIGHT UK TIME, SO THEY'RE REALLY, REALLY KNACKERED NOW)

33

BERNADETTE

From a day that started as a solo endeavour, Bernadette couldn't quite work out how it had ended with her, Hayley, Dev and Lizzy all sharing a car back to her hotel suite. What mattered was that she was loving every minute of it. This lot were a breath of fresh air. Dev was, without a doubt, one of the nicest, funniest lads she'd ever encountered. After he'd met up with Lizzy at the airport, he'd had no desire to go to the hotel where Cheryl was staying, so it had been easy for Bernadette to persuade them to come here. She'd only chatted to them on the car ride, but she could already see that Lizzy was all kinds of special. And it was patently obvious that she adored Dev every bit as much as she said in the letter. Even sweeter that it was reciprocated. Dev hadn't stopped smiling since he saw her.

In the suite, it had been easy to reallocate the beds. It turned out that one of the rooms had a king-size bed, which Bernadette was happy to give to Dev and Lizzy. The other room had two queens, perfect for her and Hayley. And no, strangely, it didn't feel weird at all to be sharing with someone she'd never met before this morning.

They attempted to switch their body clocks to St Lucia time, so they had to stay awake for the next few hours as it was barely 9 p.m., even though their bodies were claiming it was 2 a.m. the following morning and they should be horizontal. As a sleep-delaying tactic they ordered pizzas and club sandwiches on room service. Bernadette was just about to change into comfy pyjamas when her phone beeped. She took it outside on to the terrace.

It was a text from Sarah.

Got to the hospital. Eliza fine, just sore and in plaster. We've arranged to get her home tomorrow. I'm so relieved I could cry. Thank you for being so understanding, Bernadette. You're the best kind of friend. I hope you had a good flight, and you weren't too bored on the journey. I'll call you tomorrow. Love you, Sxx

Bernadette smiled as she typed her reply.

I'm so relieved all is well with Eliza. Please give her a huge but gentle hug from me. Please don't feel bad. I promise I've had the most surprising but wonderful day. I'm at the hotel now, with new friends and lots to tell. I'll fill you in tomorrow and I love you back xxx

She could hear the others chatting inside, so she took a moment to sit and watch the stunning sunset that was shooting flares of colour on the horizon. It was perfect. Beautiful. The suite was spectacular, with its white porcelain floors, cream walls, overstuffed beige sofas and the sumptuous charcoal and gold palette of the curtains and cushions. There was a sitting area, a dining area and a mini kitchen that had everything she could possibly need and more. It was bigger than her little cottage, and much as she loved her home, it did lack the champagne on arrival, the fruit basket and the chocolate-dipped strawberries that were laid out on the ebony sideboard. It was perfection. And that extended out here, to the whitewashed terrace, with the huge grey love seats and the sun loungers with cushions so thick she could probably float away on them. All of it, the room, the resort, the smell of the ocean, it was paradise. And Kenneth was the only reason she was here.

How things change, she thought. This holiday had been booked by Kenneth, as some kind of twisted gesture of love, and yet, here she was, alone, yet having seen a whole new kind of love today. Watching Dev and Lizzy come together had been an unforgettable moment and even as it was happening, she could feel something inside her shift. After Kenneth, she'd been so relieved to get away from him, so jaded with the concept of love and relationships and – God forbid – marriage, that she'd pulled the shutters down on that whole aspect of her life. No men. No flirting. No dating. It had suited her fine. She'd told herself that she'd been there, done that, got the 'I've been burned' T-shirt, and she would only be a fool to go there again.

Now she wasn't so sure.

On the shoreline in front of her, she could see a silhouette of a man, standing staring out at the ocean, watching the sun go down too. For a moment, Bernadette felt her heart quicken. He looked so like Kenneth. Same height. Same build. Same grey hair, swept back, so distinguished and the perfect style to complement the square jaw of his handsome face.

Of course, it wasn't him. His heart attack had claimed him before he could be that man, standing out there, watching something so beautiful. Bernadette wasn't sorry he was gone. Not for a moment. She was just sorry that she never got to say goodbye. And if she had…

Her mind went back to Lizzy's letter today, so honest, so brutal, so articulate in her emotions and she wished she'd had that opportunity to express her thoughts and feelings to the man who'd turned her love against her. Even when she'd left him, there had been little dialogue, just a calm explanation from her, and some furious, castigating insults from him.

She closed her eyes, so that the only things in her world were the sound of the waves and the smell of the ocean.

Dear Kenneth...

So you're gone. And not one bit of me is sorry, except perhaps the mother in me, who knows that despite everything, you were a good father to our children, and you'll always have a piece of their heart. But not mine.

In some ways, I've come so far since I walked away from you. I've built an independent life of peace and simplicity that I adore. I only allow people in my life who are caring and kind and who want the best for me, just as I do for them.

I'd be denying reality though, if I didn't admit that the awful parts of us have helped me to help other people. At work, in A&E, I'm always the first to spot signs of abuse. I don't mean the bruises and the broken bones, I mean the wounds that aren't visible: the blunt force trauma to the self-esteem, the cuts to the confidence, the footprints that show where someone stamped out the light in the victim's soul. Those are the ones I see, because those are the wounds you inflicted on me.

Today, our history seeped into the present yet again. A young woman on my flight was married to a man who reminded me very much of you. I don't need to go over that all again – you know who you were. We both do. You'd probably have been friends with this woman's husband had you met him. A surgeon. By all accounts, a very intelligent respectable pillar of society. By my own account, a reprehensible bully.

Do you know, Kenneth, thanks to you, I saw who he was. Thanks to you, I had the experience to step in and help his wife. Thanks to you, I had no fear of him, because I'd already lived with that person and survived. He was a pale imitation. An abuser who hasn't fully grown into the cruelty of his skin yet.

Thanks to you, and thanks to him, today she walked away. And I supported her. Because thanks to you, I knew what to say and what to do to help.

Thankfully, not all men are like you.

Today I met a young man who was as far from you as it is possible to be. He reminded me a lot of our Stuart. Kind, gentle, the best friend and partner in any crisis or celebration. He had many wonderful traits, but the one I admired most was his courage. No matter how many times he'd been hurt, he was opening his heart again, to love, to trust and to hope.

Maybe it's time for me to do that too.

Maybe I want to live my life having known two kinds of love. The kind that takes away and the kind that gives.

Now, I'm ready for the kind that gives, for someone who supports, someone who sees the joy in life and in the person that they give their heart to.

So thank you, Kenneth. Being with you for thirty years taught me what I didn't want. Now I feel ready to go find the life and the person that I do want.

No longer yours,

Bernadette

The man on the shore was wandering away now, strolling off across the sands. Time for Bernadette to do the same.

Invigorated, she pushed herself up from the edge of the terrace, and inhaled, exhaled, then went back inside, feeling like she'd finally said goodbye, finally turned the last page on that chapter.

As she opened the terrace door, she heard laughter, she heard chat and she heard love. And she knew it was time for her to join the party. She just wasn't sure where to start.

34

TADGH

Tadgh had insisted on getting a taxi alone with his father, and the others – Conlan, Shay, Cheryl and Cindy had found their own cabs. He wasn't sure which of them were travelling together and he really didn't care.

Tadgh stared out of the window, unable to speak. So it was true. It wasn't a mistake. That much he'd established after Cheryl's outburst. He replayed her words again and again.

'Okay, if your brother won't be honest with you, I will. Tadgh, I'm so sorry, but Shay and I have been... well, you can probably guess the rest. Forgive me, Tadgh, please – but I can't marry you.'

Shay's response played back in his mind too.

'Oh, for fuck's sake,' Shay had groaned, then spat out an accusatory criticism in her direction. 'Why the fuck would you say that now?'

It had taken every shred of discipline Tadgh had not to knock him out, and it wasn't even for sleeping with his fiancée, it was for humiliating her now, for speaking to her that way, for acting like she was the only one in the wrong. He loved his brother dearly, but shit, he was a prick, who was completely undeserving of it.

Conlan had been the first to react, poking Shay in the chest. 'But I thought you said—'

'Conlan, don't,' Tadgh had pulled his mate back by the arm of his jacket and stopped him.

Conlan had met his gaze and Tadgh saw utter shock there. Okay, so at least one friend remained. Conlan genuinely hadn't known. He'd believed Shay's story about fooling around with Cheryl's sister, Cindy. They'd both been taken for fools. Go, Shay. That was quite an achievement. But Tadgh wasn't about to have Cindy dragged into this when she had been nothing but Shay's decoy. What kind of immoral dick claims he's having an affair with a married woman to cover up shagging her sister? Jesus, this was like a Greek tragedy playing out in the middle of the arrivals hall at Hewanorra Airport.

'How long? How long has it been going on?' It was a cliché, but Tadgh had felt he needed to know. He had to understand how long he'd been lied to, how many times they'd sneaked around behind his back, made an absolute mug of him.

Cheryl had waited for Shay to answer, to take some of the heat off her, but he was standing, hands on hips, staring down at the floor.

Tadgh had waited. Refusing to fill the silence.

Cheryl had cracked first. 'Just the last couple of weeks. We've met a few times. I swear, Tadgh. That was it.'

The arrivals hall was emptying out now and their group was pretty much alone in the corner. It was probably just as well.

Conlan had shook his head, walked away, presumably to get his own cab to the hotel. Tadgh didn't blame him for wanting no part of this. Truth was, he didn't either.

So then there were five. His dad. Two brothers. Two sisters.

Cindy didn't say a word, just stood beside her sister, holding her hand. Tadgh had wished he could feel that kind of loyalty and support for his brother right now, but there was no chance – and he didn't think he'd ever have it in him to feel that way again.

That said, Tadgh's reaction had been one that he hadn't anticipated and he'd surprised himself. He'd shaken his head, feeling a strange sense of relief. 'You two fecking deserve each other.'

'Tadgh, please don't... I'm so sorry. We couldn't help it. It just—'

He'd shrugged his shoulders. 'I don't care. I don't need to know any more details. Look, you lot – sort this out among yourselves. Cheryl, I'm sorry you did this, I really am. More than fourteen years. That's a long time to throw away. But then, I'd rather know who you are now, than find out when it's too late to escape unscathed. I tell you this out of respect for the time we had together, though – good luck getting this guy to commit to you. Good luck making him stay faithful. The fucker will break your heart and he'll ruin your life, but you made that choice. Good luck with it.'

Tears were overflowing, streaming down her face now.

'And Shay,' Tadgh had swung to face his brother, who still wouldn't look him in the eye. 'Go fuck yourself, bro.'

He'd taken two steps away, when he stopped, something else bothering him. A realisation. A possibility. He turned his gaze back on Cheryl and Cindy.

'I know it's going to be a stretch to ask you two for honesty, but I met a guy today on the plane. Said he'd met you guys in London last week. Took someone from your party back to his place. But strangely, he thought the woman's name was Cheryl.'

His ex-fiancée's face had immediately swung round in the direction of her sister. 'You gave that guy my name? Why would you do that?' she'd asked, confirming every suspicion Tadgh had. They used to do that to each other all the time when they were younger. Every time one of the sisters had got themselves in trouble, they'd give the other one's name so that they could deny it later. Some habits just never changed.

'I'm sorry, I panicked. I'm married! I could have wrecked everything. You were already shagging around, so what was the problem?'

Cheryl was furious. It was difficult to feel any sympathy for her, so Tadgh had simply walked away and left them all to it. His dad had walked with him, saying nothing, just being there, shoulder to shoulder with his son. He didn't speak until they were in the taxi.

'Tell me, son. Tell me what you need me to do. You know I'm not the best in these situations. Your mam was always the one that sorted this kind of stuff out. What I will say is that Shay was wrong. As was Cheryl. What they've done is inexcusable and I'm not telling you to forgive them. To be honest, I'm just telling you that I'm sorry your mam isn't here to say and do the right thing, but I'm here for you. Whatever you need.'

A piece of Tadgh's heart chipped off right there. His dad was fifty-five years old, a man who was set in the ways of a life he loved, one that he lost when Mam died, and yet here he was, trying to fill the gap that was left when she was gone. That was love. That was the kind of man he wanted to be. Someone who loved, who cared, someone who built a world around him and didn't just think about his own happiness. That reminded him of someone else.

'Da, I need you to come with me. There's someone I want you to meet.'

Tadgh knew where he wanted to be right now.

He picked up his phone and dialled the number.

35

HAYLEY

When the bell on the suite's door dinged, Hayley felt her heart begin to race with anxiety, before she talked herself down. It couldn't be Lucas. He didn't know where she was, and he didn't have Bernadette's name, so he wouldn't even be able to grease any hands at reception to get her room number. And she'd turned off her phone locator too, just in case he decided to use it. Not that she thought for a minute that he'd want to do that tonight anyway. Right now, he'd be in the hotel bar, drinking their most expensive whisky, telling himself that he was right about everything and she didn't deserve him. Lucas wouldn't chase her yet, because he'd be sure she'd be back in the morning. That was a whole lot of arrogance. It would be followed by rage when he discovered she was gone for good, but she would deal with that later. Right now, she was happy just to relax, enjoy her surroundings, to let him believe that he was right. In some ways, he was. She didn't deserve him. She deserved someone a whole lot better.

If she'd ever thought about this moment, she'd have anticipated that she'd be devastated, distraught, beside herself and falling to pieces, but no. All she felt was a strange sense of calm. Of peace. Of thanks for the people she'd met today, who had deliberately or inadvertently helped her make the decision to leave her marriage. And of happiness that grew as she realised who was pressing the doorbell.

'No, no, you two sit there! I'll get it,' she teased Dev and Lizzy, both of them showing absolutely no signs of getting up to answer it. They'd been on the sofa, intertwined, staring at each other with goofy smiles pretty much since they got back from the airport. They'd only broken off to consult the room-service menu, to grab a couple of beers and to fill Hayley in on the letters they'd exchanged and all the other stuff she'd missed on the plane because she'd been too busy living in the bubble at the other end of the row. Dev and Lizzy were swelling her heart though. This is what love should look like. It had been a million years since she and Lucas had looked at each other like that.

Bernadette, meanwhile, was in the shower, freshening up after the long flight. Hayley knew she would never stop being thankful for whatever miracle had brought Bernadette her way today.

The doorbell rang again just as she reached it and she felt almost shy when she opened the door and saw Tadgh standing there, that easy, chilled smile on his way too gorgeous face. In a strange way, this meeting was out of context for their relationship so far. A bubble in a plane, just the two of them, with dim lighting, and the rest of the world on mute was one thing. Seeing each other on solid ground, interacting with other people, felt a bit... different. More real. And she liked it.

'Hey,' she said, matching his grin with her own. 'Come on in.'

He stepped into the doorway, and his height almost filled it. That's when she noticed the other person at his side. Of course. That had been the reason for his call to her. And not at all what she'd expected.

It was only half an hour ago that he'd rang her. She almost hadn't answered it, because it was an unknown number, but at the last minute, she'd picked up.

'Hey Oprah, this is Tadgh.' His voice had made her smile and there was something going on in her stomach that she couldn't quite put her finger on. Was it suddenly hot in there? Had the air conditioning switched itself off?

'Hey. How are you? How did it go with Cheryl?' She'd felt herself hold her breath as she waited for the answer.

A sigh. 'Not great. She's been seeing Shay, right enough. It's pretty safe to say that the wedding is off and I'm feeling like I might want to be an only child.'

'I'm so sorry,' she'd said, meaning it.

'I don't think I am though. At least about the wedding part. It feels like it was just meant to be this way and I'm cool with that. What about you? How are things going with Lucas?'

Of course, he wouldn't know. He was already gone when she'd had the showdown with Lucas at the baggage area.

'It's over. And not that I want to steal your lyrics, but it feels like it was just meant to be this way and I'm cool with that.'

His low, sexy – yes, sexy – chuckle came down the line to her, followed by, 'Where are you now? Do you need somewhere to stay?'

'No, I'm staying with Bernadette. She was supposed to be here with a friend and they'd booked a two-bedroom suite, so I am absolutely slumming it in a five-star resort. This heartbreak stuff is hard work.'

That had made him laugh again. 'I hear you. But actually, I'm glad you're there because that was why I called... to ask for Bernadette's number. I was hoping to catch up with her tonight.'

'Oh.' Hayley had hoped she'd somehow managed to cover up the disappointment in her voice. He hadn't been calling to speak to her, he'd been calling for Bernadette's number. She'd suddenly felt like a bit of a fool, but why should she expect anything else? She'd known him for one whole plane journey, he'd just found out that his fiancée had been unfaithful, and he knew she was a married woman. One of those situations could put her in bargepole territory, but all three made any contact highly complicated. Still, that didn't mean she couldn't be polite. 'Tell me something, have you eaten?' Chipper and friendly, that's what she was going for. Chipper and friendly.

There had been a pause, as if he'd had to think about his answer. 'Actually no. Not since the plane, and we barely touched our food on there.'

'Well, we've just ordered more room service than a football team could eat, and you're welcome to join us. Dev and his girlfriend, Lizzy, are here too...'

'His girlfriend, Lizzy? What about... Cheryl. Or the person he thought was Cheryl. It's a long story, but I think I can clear some things up with that.'

'I don't think it matters. He realised when he landed that he was actually in love with his best friend, Lizzy, and she was on the plane the whole time. He had no idea she'd got a last-minute, stand-by seat. It was one of those amazing romcom moments. I think it might actually have restored my faith in the good guys winning.'

'In that case I'll come over. I could do with some of that faith myself. Just one thing though, is it okay if I bring someone? That's what I was calling Bernadette about.'

Hayley's heart had sunk. He was bringing someone. 'Of course you can. That'll be great.' Her tone was probably high enough to crack windows. She'd immediately chided herself. Why should that bother her? For God's sake, she'd been separated for about five minutes and her husband hadn't even accepted it yet. Why was she having any sort of reaction to any other man at all?

Now, half an hour later, as she let him in, she saw the other person. In fact, the man held his hand out to introduce himself. 'Hello there. I'm Jack. Tadgh's father. Terrible business all this. It was very kind of you to invite us over. Probably best that we're out of the way for a while.'

Hayley melted yet again. It was obvious where Tadgh got his looks from. His dad was as tall as Tadgh, over six foot, with the same broad shoulders and twinkle in his brown eyes. 'You're so welcome. It's lovely to have you here. We've just ordered food, so I hope you're hungry.'

She stood back to let them pass, thinking that, if nothing else, there was another nice person to add to her memories of this trip. She still hadn't decided how long she was going to stay for, but maybe if she kept Bernadette company for a few days, they could have a drink with Tadgh and his dad. Or was she overstepping and intruding on their time?

Tadgh clearly wasn't interested in spending time with her. He'd only called because he wanted to speak to Bernadette. It was nothing to do with her at all.

Tadgh's dad passed her and followed her gesture to the door through to the lounge.

Okay, just be cool. Friends. Friends is fine.

But instead of walking past her, Tadgh stopped, rested his gaze on hers.

'I like the sound of the good guys winning,' he said, and she could feel his breath on her skin as he spoke.

She moved a little closer. 'Me too.'

Their eye contact remained unbroken and she felt like neither of them wanted this moment to end. How could that be right? How could there be some kind of bond there, given that they hadn't even know each other for a whole day, and in the hours they'd been together, they'd both had their hearts shredded?

'Maybe, if you're going to be around for a couple of days we could hang out and find out if that's true?' Tadgh suggested.

Hayley nodded slowly. 'I think I'm free.'

36

DEV

Dev managed to drag his eyes away from Lizzy's face when Tadgh and his dad came into the room. So this was what being in love felt like. Not casual love. Not friendship love. Not shagging the bloke from Fake Twat love. Real love. Forever love. In-freaking-credible love. The only way to describe it was that it was like a dam breaking, causing a tsunami. Lizzy had knocked one brick out of his wall and suddenly it had crumbled, and he'd been carried along on a wave of sheer fricking delight.

She loved him. He loved her. It couldn't be more obvious. And it couldn't be more perfect because it was real. There was no pretence, no acting, no fake crap that turned up later. They already knew everything about each other, so they didn't even have to worry about there being ugly surprises down the line. Although... the fact that Lizzy had covered her feelings up for a lifetime was a bit of a concern. She'd done it so well he was fairly sure she could be a Cold War spy and he wouldn't have a clue.

He climbed off the sofa and shook Tadgh's hand, then did the same with his dad, before introducing Lizzy.

'Holy crap, are you the guy from Home?' she gasped, wide-eyed.

Dev groaned on the inside. Of course, she knew him – Dev had sent her a link to the band's website earlier and she'd thought he was gorgeous. Great. He'd just realised she was his forever love and now she'd met someone who was exactly her type, with that whole rock guy image and…

He stopped himself. He wasn't doing this. After nearly thirty years of knowing each other, Lizzy had declared her love for him. He was enough. They were good. She wasn't suddenly going to run off with a rock guy because he had good hair. Besides, if he wasn't wrong, there was definitely some chemistry between Tadgh and Hayley.

'Yeah, I am. Or I was. I think I just decided to go solo.'

Tadgh and Jack sat on the sofas, gratefully accepting a couple of beers from Hayley, then Jack spotted the view of the setting sun on the terrace and went to investigate. There was no awkwardness, just easy chat, until Tadgh said, 'I don't know if you care, but I can tell you what happened with the whole Cheryl thing?'

Dev didn't even get a chance to answer, when Lizzy jumped in, 'Yes! Or to be honest, he doesn't really need to know, but I do because I'm shallow and nosy and generally think people are weirdos. What's the story?'

'It wasn't Cheryl, it was her sister, Cindy. She gave you Cheryl's name because she felt guilty – she's married.'

'Shit,' Dev whistled. 'I should have known. It was all too good to be true.'

Lizzy nudged him with her elbow. 'Eh, I'm too good to be true, thank you very much.'

'You are, babe,' he agreed, nuzzling into her neck. He still couldn't believe this was happening. He was nuzzling Lizzy Enid Walsh's neck and she wasn't threatening to break his legs or burn his Tottenham Hotspur poster collection. This was love. True love and devotion. And there hadn't been a single minute in his life when he'd been happier.

'Tadgh!' That came from Bernadette as she came out from the bathroom, her newly dried red hair wavy, her eyes bright.

Dev watched as Tadgh got up to greet her with a hug.

'Okay, give me bullet points because I don't want you to have to repeat yourself and I caught snippets of what you said from the shower. Cheryl?'

'Over,' he replied, and Dev thought it interesting that there didn't seem to be any sadness there. It obviously just wasn't meant to be. Not like him and Lizzy. And if that sounded smug, he'd be suitably repentant just as soon as he stopped feeling like the luckiest guy on the planet.

'Are you okay?' Bernadette asked him.

'Surprisingly fine,' Tadgh answered.

'Excellent. Well, welcome to the Surprisingly Fine Club. I just made that up, but it's pretty apt. You. Hayley. And I'm even remarkably fine, considering I got stood up and I'm not here with my best friend.'

'Actually, that's what I wanted to talk to you about. So, I don't know what your plans are, but I figured you might have a bit of free time over the next two weeks, and I know you said that you didn't fancy doing much on your own...'

'How come I've got a feeling this is leading somewhere, Tadgh?'

'Because I was just thinking that... if I stick around for a few days, and Hayley does too, then maybe we could plan some stuff.'

Bernadette smiled at his suggestion but shook her head. 'That's very lovely of you to think of me, but I'm not going to be the old dear traipsing round in the middle of you young ones.'

'But that's the thing,' Tadgh argued. 'You wouldn't be in the middle because...' He searched behind him, to each side, then grinned as his father came back in through the terrace door.

Beside him, Dev could feel Lizzy almost fizz with excitement as she saw exactly what was going on here.

Tadgh held his hand out, gesturing to his dad. 'You won't be in the middle because my da would be with us too. Bernadette, this is Jack Donovan. Da, this is Bernadette.'

'Very pleased to meet you, Bernadette. And if you don't mind an old git like me spending some time with you all, I'd love to join you for a day or two.'

Dev couldn't take his eyes of Bernadette's face as it transcended a whole range of reactions that, if he was reading it right, went from surprise, to interest, to appreciation, to agreement. And somewhere in there, he was pretty sure that she probably registered that Jack Donovan seemed like a very attractive, very engaging, very friendly guy. Classic romcom opening. Dev made a note to include it in his book. Not the one he was writing before. The new one, where the guy chased the girl, then discovered that his best friend was the right one for him all along. Yes, it had been done before, in almost every romcom ever written, but at least this time he got to live the ending instead of just watching it.

Besides, this ending came with definite perks, one of them being a suggestion Lizzy had come up with about half an hour before, when the sun first started to go down.

'I think there are quite a few interesting things going on here in the next week or so,' he hinted to Bernadette, Hayley, Tadgh and his dad, drawing them in.

'Really? What kind of things?' Bernadette asked brightly, her demeanour so different from the drawn stressfest she'd been when she'd boarded the plane that morning.

'Well, Lizzy and I were just thinking about putting a small

dinner party together. With a bit of live entertainment thrown in. So if you're not doing anything next weekend...' He did the romcom pause, the one where everyone knows what's coming but they milk the ending for dramatic effect. 'We just wondered if you fancied coming to a wedding?'

EPILOGUE

TWO WEEKS LATER

Bernadette glanced up at the board. The flight back from St Lucia to London had a two-hour delay. Her first thought was that she didn't care one bit. It gave her two hours longer to sit in the bar and pass the time with Jack Donovan.

Not that they weren't going to have the opportunity to do that on the plane and when they got back home. He'd already changed his flight back to Dublin for Glasgow instead and was going to spend the next few days with her at her cottage. Lizzy had explained to her what the phrase 'all the feels' meant and that's exactly what Bernadette had. All of them. She was excited, thrilled, terrified, nervous, giddy. Most of all, though, she was just happy. Happier than she could ever remember.

The last two weeks had been... Oh, it was hard to put it into words. Spectacular. Yes, that just about covered it. The six of them, Bernadette and Jack, Tadgh and Hayley, Dev and Lizzy, had stuck together most days, sometimes touring the island, other times just lying out on the golden sands of Bernadette's terrace, chatting, laughing, singing, just, well, happy to be there. She'd connected with Jack straight away, this sweet man who didn't need to be the loudest in the room, but who could make all the noise fade into the background just by catching her eye.

It had taken him a week to hold her hand, then a couple of days more before he'd stopped her as they walked along the beach at dusk.

'You know, all this is new to me,' he'd told her, and she'd known exactly what he meant. They'd already talked about how they'd both had one partner in life, and couldn't quite get to grips with finding another. Though for very different reasons. Jack had adored his wife, and Bernadette had hated her husband. They both had those barriers to break down. Every day, she'd felt that happening though. That night, she'd watched his face, so earnest, but with a twinkle in his eye that had got brighter with every moment that passed. He'd leant down and slowly, almost hypnotically, he'd moved his face towards Bernadette's and kissed her.

Lord, bits of her that hadn't been ignited since 1984 were suddenly limbo dancing across the sands, while shooting fireworks into the sky and shaking maracas. All the feels and a few more new ones that she hadn't quite found a name for yet. And maybe, just maybe, when they got back to her home, they'd discover a few more.

The irony wasn't lost on her that, in some ways, this was all down to Kenneth. He'd booked this holiday to try to manipulate her. Instead, he'd given her the chance of something special with the man who was standing next to her right now, his hand shyly grazing hers. Kenneth's chapter was closed, but she was pretty sure she'd just flipped open the first page on a brand new one.

'Bugger, it's delayed,' Lizzy declared, as she reached Bernadette and Jack. 'You know what that means, don't you?'

Bernadette couldn't wait to find out. This young woman had been a source of constant entertainment over the last fourteen days.

First up. Last to bed. And just so much fun and laughter in between. Thank the heavens that the lad had come to his senses.

'It means I'm going to have to drag my husband to the bar and make our honeymoon last a bit longer.'

'Did I hear my name being mentioned there?' Dev asked, as he and his suitcase came to a stop beside them.

Dev was fully aware that he hadn't stopped grinning in two weeks. This was serious romcom stuff. He and Lizzy had tied the knot a week after they arrived. He'd felt it was imperative to make it legal before she came to her senses and changed her mind. Bernadette had offered to let them stay in her suite, but when they expressed the need for a little pre and post-marital privacy, she had managed to wangle them an absurdly good rate on a room a couple of doors down from hers. Dev had, of course, cancelled his room at The Sands. He'd heard it was pretty miserable over there. A lot of unhappy faces at the pool every day. Same couldn't be said at The Sugar Beach. There must have been something in the water of the sparkling ocean, because there was nothing but joy, not just for him and Lizzy, but if his newfound powers of perception were to be trusted, for Bernadette and Jack too.

'I was just saying that we need to go to the bar and make the most of two more hours that have just been added to our honeymoon.'

'Dammit. And we don't even have a lilo,' he'd murmured in her ear, before kissing her.

Wow, she was spectacular. Over the last two weeks, he'd found himself too excited to sleep, so he'd been writing his novel instead of lying awake staring at Lizzy's gorgeous face. He was trying to lose the stalker tag. He already had forty thousand words and the second half of the story mapped out. It didn't have a title yet, so for now he was using the working title – Lizzy Enid Walsh Got On The Plane. It needed work, but the celebrant at the hotel had said he had loads of time. Something to do with Until Death Do Us Part. If he ran out of storylines, he could also throw in some stuff about an Irish rock star and his fledgling romance. Dev's newfound romance alert pinged in his head as his gaze went to the couple walking across the room. There was another romcom just waiting to be written.

Tadgh took Hayley's hand as they headed to the bar. He glanced around for any sight of Shay and Cheryl, or Cindy and Jay. Cheryl had called him a couple of times in the first few days after he'd got here, but he'd ignored the calls. There was nothing to say. He'd ignored a few calls from Shay too. Nothing to say to him either. Maybe one day, but not yet. Not to either of them. He'd spoken to Conlan, who reported that Cindy hadn't fessed up to her husband about the one-night stand, but Jay had suspicions. He'd also had a long chat to Conlan about the future of the band. Conlan was going to stick with it for now, but he was totally cool and understanding of Tadgh's decision to leave. Going solo was definitely his best move, at least in his musical life. On the personal side, he was definitely part of a duo now.

'What are you grinning at?' Hayley asked him, her fingers snaking into his.

She didn't have to worry about Lucas coming across them. He'd called her on the second day of the trip to announce that there had been some work emergency – a very famous celebrity requiring his immediate attention. He'd demanded she go with him and had been apoplectic when she'd refused. It was all she needed. As soon as he was gone, she blocked his calls and had a lawyer friend notify him that she was starting divorce proceedings. She hadn't heard from him since. It was over. Done. A child wasn't in her future, it might never be, but instead, she'd found someone else, the woman she'd used to be. And that woman had spent the last two weeks surfing, swimming, drinking, having fun and discovering a different kind of love, one that came in a bubble with the most beautiful man she'd ever met.

Tadgh had played her 'Everywhere Without You', the song he'd written about his mam's passing and his da mourning for their life together. Last night he'd written a new one for her called 'Everywhere With You'.

And that was exactly where Hayley wanted to be.

When they got over to the big wooden table in the corner of the bar where the others were sitting, Hayley took a seat on the same side as Dev and Bernadette, while Tadgh sat across from her, next to Lizzy and his dad.

'So... I propose a new tradition,' Dev said, raising his glass and waiting for the others to follow before going on. 'Every year, a weekend, the six of us, to celebrate the wedding anniversary of me and this woman who was daft enough to take me on.'

'I just checked my diary and I'm free,' Bernadette joked. She didn't need to check anything. She would always show up for this lot.

'Aye, I reckon I'm in,' Jack agreed, winking at Bernadette.

Tadgh nudged his dad's shoulder with his. 'I'm right there with ya, Da.'

'Ah, sorry, I can't make it,' Hayley piped up and the others all spun their heads to face her. 'Kidding,' she shrugged, giggling. 'Look how much has changed in a fortnight. I can't wait to see what happens in a year.' As her glass clinked with her new friends, Hayley made a toast. 'This is for you, Dev. And Lizzy. Sod it, it's for us all. Here's to happy ever after.'

Tadgh watched her, a slow easy smile on his face. That was happy ever after, right there.

MORE FROM SHARI LOW

We hope you enjoyed reading *One Last Day of Summer*. If you did, please leave a review.

If you'd like to gift a copy, this book is also available as an ebook, digital audio download and audiobook CD.

Sign up to Shari Low's mailing list for news, competitions and updates on future books.

http://bit.ly/ShariLowNewsletter

Explore more from Shari Low.

ABOUT THE AUTHOR

Shari Low is the #1 bestselling author of over 20 novels, including *My One Month Marriage* and *One Day In Summer,* and a collection of parenthood memories called *Because Mummy Said So.* She lives near Glasgow.

Visit Shari's website: www.sharilow.com

Follow Shari on social media:

facebook.com/sharilowbooks

twitter.com/sharilow

instagram.com/sharilowbooks

bookbub.com/authors/shari-low

Boldwood

Boldwood Books is an award-winning fiction publishing company seeking out the best stories from around the world.

Find out more at www.boldwoodbooks.com

Join our reader community for brilliant books, competitions and offers!

Follow us
@BoldwoodBooks
@BookandTonic

Sign up to our weekly deals newsletter

https://bit.ly/BoldwoodBNewsletter